Passport to Danger

A World War II
Spy Adventure

William F. "Bill" Kelly

William F. Kelly

Barringer Publishing, Naples, Florida
www.barringerpublishing.com
Cover, graphics, layout design by Lisa Camp
Editing by Carole Greene

Thank You…
To Polly, for telling me what I needed to hear
in spite of me not wanting to hear it.
To Susan Murphy, for helping me put more meat
on the bones of my protagonist.
To John Wright, Jr., for his suggestions and encouragement.

ISBN: 978-0-9891694-1-7

Library of Congress Cataloging-in-Publication Data
Passport to Danger / William F. Kelly

Printed in U.S.A.

Chapter One

The letter that would change Billy's life rested deep in a large canvas basket in a corner of the post office on board the *Queen Mary*. It would be another day on the Atlantic Ocean before it would arrive at the New York Post Office. Several additional days would be required before being delivered to the home of the Schmidt family in Northport on Long Island.

At that moment, unconscious and in distress, Billy lay sweating in his bed while the doctor examined him for the third time within twenty-four hours. Billy was still struggling for air. His family was led to believe that every hour he survived was positive for his recovery. Yesterday there was concern as to whether he would make it through the night. Now the doctor dared to suggest that he may have seen the first signs of improvement. Doctor Norton had his mother refill the humidifier in the room while he administered the medicine by injection.

The doctor met with the parents outside the patient's room while his sister, Greta, remained at Billy's bed-side. "I believe he has a fifty-fifty chance to make it. There is nothing more we can do. He is young and strong. I'm encouraged that the worst may be over."

"He vill live…yes, Doctor?" asked his mother.

"If he survives the night, he'll be up and around in several days. Call me in the morning. I'm encouraged," he said as he reached for the railing and started down the stairs.

The family took turns sitting with him through the rest of the night. Usually two would sit in the room, just in case one fell asleep. Even when they took a break and slept, it was only for an hour or two. The long night ended, morning came and Billy opened his eyes.

His breathing was slow and shallow but steady. Color was returning to his cheeks. His family fervently hoped that he was on the road to recovery. All that day and the next, Billy held his own. Finally they noticed deeper breathing, and the patient actually smiled.

Two days later, Billy adjusted his pillow and scooted up in bed to keep the setting sun from his eyes. It had been a good day. The humidifier and medicine were finally providing relief. Just being able to breathe was a wonderful experience.

Billy was aware that these asthma attacks usually happened in the summer and fall with the increase in pollen and ragweed. Playing in the fields and especially the woods seemed to bring on an attack as it did when he'd spent the afternoon last weekend playing with his friends near Moore's Pond. The pollen count was high, although he had no way of knowing. They were having fun fishing for bream and carp. He hadn't had an episode for several years, and he thought that maybe he was over them. That evening, as Billy was bragging about the fish he caught, he experienced a shortness of breath. He would just have to avoid the woods.

"How are you feeling?" his mother asked when she visited him to pick up his soup bowl.

"I would like some more of the chicken soup. That tasted good. I think I'm breathing easier." He paused, "When I breathe out…it feels better."

Billy's mother took good care of him, bringing him his meals, keeping the house quiet and keeping the humidifier filled, especially at night. It was now the fourth day since the onset of his difficulty breathing, and he was finally feeling that his lungs were expelling enough air, making it more comfortable to rest. Perhaps in the morning he would be able to get up and walk around the house, he thought. He hoped that he would feel well enough to eat his meals at the table and sit on the porch. Those would be his next short-term goals. Hilda, his mother, brought the chicken soup up to him just as the sun was beginning to set over the hills across the harbor. She pulled the shade to keep out the hot sun and turned on the light next to his bed. Then she propped him up with a second pillow.

"Greta wants to know if you're up for throwing the baseball. I told her I didn't think so," said his mother.

Billy, observing his mother, noted just how tall and thin she was. When they came to America in 1928 she couldn't speak but a few words in English, wore her black hair long, and was warm and compassionate. They all became citizens seven years later. Now it was the summer of 1937; her gray hairs were noticeable and her English had improved but she still retained her accent along with her warmth and compassion.

"I'm feeling much better, but I'm not ready to throw any fastballs just yet. I'll bet I'll be ready to play with her tomorrow," Billy replied. His sister often played catch with him. She caught well and got the ball back to him with some velocity, but it wasn't her choice of play. He was proud of the fact that she didn't throw like a girl. She would have much rather challenged him to a game of chess. Playing with Greta allowed him to keep his arm loose between baseball practices at the high school. He was on the varsity team, played short stop and batted in the clean-up spot. His dream was to one day play short stop for the Brooklyn Dodgers. He figured when he was old enough, it would be about time for Leo Durocher to retire.

"Greta vill be up to get your tray and you can tell her then. She'll understand," said his mom with a sunny smile.

As Hilda returned to her chores downstairs in the kitchen she thought of the many episodes of asthma Billy had endured in the past. She said a little prayer, thankful that once he turned fifteen, the severity had diminished, except for this episode. That wasn't to say that she didn't worry and feel sorry for Billy when he was struggling to expel air. She remembered the times when he was a baby and she wasn't sure he would survive to take his next breath. It had been much worse in the past, but this event brought back just how bad his asthma could be.

When Greta came up for the tray, she sat on the end of the bed for a minute. "You look much better today. Yesterday you were pale. But you look good today. Maybe tomorrow we'll throw the ball around."

Greta settled herself on the edge of the bed and talked with Billy for a while. "Do you need anything? Would you like me to get some fresh water?"

"No. I'm fine. I'm gonna listen to the Dodgers game on the radio for awhile. If I fall asleep, please turn it off when you come to bed. I don't like waking up in the middle of the night to static."

"I will. See you in the morning."

Chapter Two

Greta and Wilhelm easily adapted to America. Greta was only eight and Wilhelm six when they'd landed at Ellis Island. Billy remembered that first view of the Statue of Liberty. Like everyone else, he was on the deck hanging on the portside rail and straining to see in the early-morning fog. All of a sudden, the fog lifted and he saw her, shining in the morning sunlight. The postage stamps of Lady Liberty that he had saved as a child were now a reality. He was not only breathing clean free air, he was experiencing what it was to be free. He had previously memorized the words at the base of the statue that cried out to him, "Give me your tired, your poor, your huddled masses, yearning to breathe free." He read them now as he stared at the symbol of freedom. He and his sister jumped up and down, Billy shouting, "Greta, we're here. Isn't she beautiful?"

Hilda had a different recollection of their early days in America. Their family knew a German family that had moved from Saarbrucken several years before. That contact helped them find an apartment and get settled in Brooklyn. They lived on the third floor of an extremely small apartment and shared a bathroom with another family. Otto worked in a grocery store in the neighborhood, most often seven days a week and usually ten hours a day. Hilda helped out when they needed her. They lived in an area known as Flatbush, only a very short distance from Ebbets Field, the home of the Brooklyn Dodgers. This nearness to the ballpark led to a love affair between Billy and the Dodgers. Hilda didn't understand the game or why he wished to be a ball player, but watched as becoming a ball player became Billy's consuming passion.

Billy remembered how difficult it was to adjust in this new land. Yet he loved the crowded streets, the vendors selling produce on the avenue, the noise, and the sounds of numerous languages. He heard French, German, English, Spanish, Dutch and Yiddish often in the span of one city block. This new country was exciting and alive.

"Vegetables...get your vegetables here," was shouted with strange accents by the vendors, who pushed their carts up and down the streets. Windows opened and women yelled down to the vendors to wait till they could reach the street. The carts were pictures of color, with ripe red tomatoes, dark green watermelon, orange carrots and light green lettuce. Ask for a dozen of anything and the vendor always counted to thirteen. What a wonderful country.

Hilda remembered the problem the family had with the two Irish boys who hogged the bathroom they were forced to share with neighbors. Then when the bathroom was finally free they would return and insist that it was an emergency. They also liked to wait until Greta took her turn and they would wait outside, knocking on the door and telling her to hurry. She ignored them as best she could, but they made the task of sharing unbearable.

Otto remembered the long hours in the grocery store, carrying boxes of fruits and vegetables from the truck to the store. Sometimes he didn't get to eat lunch until mid afternoon. He often returned to the apartment tired and cranky because his back hurt and his legs were crying for rest.

He remembered how wonderful it was when, several years later, he got a job with an import/export company in Huntington on Long Island. After several months, the family moved from Brooklyn to Northport, a few miles from his work. His language skills and his accounting ability made him a real asset for his new company, and the money they made from selling their house in Saarbrucken was finally deposited in their bank account. It was less than Otto and Hilda thought they would realize, but it would do. They were looking forward not backward.

The children, Greta and Wilhelm, already spoke German and almost perfect French before they arrived and quickly learned English. Greta remembered living in Saarbrucken and both she and Wilhelm understood that Saarbrucken was a border town between Germany and France and had been occupied by both countries over the centuries. Both languages were acceptable and both were spoken. The children were gifted students, although Greta got all the awards because she applied herself. They, unfortunately, developed an undesirable Brooklyn accent. They had a tendency to drop the "er" and put "ah" in its place with such words as mother and father. Then with words that ended in an "a" they substituted an "er" as when they said idea or china. While such pronunciations were not correct, they spoke like all the other children in the neighborhood.

One of the first things Wilhelm did when he came to America was to change his name to Billy. He had been planning this since he first heard that they would be moving to America. He told the teacher his very first day in school that his name was Billy, and he wanted to be called Billy. The teacher had no objection, so the name stuck. He didn't tell anyone that he knew all the stories of Billy the Kid and Wild Bill Hickok. He told everyone that he admired Wild Bill Hickok, but secretly he loved the stories of Billy the Kid. He read about him from a book in the library and from some dime novels, becoming aware that many of the stories were legends, and probably untrue. Billy was determined to learn the truth about "the kid," and the more he learned, the more he realized that the life he was reading about was seriously exaggerated.

Greta was happy with her name and left it alone. Hilda adapted slowly to the name change and had a tendency to call him "Willy"—sounding like "Villy." But Billy patiently corrected her and she soon learned to call him by his preferred name.

The entire family became citizens in 1935, after spending many evenings learning about United States history. They all easily passed the written test to become citizens. On Thursday morning, the fourth of July, they stood in the crowd and observed the parade marching down Main Street. Few villagers remained home. In some places, the crowd was three and four deep. Soldiers from the World War walked proudly in front of the high-school band. Firemen and police struggled to keep their lines straight, brought on by a lack of practice. All the fire trucks drove in the parade as well as trucks from the public works department. The crowd was enthusiastic, with little ones sitting on the curb or on their fathers' shoulders, many waving red, white and blue flags. It was a wonderful sight.

They drove that afternoon in their new 1934 Ford Sedan to the county courthouse in Riverhead. There, with about fifty other people, they swore their allegiance to the United States of America. The family returned home, ate a meal of hamburgers and French fries on the back deck and stayed up to watch the fireworks over the town dock.

The following morning they took the train to Pennsylvania Station in New York and a cab to the pier on the west side. The Schmidts spent the day on the Hudson River Day Line on a boat named the Peter

Stuyvesant. The boat was named after a governor of what was the colony of New Netherlands under the control of the Dutch. They traveled to Indian Point on the Hudson River, where they enjoyed a picnic at one of the many tables on the side of the hill overlooking the landing and the river. The beautiful grounds provided them with a place to walk and take pictures. Their first full day of being American citizens couldn't have been more pleasant. It turned out to be a day the entire family would never forget, each for different reasons.

The boat returned to Manhattan in the early evening. They retraced their route by cab to Penn Station and took the Long Island Rail Road back to Northport. They arrived home just before midnight, the end of a long and memorable day. Otto didn't think a happier family was on that boat. Nor was any family prouder to be Americans. Billy made a silent promise that he would always be true to his new country. He would serve in the military, if they would have him and his asthma didn't interfere, and he would always be proud to be an American.

Chapter Three

Billy awoke in the morning feeling considerably better. He felt strong enough to walk to the kitchen, where his mother was setting the table. "Billy, you look good. How do you feel?"

"Fine, Mom. I'm starting to get my strength back and I can breathe."

"Good. Would you like a nice, big breakfast?"

"No. But I would like an egg and two pieces of toast with marmalade."

"That will take a few minutes. Sit down and I'll fix it."

His mother went about the task of boiling water, putting in the egg and dropping two pieces of bread in the toaster. Billy sat at the table and read the newspaper. He first went to the sports section to see if the Dodgers won last night—since he fell asleep before the game was over. Finding that they lost, he turned to the headlines.

Billy's bouts with asthma weren't his only problems. He was born with his left leg shorter than the other, giving him a limp. As a child, it was more a detraction to him than anything else, but when he became a teen he suspected that some of his fellow students avoided him because of his limp. He was called "gimpy" and "peg leg." These nicknames didn't bother him but he didn't like to be avoided or ignored. The limp didn't keep him from doing anything, except he felt a bit awkward when he danced. He knew the steps, but the limp made him appear less than graceful. As far as he was concerned, if it didn't interfere with him playing baseball, it wasn't a problem.

His mother served him the egg and toast and went about her usual routine while Billy ate and read. When he finished, he put his plate in the water in the sink and walked out on the back porch to see what was happening in the harbor. The smell of the harbor air was always pleasing to him. He enjoyed watching the yachts and sailboats beginning to stir in the early-morning July sunshine. Binoculars were kept handy to get a closer look at a particular yacht.

The Schmidt home on Fox Lane ran parallel to Woodbine Avenue and overlooked Northport harbor. As Billy looked out over the harbor, he recalled his first visit to this home. He loved the view but noticed the small back yard because the property was so steep. It was an exciting place with plenty to watch during the summer. Billy especially liked the wavy water patterns that would form on the walls and ceilings for several hours on sunny summer afternoons. The setting sun would reflect off the water and leave patterns, making the house appear alive.

Billy read about the history of Northport in a book in the school library. He learned the town of Northport was a quaint village on the eastern side of the harbor on the north shore of Long Island. Hills, left by the glaciers of the latest Ice Age, rose up on both sides of Main Street. The main shopping area was the first five blocks of Main Street, starting at the park and town docks. The stores near the dock catered to the many yachts that filled the harbor, providing ice, take-out meals, liquor and beer. In the summer it was a bustling little town. In the winter it was quiet. The locals seemed to like it that way.

Billy didn't see the mailman when he delivered the mail to the Schmidt house but heard a neighbor greet the postman. He waited a few moments before his curiosity got the best of him. He walked to the front door and gathered the mail that was dropped in the slot, placing the letters on the dining-room table. The letter from Germany stood out from the rest because of the stamps. The stamps were of boats sailing the high seas. Billy thought that was significant. He saw that it was addressed to his mother. He took the mail into the kitchen, where he found her.

"Mom, there is a letter from Aunt Ursula."

"Wonderful. Let me open it and we can read it together."

The two sat at the kitchen table. Hilda slit the envelope with a kitchen knife and read the letter aloud. It was in German. Billy had no trouble understanding what his mother was reading even if he had trouble reading the words his aunt had written in script. There was definitely a difference in the way Germans and Americans wrote in cursive.

69 Turnerstrasse
Saarbrucken, Germany

My dearest Hilda,

A day doesn't go by that we don't think of you and wonder how you are doing in your new country. I hope that all is going well for Otto in his job. It was so difficult for him to leave the wonderful position he had in Saarbrucken to work in a grocery store until you could get settled and he could find a good job. Tell him we're happy for him.

How are the children? I call them children, yet I know they are almost grown up. Greta must now be seventeen and Wilhelm fifteen. Am I right? It seems like yesterday that they were babies.

This summer Frederick will be taking some classes at the university and will not be able to entertain Wilhelm this year. He is really disappointed and wants to cancel his studies. We don't think that would be wise, not with the situation in the country. We promised him that Wilhelm can come next year. Tell Wilhelm to get his passport now so he'll have it when needed. Frederick is terribly disappointed that Wilhelm won't be coming but is planning lots of things for next year. This year Frederick has been directed to be at the Hitler Youth Rallies at the stadium, and if he isn't there they come to our house to ask why. Frederick's excuse is that he had to work. The official was none too pleased but told him that it shouldn't happen again. Next year things will have changed and it will be easier for Frederick to take a holiday.

Make plans for August, Wilhelm. Frederick will do the same.

Hilda, write me as soon as you can. I so enjoy hearing about your life in America.

Frederick sends his love with mine as well as young Frederick. Till we hear from you,

Best wishes,

Ursula

"Can I go next year?" said Billy. "Write back and tell Frederick that I'll get my passport and will start making plans for next year."

Hilda was slightly upset by the letter. While she didn't totally understand politics, she did not like what she was hearing out of Germany and was convinced that what was happening was bad. She didn't like Hitler and his gang in Berlin and especially didn't like the way he was organizing the youth in the big cities like Munich and Nurnberg.

But those cities were a long way from Saarbrucken, where Frederick and Ursula lived, and Billy would be safe with them. The paragraph about the official coming to their house was disturbing.

"Your father and I will have to talk it over. It is still a year away and a lot can happen in a year," said Hilda.

"I know, Mom, but I would like to see Frederick. He and I have always been close friends. He's fun to be with."

"Billy, I know you want to go. And I trust your cousin. He has always been very levelheaded. And Uncle Frederick and Aunt Ursula would like you to visit."

"I'm excited already. It gives me something to look forward to."

"In the meantime, we'll get you a new passport and you'll be ready if we can work it out. First, I have to talk with your father."

"I know, Mom. I'll be patient."

Hilda sat in the living room and closed her eyes, putting herself in Ursula's kitchen as Ursula was writing the letter. She thought that she wouldn't want to live in Saarbrucken now that the Nazis were running things. She was afraid that she might say something that would get them thrown in jail. Sometimes she was too outspoken, saying things that were ill advised.

She remembered how she and Otto had wanted to come to America right after the World War. They applied for immigration papers at that time. It was several years before they were selected. In anticipation, they had saved up a considerable amount of money. Otto was a Customs officer and made a good living. He also spoke German and French on a daily basis and learned English because so many British and Americans were visiting the country during the "roaring twenties." One of the reasons for Otto's big promotion was because he was tri-lingual. When they were chosen to come to the United States, they didn't hesitate.

Billy yawned his way to bed early that evening, as he was tired after spending his first full day out of bed after his illness. He fell asleep thinking of the good times that he and Frederick would have next year. They could swim, ride bikes, visit friends and enjoy each other's company, as they had as children and young boys. He liked Frederick and looked forward to his trip to Germany next year.

Chapter Four

Billy's recovery continued the following days, and a week later he returned to normal activity. He liked to swim and often hiked to the Town Park and beach that were about a half mile from their home. He would usually walk to the beach but during high tide he would use a neighbor's dock and swim from there. The neighbor was Thomas McCann. He owned the home immediately in front of the Schmidt's. Billy could sit on his deck and see the McCann house beneath him. Sometimes he would catch a glimpse of Mr. McCann pacing on his deck.

Billy would take a short cut through the McCann property when he wanted to use their dock. He was given permission to do so. Mr. McCann was his friend.

Mr. McCann's home on Woodbine Avenue was across the avenue from steps that zigzagged down to his dock. It was exactly fifty-two steps from the street to the dock, and because of his age it was almost impossible for Mr. McCann to make the trip. Being overweight didn't make the task easier. Billy knew his friend was now in his seventies and climbing stairs put a strain on his legs and hips as well as his heart. He sometimes asked Billy to fetch something from the dock or from the boat locker that was located on the dock. Billy was told where the key to the lock was hidden and would get whatever Mr. McCann needed. In return, Billy had use of the dinghy that was tied up to the dock. Nor did Mr. McCann mind if Billy used his dock to swim. It was a nice arrangement.

On this day it was about an hour before high tide when Billy left his towel hanging over the railing. He loved the smell of the sea, especially at high tide when the fishy smell wasn't too strong and the salt water filled the cove. Today he was anxious to join his friends at the town beach. He dove into the water and, with long strokes and a steady kick, made his way toward the strip of land that reached out into the harbor. His gimpy leg wasn't noticeable in the water.

He aimed for a sailboat and, when he got to it, aimed for a small yacht that was in the general direction he wanted to go. When he tired of the crawl, he switched to the breaststroke, then to the sidestroke and finally did the last yards using the crawl. He went from boat to boat in case he developed a cramp or got into some kind of trouble. He believed, with the confidence of youth, trouble like that would never happen. Nevertheless, he promised his parents that he would do it anyway; in his heart he knew they were right.

The beach had two floats, approximately twelve feet square. They were about sixty feet from shore and one hundred feet apart. Swimmers were expected to swim within the boundaries marked by buoys. A lifeguard would blow his whistle if anyone strayed past the buoys. Billy swam to the first float and climbed up the ladder.

Virginia was on the float, waiting for Billy when he came out of the water.

"I watched you swim from McCann's dock. What happened, did you get tired doing the crawl?" she kidded.

"Hey, what's the rush? I like to practice all my strokes and save my crawl so I can beat you."

"Not going to happen. Not this summer."

Virginia was seventeen, a big girl. She was going into her last year of high school. She always beat Billy when they raced, but he was definitely competition for her this year. None of the other boys would race Ginny, as she was called, probably because they knew she would win. They couldn't stand the razzing they would get. Billy liked having someone who would challenge him since he believed he was on the verge of beating her. He was experiencing a growth spurt; when it was over he felt that he would have the edge. For now, it was her title, but he aimed to take it away.

After a while, Ginny gave her usual challenge, which Billy accepted. They asked one of the boys on the float to start them off. The finish line was the other float. The competitors waited until no one was in the water between the two floats before the boy yelled his command of, "On your mark, get set, go." Ginny, as usual, got the better start, and although Billy closed the gap, he lost by an arm's length. He knew he was getting faster but was annoyed with himself that he couldn't beat her. They sat on the float to rest for a few minutes before Ginny cleared her throat.

"Do you really want to beat me, Billy?"

"Yes, and I will."

"I'll tell you how."

"Whata'ya mean, you'll tell me how?"

"I know something you're doing that's slowing you down. Do you want to know what it is?"

"Would you really tell me?"

"I just might. Probably by the end of the summer you'll beat me anyway, but you do something that really puts you at a disadvantage."

"I'd like to have you tell me." After a pause he continued, "That would be very nice of you. Why would you do that?"

"Because I like you and we probably won't have many more days here at the beach. I've known for sometime how you could easily beat me. If you had just a little coaching, you would be the faster swimmer."

"If I beat you, I promise I won't rub it in."

"No gloating?"

"No gloating.... I promise."

"OK. Here's how you can win. When you dive, you raise your head just as you hit the water. It slows you down dramatically. Then you spend the rest of the race trying to catch me. If you were even with me after the dive you would easily win."

"Are you sure I lift my head. I'm not aware of it."

"You lift your head," she said with conviction. "Take my word for it. Go ahead, dive in and pay attention to your head."

Billy dove in and upon coming to the surface he immediately turned around to face Ginny. "I do lift my head. Holy cow! I wouldn't have believed it. Let me see if I can keep it down," Billy said as he swam back to the float and climbed the ladder.

He dove off three more times, each time concentrating on keeping his head down. He could feel the difference. His dives were smooth, he went farther and he didn't lose momentum as he returned to the surface.

Ginny had a big smile on her face. "We've come to the end of an era."

When they raced back to the first float, Billy did win but only by a short distance. They both wore big smiles on their faces. Some of the boys on the dock were putting Ginny down and congratulating Billy, but Billy whispered a quiet thank you to Ginny just before she climbed the ladder.

Back on the beach, Billy dried his face with Ginny's towel. After she was dry she sat on the towel and offered half to Billy.

"I'll sit in the sand. I don't mind."

"Billy, Monday I start a job for the rest of the summer. I'm going to wait on tables at the Mariner Inn. I could use some money before going back to school. I'm going to miss swimming with you at the beach."

"I'm going to miss you, too. It won't be as much fun with you not being here."

"Oh, yes it will. You'll have the attention of all the girls. Believe me. They are avoiding you now because I'm here and they know you're interested in competing with me. Next week, all the girls will be chasing you."

"I might have to go to the Mariner Inn for some advice."

They talked for a while longer before Ginny excused herself to walk home. Billy had the long swim back to McCann's dock. He had a lot to think about. He was sorry Ginny would no longer be at the beach. He liked Ginny. She was a true friend.

Chapter Five

Frederick was annoyed with his mother for not telling him what she had written to his aunt in America. He kept asking his mother what she had written, but she repeated that it was a private letter and none of his business. To calm his curiosity, she gave him a crumb.

"I did tell Aunt Hilda that you were busy this summer taking courses at the university and that you would not be able to entertain Wilhelm this year."

"Mom, you know that isn't the truth. You don't want Wilhelm to come because I might miss the youth rallies and the Nazis would think you and Dad were against them," said Frederick. "I hate those stupid youth rallies and I want Wilhelm to visit us. We may never get a chance to do this again. Please. I really want him to come."

Ursula hated to admit it, but Frederick was right, even though he was acting like a spoiled child instead of seventeen. She had been visited by one of the Nazi officials, who told her that if Frederick didn't attend the rally it would throw suspicion on the entire family. The party might believe they were not patriotic Germans. It might even be presumed that they had Jewish leanings. Ursula tried to explain that her husband was an influential businessman and they loved Germany, but the official wasn't having any of it.

"We'll see just how much you love your country. Frederick will be at the rally on Friday night. See to it," was his parting remark.

That evening Ursula and her husband, whose name was also Frederick, spoke about Wilhelm coming to visit. "It might be okay for Wilhelm to come to Germany if he stayed out of sight and spoke only German. If Frederick were to go to America, some of those officials might see that as treasonous."

"I'm afraid of that youth rally official. He said that if Frederick didn't attend, it might be because we had Jewish sympathies. I don't like that guy," said Ursula.

Ursula told her husband what she had written and he agreed that this year was not a good time for Wilhelm to come for holiday. Both agreed that by this time next year the situation would be quite different, making a visit possible.

Frederick worked at his father's factory when he wasn't in school. They made gears for machinery. He did some menial work, such as cleaning up at the end of each day, but also spent time with his father learning the business. He would frequently make calls to suppliers when an order was late to inquire when it would be delivered. He understood it was important not to allow suppliers to be tardy. He would insist that they deliver when they said they would. He seemed to have no trouble understanding the accounting and the significance of the figures. He had the ability to remember last quarter's totals and knew if the new figures were higher or lower than previously. The numbers told Frederick if the company was ahead or behind and in what areas. His father told him that he would be a good businessman and Frederick believed him.

When it came time for the next youth rally, Frederick asked his father if he could work in the factory for the evening. His father told him that he understood how Frederick felt but this would soon pass and it was best to cooperate for now.

"If I go, I'm not going to wear that brown shirt with the red armband and black swastika," insisted Frederick.

"That's fine with me. Just tell them you had to work late and you came right from work."

"Maybe that will get me off the hook. I'll tell you all about it tomorrow."

That evening Frederick attended the rally and tried to appear invisible by sitting with some of his friends from school. Most of them were decked out in black shorts and the brown shirt with the swastika armband. They clapped and yelled at the appropriate times but were more interested in how big busted Inga had gotten since last summer, or if anyone thought Marlene was still a virgin. They acted like typical immature teens. They listened to speeches that spoke of the future glory of Germany and of the wonderful plans Hitler had for them. Most of the boys paid little attention. Yet when it was time to throw their arms out and shout "Heil Hitler," they thought that was great fun and went through the ritual with gusto.

The music was loud and the speeches enthusiastic. The young people were urged to be strong, to be faithful to their leader and to make sacrifices for their country. It was as if mass hysteria possessed all the young people, each trying to be more patriotic than his neighbor. It was frightening to Frederick that so many young people could be made to conform. Conformity, he understood, was not a quality youth naturally embraced.

The next day Frederick gave a description of the rally to his father. He told his father what was said in some of the speeches and that he felt most of the youth who attended did so because they were afraid not to. "No one was really listening to what was said, but it was repeated so often that it had to have an effect. What scared me most was that those clowns on the platform were serious. They could hardly complete a thought without blaming the Jews. And the music! It was so loud it hurt my ears."

"I think Hitler is gearing up for a war," said his father. "Our little factory probably won't be involved, but many of my fellow businessmen will be. They are concerned. We will have to pay attention to what is happening. Maybe, if we stay busy and don't make trouble, we can avoid being taken over by the party. Now let's see if we can make some more gears," he said as he arose from his chair.

"Ursula, do you wish we applied for immigration when Otto and Hilda did?"

"Now I do. At the time, I thought they were foolish giving up all that they had in Saarbrucken for a difficult life in a new country. Especially Hilda. She couldn't speak English."

"We didn't know that this madman would be running our country and would want to get us back into war."

"If we had known this, we would have applied also. Now I'm sorry we didn't.

"Since Otto got that job with the import/export company, they've been able to buy a nice house and put some money aside for college. The main thing is they don't have to be afraid to speak their mind without fear of being put in jail or sent to a work camp."

"Maybe things will be better by this time next year. I sure hope so."

Young Frederick kept a low profile, attending the rallies when he couldn't avoid doing so. He sat with a large number of young people who were enthusiastic. He wished he could make himself invisible. He was glad when school began in the fall and the number of rallies dropped off. When he had a chance to daydream, he thought about some of the things he and Wilhelm would do when his cousin visited next year. He knew Wilhelm liked to hike and so was planning a trip to the Idarwald near Trier. They could also swim in the local outdoor pool, and Frederick would introduce him to many of his friends. He had a special girlfriend named Irma and she had a friend just a year younger that he was certain Wilhelm would like. Her name was Elizabeth. It was all going to be a wonderful holiday. Next summer.

Chapter Six

In low tide, Billy would occasionally dig for clams. It was Mr. McCann who told Billy how to be a clam digger and where he should dig. He also let him use the dinghy to row across the harbor to the area where most of the clams were untouched. The bottom was also sandier on that side of the harbor. He could go where the clams hadn't been harvested and bring more back with him in a shorter time. Billy would tie the painter around his wrist and use his toes to locate the clams. Then he would dive into the shallow water and come up with a handful, depositing them in the dinghy. He got littlenecks, cherrystones and chowders. Mr. McCann taught him the chowders were the biggest and the littlenecks the smallest. Littlenecks and cherrystones could be eaten raw on the half shell or steamed. The chowders were used in soup.

The smell of the clams, the fresh, salt sea air and the warmth of the sun on his back and shoulders made Billy feel as if he was the luckiest young man in the world. The gulls screeched their request for food, providing music as they circled overhead. Occasionally, a gull would swoop down, attempting to frighten him. He was in his element, enjoying a life few were privileged to know. He wanted this summer to last forever.

When Billy returned to the dock, he put the clams into buckets. He set aside for Mr. McCann a full bucket with some of each. He kept two buckets for his family. He first used one of the buckets to wash the mud out of the dinghy, using a sponge to remove the water. When the dinghy was dried, he tied it up to a post set about four yards out from the dock. The painter was tied to a cleat on the dock. During low tide, the boat would sit in the mud. He put the oars in the boat locker, locked the door, hid the key and made the first of two trips up the stairs. Climbing fifty-two stairs with two heavy buckets was a challenge, but being fifteen and strong, he found this activity presented no problem. In fact, he liked the challenge. Mr. McCann thanked Billy and told him that he was most generous.

As Billy and Mr. McCann sat on the swing on the porch overlooking the harbor, Billy told his friend how good the clamming was and how he appreciated having the dinghy to get to the mussels. Sitting with Mr. McCann and talking with him was something Billy liked to do.

"Ya know, Mr. McCann, you never talk down to me. I like that." Billy rubbed his hands along his thighs, searching for the right words. "Are you all right? Is something wrong?"

"My son is having trouble with his boss. He may be fired because he told the boss what needed to be done to improve the business."

"That's what a good employee should do. Only an insecure boss would resent a suggestion from an employee."

"Billy, when you get in a position of authority, ask your workers what needs to be done to improve things. They then have a say in the solution and will more likely support the decision. If I've learned anything in my years of work, it is that the workers usually know the problems better than management. Many times they will also know the solution. Don't forget that and you'll be a successful manager. Besides, people will think you're wise."

"That just makes sense," said Billy.

"Then why is it so few managers ask their employees how to improve things? Remember to do that and you'll be successful in whatever you choose to do."

"I'll remember. It makes sense to me. And I'll remember when I become a manager." Billy knew that he would always remember the man who gave him that wise advice.

Billy made a second trip to the dock to get the rest of the clams for his family. When he returned home, he put the mussels into a galvanized tub and trickled water over them to wash them and get any dirt out of their system. After a day or so, they would be ready to be eaten. The family felt like royalty, being able to eat half a dozen clams on the half-shell or to have steamed cherrystones. Hilda learned to make both New England chowder and Manhattan chowder from the larger clams. The family liked the New England chowder best. Billy learned from Mr. McCann how to make a sauce to be eaten with the raw littlenecks. It was made with ketchup, horseradish, Tabasco and lemon. His parents never failed to enjoy their clams with a good Mosel wine, and Greta and Billy were invited to share a half glass with them.

As this glorious summer was coming to an end, Billy tried to get in as much swimming as possible. It was at the beach where he met Trish. Patricia was one of the girls who made a move when Ginny wasn't there, just as Ginny promised the girls would. The first day he went swimming without Ginny, Patricia swam up behind him and dunked him. He didn't know who it was. He saw someone swimming away, caught her and returned the dunk. On the float several moments later, he was embarrassed. She was wearing a two-piece bathing suit that probably didn't fit her last year and now left little to the imagination. She was going into the eighth grade and was either thirteen or at most fourteen. Billy overheard one of the guys call out, "Boy, is she stacked."

Trish was Irish, with strawberry-blonde hair. She was short but with a full figure. She was young but acted much older than Billy. She didn't seem to be at all embarrassed that her bathing suit was skimpy. Nor was she the least bit self-conscious. He recalled one day, soon after they'd first met, when she came up behind him while he was treading water near the float and dunked him from behind. He reached his arms over his head and pulled her down as he turned around and found his face smack in the middle of her breasts. He released her and his face reddened as he came to the surface. She just laughed and swam away, enjoying his embarrassment.

His face reddened again, just thinking about that incident.

Several days later they were sitting on their towels after having just had a swim. Billy leaned back on his elbows and stretched his legs out. "Seen any movies lately?"

Trish stretched out to match Billy's posture then turned her head toward him. "No. I don't get to movies much. How about you?"

"Not too much." Billy was waiting for the right moment to ask her, but it didn't seem that there was a right moment. "If I were to ask you to go with me to the movies, would you go?" Billy felt stupid for being so cowardly.

"I just might. It depends on what night I'd be free."

"How about tonight? I can pick you up at quarter to seven. Is that okay?"

'I'd like that. Pick me up at the foot of Grove Street at ten to seven. Wait for me there."

She was coming down the path from her house when Billy arrived. She had a textbook in her hand that she placed in the crook of a tree. They walked the short distance to the theatre and sat off to the side and near the rear. Trish chose the seats. They held hands and enjoyed the movie. When the movie was out at nine, Billy walked her back toward her home. When they got to Grove Street and the path, she retrieved her textbook.

"I'll walk by myself from here."

"I always walk a girl to her door. That's what my parents taught me."

"You're not going any further," Trish insisted. "No one knows I went to the movies and I'm not allowed to go out with boys. I'm supposed to be studying with a girlfriend at her house, and I'll get yelled at for being home after nine. Don't make things worse. Thanks for the movie," she said as she gave him a peck on the cheek and turned abruptly toward the hill.

Billy watched her make her way up the hill. She was a beauty. He thought that maybe she was just a bit too young. On the way home he could think of nothing else but Trish and the incident when she dunked him. He resolved to get involved only with girls his own age. He didn't think he could handle those older or younger.

Chapter Seven

Frederick wrote a letter to Billy shortly after school started in September. Billy got his mother to read it since he had trouble reading German script. Frederick apologized for being engaged in studies and work during the summer and assured Billy that next year he would have a full month off for holiday. He wrote about some of the trips they could take and what they would do when he came. There was even a brief description of Elizabeth. Billy looked forward to meeting her. He realized that a year was a long time to wait, but it gave him something to anticipate.

Frederick sent a picture of himself with his letter and Billy was surprised at the resemblance to himself. Frederick was almost two years older and had the same coloring: brown hair and blue eyes. He looked more mature, but in a year or two there would be little difference. They both had the same grandparents on their father's side and the boys were named after their grandfather. One was Frederick Wilhelm and the other

Wilhelm Frederick. A family resemblance wouldn't be so unusual.

Hilda got a glass of water before she continued reading Frederick's letter.

Wilhelm, I have some things to tell you about our life here in Germany. Because I wouldn't want a Nazi official to read what I will be telling you, I'm having a friend post this in France.

The Nazis are making changes in Germany, many disliked by the small businessman. The factory owned by my father now belongs to the state. We are still making gears but the factory has been converted so we can make ball bearings as well. The old equipment for making gears has been unfastened from the floor and moved closer together, causing the workers to have less room to work. The increase in the noise level, besides being annoying, has already caused an increase in the number of accidents.

Father has no say in the changes and hated having someone come in and tell him how the business would be run. Especially someone who didn't know the business. After several attempts at making improvements, they were ignored; Father was forced to go along. I told Father that it would do no good to antagonize these people. I was afraid they would call him subversive and threaten to send him to jail or a work camp.

I continue to work in the factory after school and on weekends, but my heart isn't in it. I told Father that we are not making sufficient profit to sustain the business and replace the old equipment. He was told that it was his patriotic duty to keep the cost low so the Third Reich could prosper. Father told me they would soon be cutting salaries so the country could prosper. This past week they cut salaries again and workers, as well. Those that were let go were immediately conscripted into the army.

There was a rumor among businessmen that Hitler had drawn up war plans and Germany would be at war within a year. We hope that will not be so. In any case, a lot can change in a year and we believe that things will be better and we can spend some time together.

Frederick finished his letter by telling Wilhelm that his mother and father were looking forward to his visit and that they would write again near Christmas.

Billy and his mother discussed the letter and Hilda voiced her concern over the control that the Nazis had over ordinary citizens. "It wasn't like that when we lived there."

"By this time next year, things will be much better. You'll see, Momma." Billy used the word "Mutti" as a sign of affection and to let her know that he understood. Other letters described how the holidays were celebrated as usual except that they were a lot more sober this year. The Schmidts went to Midnight Mass at Saint Nicholas Catholic Church in Saarbrucken and opened their presents when they got home. The three of them had a nice breakfast in mid morning and a goose for the evening meal. They knew that all Germans weren't as fortunate as they.

After reading one letter that arrived in May, Billy conjured up an image of how the discussion at his cousin's house might have gone. In March of 1938, when Ursula and Frederick were considering having Wilhelm for a month during the summer, there was news that Hitler announced "Anschluss" or union with Austria. They weren't sure what such a union meant, but it gave some Germans hope that Hitler wasn't contemplating a war. One evening, Frederick, Ursula and young Frederick sat down to discuss if it would be wise to invite Wilhelm to visit for the month of July.

"The only question I have," said the elder Frederick, "is whether Wilhelm will be safe." They always called him by his German name.

"I think he'll be safe if he speaks German," said Ursula.

"And I'll make certain he doesn't let on that he's American," said Frederick.

"If he speaks German, tells everyone that he is German and avoids any political talk, I think he'll be safe," said the father.

"Can I write the letter?" young Frederick asked.

"No, at least the first letter should come from your mother to Aunt Hilda. When they agree on the visit, you and Wilhelm can write to each other."

"I'll write it in the morning and let you both read it tomorrow night. If it covers everything and we all agree, we will post it the next day," said Ursula.

Billy was pleased to get the news. He had been looking forward to spending time with his cousin and eagerly looked forward to this visit. He already had his passport.

His father called a travel agent to arrange the trip. They knew that it would be by boat because of the prohibitive cost of air travel. He would sail from New York to Le Havre, France and take a train to Paris. A night in Paris and a train ride to Saarbrucken the following day would complete the journey. His knowledge of French would be useful as well as his ability to speak German.

When the arrangements were complete and Billy had an itinerary in his hand, he wrote to his cousin, giving him the dates. Billy would leave New York on July 6 and arrive in Le Havre on July 11. He would overnight in Paris and take the train to Germany in the morning. Frederick wrote back telling Billy that he would be met at the Saarbrucken *Hauptbanhof.* His train was due to arrive July 12 in mid-afternoon. Billy could stay until August 10, when he would take the train to Paris and Le Havre to depart on August 11. He would then arrive in New York on Wednesday, August 17. The travel agent also arranged rail travel as well as a room in Paris across the street from the railroad station. The train from the *Gare de'l'Est* would leave in mid-morning for Saarbrucken.

He carefully folded his letter and slipped it into an envelope. He wrote his cousin's address on the front. He'd have to take it to the post office for the overseas stamp. Then he stared at the itinerary, wishing the time would zoom by.

Billy was so excited he could hardly contain his joy. Greta had no female cousin in Germany and didn't have any close girlfriends, so no plans were made for her to travel. She did have a little bit of envy for her brother but was happy for him at the same time. In all honesty, Greta admitted she didn't want to go back to Germany, even for a visit.

That year, Greta was taking typing classes in high school. She bought a Smith Corona typewriter with the money she made from babysitting, so she could practice at home. Billy watched and was intrigued by seeing beautiful letters appear on a clean white page.

Billy stared at the address he'd just written. His handwriting was atrocious. He figured that whatever gene decides how you write was missing from his make-up. He could print passably well but couldn't read his own writing in cursive. He decided that he would also like to learn to type. He knew that most boys never learned to type as most secretarial positions were saved for women, but he wanted to learn. He asked his sister for help and she was pleased to teach her brother. When Greta wasn't using the typewriter, Billy was. He prided himself on his accuracy even if his speed was half that of his sister. He knew that if he ever had to type on a daily basis, his speed would increase.

Several months earlier, Billy and Greta had both applied for their passports. The passport they used to come to the United States was of two young children, six and eight years of age. Now they were almost expired. They had to bring their German birth certificates and their proof of American citizenship. The only trouble they had was when Billy wanted Billy to be his name on the passport, while all his documents said Wilhelm. The woman who was assisting them spoke to her superior, who told her that it was a formal document and would have to say Wilhelm. Then Billy got his back up and wanted his middle name to be listed as Fred not Frederick. The lady said that she couldn't do that, either.

"Billy, Wilhelm is a fine name and the name Wilhelm Frederick Schmidt is elegant. Besides it will be less conspicuous when you go to Germany. How could anyone not like that beautiful name?"

Billy didn't like admitting that she was probably right, so he just pouted a bit and decided he should cooperate. Really, what choice did he have?

Chapter Eight

He heard they needed a dish washer at a local restaurant and he applied. He didn't like the interviewer, who turned out to be the boss, but said that he could work when they needed him—all day Saturday and Sunday afternoon and evening. The pay was minimum wage, but it gave him the pocket change he needed to buy an ice cream cone or go to a movie.

The work was repetitive and endless, especially on Saturday night when they had their biggest crowd. The waiters would come in and ask him to wash the blue plates while the cooks would be yelling at him to wash certain pots and pans. They needed two people but the boss wouldn't hear of it. Billy worked as fast as he could and tried to accommodate everyone but knew that the situation was impossible. The kitchen was hot; perspiration would pour off him. Yet he didn't mind that part of the job. What he didn't like was being yelled at for what was not his fault and then not being offered any way to improve the situation.

What especially irked him was when he was washing blue plates and the waiters needed six or eight and he had washed only two or three. The waiters would take the plates from the pile of dirty dishes, wipe them off with a towel and take them to the chefs as if they were clean. They were still unsanitary; even though they looked clean, Billy knew they weren't.

He worked several weeks under these circumstances. One Sunday afternoon when it wasn't too busy, he had a chance to talk with the boss. He told him that they needed two people on Saturday night. They could accommodate many more customers if they had a second dishwasher. He told the boss that people didn't like to be kept waiting for their meal. The boss listened as much as he wanted to listen then, without saying a word, walked away. At closing time that evening the boss handed him his check and told him that his services would no longer be needed.

Billy didn't feel too bad when he walked home except that he didn't like the fact that he was fired. As he passed the town docks he realized that the boss was insecure and didn't know how to be a good boss. He sure didn't like someone half his age telling him how to run his restaurant.

Billy made a list of the clothes he would take to Germany and asked his parents to help him so he would not forget anything. He found it hard to believe it was mid-June already; soon he would be leaving for Saarbrucken. He had his ticket on the *Queen Mary* and was assigned a cabin. He would have liked to be in a cabin with a window but would have to settle for a porthole from which he could see the ocean. At least, that's what the travel agent told him. The trip was expensive enough, as it was. He really liked being in third class since he wouldn't have to dress up for dinner every night and there would be people his own age traveling in third class. He saw a picture of a third-class cabin and thought it would be fine, even if it was small. He had his passport and was pleased that the picture on it made him appear mature. Maybe he was growing up.

School was out on Wednesday, June 22, except for the seniors taking Regents exams. As the first day of summer vacation was warm, Billy spent it at the beach. The water, however, was cold. Only a few people were basking in the sun, and as yet no lifeguard was on duty. He thought about his trip to Germany and how much money he would need while there. He was glad he'd saved some money from working at the restaurant, even if it was a bad experience. Since so few people were at the beach, he walked down to the docks to see what was happening there.

Whenever he walked by himself, he was acutely aware of his limp. Even though he had a special shoe made that was slightly higher than the other shoe, he couldn't completely eliminate the limp. He shrugged. He would just have to learn to live with it.

At the dock, he never failed to find a yacht that he hadn't seen before, and the sailboats always got his attention. There was usually an old man or two sitting on the dock, fishing. He saw them catch flounder and eel. When an eel would get on the line, most of the fisherman would just cut the line and put on a new hook rather than mess with it. Billy liked talking with the fishermen, finding them all friendly and loquacious.

This day Billy was admiring an especially large yacht that took up a huge portion of the dock. A man dressed in white pants, a blue blazer and white captain's cap came out on deck and spoke with him.

"Do you know where to buy 'pigs in a blanket'?"

"Sure. On Main Street there is a restaurant."

"Would you please buy four for me and bring them to the yacht? Here's a twenty. Will that be enough?"

"I think that will be more than enough. I'll be back shortly."

He returned with the "pigs in a blanket" with a pickle and fries. The sailor told him to keep the change from the twenty, about eight dollars.

Before he went below, he asked Billy if he would like to do another chore.

"I sure would. What can I do?"

"Here's a five dollar bill. I need two bags of ice. Please bring them here and put them in the refrigerator in the galley. Keep the change."

It took about ten minutes for Billy to complete that chore. While he was in the galley he looked at that portion of the yacht and could not help but be impressed. It was elegant.

Billy stood still until the captain noticed him. "Sir, do you have any other chores I can do?"

"I'm afraid that will do it for today. But I'll keep my eyes out for you, and I'll call if I think of something."

"Thanks. I like your boat."

"You're welcome. So do I."

Billy felt he'd had a wonderful afternoon. He'd made more money in an hour than he would have made had he worked all weekend at the restaurant. He would have some money for a soda or popcorn at the Fourth of July concert in the city park just across from the town dock.

When the holiday came, Billy waved to his parents and set off for the park. The concert from the gazebo in the park was a medley of show tunes and patriotic band music. He bumped into a classmate by the name of Rudy, and the two sat on the grass together listening to the music. "Stars and Stripes Forever" always had a dramatic effect on Billy. When the show closed with that number he had to reach for his handkerchief to wipe his eyes. The gesture wasn't lost on his friend, yet he didn't say a word. Billy was so proud to be an American, sitting here on the grass of a quaint little town on Long Island. It was the anniversary of his becoming a citizen.

Earlier in the evening, before the band started playing a medley of show tunes, Billy spoke of his upcoming trip to Germany and what he and his cousin had planned. He told Rudy that he would be hiking in the mountains and swimming in the local pool. Before they parted and went to their own homes, Rudy said, "I know you're happy to be seeing your cousin and your aunt and uncle, but if I were you, I'd be afraid. It's not safe there these days."

Those words remained in his head long after he returned home.

Chapter Nine

They departed on the 12:16 train from Northport to Manhattan on July 6, 1938. Just Billy and his father were making the trip. The night before, he said his goodbyes to his mother and Greta and gave each a big hug. He told them he would miss them even if it were only six weeks. Once they arrived in New York, they took a cab from Pennsylvania Station to the pier where the *Queen Mary* was docked. There was a bar near the pier where father and son had a ham and cheese sandwich on rye with a kosher dill pickle and chips. Otto had a beer with his meal and Billy, a Coca-Cola.

It was two in the afternoon when the two decided it was time to board. They walked the final block from the bar to the pier and boarded immediately. Billy carried a small knapsack that held his tickets, travel information, a book, passport and money. Otto carried the duffel bag containing his clothes. Both were anxious to see Billy's accommodations.

The cabin was several flights below the promenade deck and had a card with the name Schmidt on the door. Billy noticed that most of the cabins had two names on them. It appeared that he would be the only one in his cabin. The room was small, but they'd expected it would be. It had a bed built in and a bunk above it with a ladder to reach the upper berth. There was a small built-in chest of drawers and a tiny table with two chairs. In the corner was a sink with a mirror above it. The porthole allowed Billy to look outside and a small amount of light to enter the room. Nor was the ceiling light any too bright.

"It's cozy, Son." His father threw the duffel bag on the upper bunk. "You can take out what you want later."

"I will. It sure is cozy. I'm glad I'll be living here alone. It would be a bit tight if I had a roommate."

"They didn't spend too much money on bright lights either. I guess that's so the generators can provide lots of light for those in first class."

"I suppose so. When we arrive in Le Havre, those in first class won't be there any sooner, will they?" Billy said, grinning.

"No, they won't. You'll all arrive at Customs together."

Down the hall was a large room with many tables. This was the dining room that would accommodate all those in third class. The kitchen was off the dining room. There was no outside light below deck, so light fixtures provided the only light. While they were adequate, they made the accommodation look a bit drab.

Billy didn't think he would lack for company on the trip and was convinced he would be much more comfortable in third class than if he had to dress for meals. Besides he would have nothing to say to all the rich people in first class. Maybe tourist class would be all right, but he felt that he would be happiest in third class. He'd already noticed more young people.

"Well, Son. It looks like there will be a good number of young people on this deck."

"It does, Dad. They all look a bit older than me. That's okay."

"That young man looks like he's having trouble adjusting to the slight swaying of the ship."

"He does. I'm glad that we live around the water and I won't get seasick."

"Don't be too sure. Remember, storms on the Atlantic can be brutal and last for days. That would make anyone sick."

"Let's hope we have clear sailing."

"I'm looking forward to meeting some of these people. We'll probably meet over dinner." The two continued touring the ship. Otto saw that Billy was adjusting just fine. "I'm really excited about this trip to Europe. It's my first experience being away from home and meeting so many interesting people. It will be an adventure."

"I'm glad you're comfortable about the weather. I think a lot of people get seasick because they're anticipating that they will."

"If I get bored, I'll write in my notebook or read one of the Zane Gray Westerns I packed in my knapsack. If I finish those two novels, I'll trade them with someone."

When Otto felt that Billy was comfortable with his new home, it was about an hour before the ship was scheduled to depart. "Son, I'm leaving now so I can get home at a reasonable hour. You never know about those trains. Here's a few dollars that you can buy something for Frederick,…lunch or some '*Kuchen*.'" Otto had the money folded and put it in the side pocket of his son's jacket. Give my love to Aunt Ursula and Uncle Frederick."

"I will, Dad. Thanks for making this possible. See you next month."

They walked together down several flights of stairs until they arrived at the gangway. "Thanks, again, Dad. I hope the trains are on time." They hugged each other. Billy was surprised that his father didn't want to let go. Finally, Otto wished his son a good trip. He slowly walked the gangway, stopped when he reached the pier and waved. He blended into the crowd. Billy quickly lost sight of him.

Otto found the bar where they'd had lunch and ordered a beer, drank it slowly, then returned to the pier to watch the ship prepare to leave on its trip to France. Finally, with whistles blowing, streamers flying and lots of fanfare, the huge vessel slowly made its way from the pier into the Hudson River. Otto saw his son looking over the side of the ship on the upper deck. He was waving at all the people below. Otto waved back but knew his son didn't know he was there.

The ship then began its journey through New York Harbor. Otto knew it would cruise past the Statue of Liberty and head for the open water of the Atlantic. He stood on the dock until the ship was out of sight, becoming the only person left on the now deserted pier. He walked several streets before he was able to hail a cab to take him back to Pennsylvania Station.

He didn't know why, but his heart was breaking.

Billy walked to the starboard side of the ship to get a perfect view of the Statue of Liberty. He couldn't help but remember the first time he and Greta saw her in the fog and remembered how beautiful she looked. Now, in the late afternoon sun, she was reflecting the sun in all her glory. Thinking of his bout with asthma a year ago, he was reminded of the words on the base of the statue. "Give me your tired, your poor, your huddled masses, yearning to breathe free." Billy walked slowly toward the stern, to be able to see this symbol of freedom until she was out of sight. He watched her disappear into the distance.

Within the first hour on board after he went below deck, Billy met several young men his age and a bit older. He sized them up quickly and decided to carefully choose with whom he wanted to spend time. At supper that evening, he discovered a good number of students traveling to Europe for vacation or to visit relatives or friends. There were more adults than students; these sat at their own tables. The students gravitated toward each other. Tables were moved together to accommodate others as they arrived. For the most part, this was not the first crossing for many of them. Billy did meet several for whom it was their first Atlantic crossing, so he didn't feel like he was such a newcomer. He knew he was one of the youngest even though he looked much older than sixteen.

At his table were four young men besides himself, and two young women. Everyone had a chance to tell everyone where they were from and their reasons for going to Europe. First they introduced themselves. Billy was definitely the youngest, just having turned sixteen, but because he was tall and had a light beard, the group took him to be older. Several asked him what college he attended and he told them he was still in high school. He shook hands with a twenty-year-old college student who was studying art. He reported he was on his way to Paris for the summer. His name was David, but he wanted to be called Dave. He was the unquestioned leader of the group. Henri, sitting next to him, was visiting his father, a businessman in Paris. Charles was returning home to Lyon after a year of school in Chicago.

The two girls, Bea and Charlene from Rhode Island, were traveling together and were being met by Bea's aunt in Le Havre. She was going to show them Paris and take them by train to southern France. The final person at the table was a quiet eighteen-year-old boy who was being shipped off to live with a relative who owned a vineyard near Bordeaux. His name was Joseph and he was painfully shy. Billy was most interested to speak with him when he had a chance. Everyone spoke English and another language, usually French, and one or two spoke German. Billy thought it would be good practice to start using his German as well as his French. It had been several years since he'd spoken German exclusively. Dave spoke fluent German and French.

After supper, he joined several tablemates in a stroll on the deck. Several paired off to watch the sunset and others wanted to see the engine room. Joseph excused himself to return to his quarters. Billy eventually ended up as the only student walking with Dave. Their conversation was pleasant and Dave had a way of steering the conversation back to what Billy was doing or liked to do. He found himself talking about Northport and the wonderful summer he was having and how he was looking forward to spending a month with his cousin.

"Be careful that those Germans don't recruit you into their German Youth Program," Dave chided.

"Of course not. My cousin wouldn't let them."

"Don't be too sure. They make it difficult to say no and they accuse you of being a Jew lover if you don't join."

"I'll be careful, but I'm an American citizen and they have no control over me."

"Yes, that may be so, but they can harm your cousin and his family. All I'm saying is that you need to be careful and wise. This is not a good time to be going to Germany. I'm Jewish and I wouldn't even consider going there."

"Do you think I'm in any danger?"

"Not if you can stay away from the politics. Don't go to the youth rallies; don't get into arguments about Hitler and his idea of a master race; don't advertise that you are an American."

"We'll take a few hikes and ride our bikes and maybe spend some time at the local pool," Billy ventured. "Maybe we'll do some sightseeing."

"Just be careful. For goodness sake, don't speak English. For this month, you are German."

Dave and Billy strolled around the deck several times. Both commented about how cool it had become since they started their promenade and it would get cooler once the sun went down. They made their way back to their quarters and retired for the night. Billy had a strange feeling when he thought about what Dave had said. He concluded that he was exaggerating the danger. After all, Dave was speaking from a Jewish perspective. Billy spent ten minutes writing his thoughts for the day in his journal and then began to read his western, *West of the Pecos.*

Maybe it was the tension or the length of the day or the sea air from their stroll around the deck, but it wasn't but a few minutes before his eyes got heavy. He turned out the light and was asleep in minutes even though it wasn't much past eight and light still streamed through the porthole.

Chapter Ten

Billy woke to the sound of the huge engines propelling the ship through the water. Below deck, the noise was louder than topside but the sound didn't bother him. In fact, it had been instrumental in lulling him to sleep the night before. He considered his cabin relatively quiet.

He dressed and headed for breakfast. In the dining room, he saw only one person from his table the night before. That was Charlene, now sitting with another young man who looked like he was getting ready to leave. She waved Billy over and introduced him to Michael.

"Michael just finished his third year at Princeton and is studying mathematics," said Charlene.

"Swell," said Billy. "I hear that Princeton is a good school."

"I think so. If you'll forgive me, I have to meet someone and I'm late. Maybe we can have lunch together later."

"I'd like that," said Billy.

He sat next to Charlene and asked her about breakfast.

"The buffet is fine. Get your breakfast and we can talk. I'm not rushing off."

Billy got a cup of coffee and orange juice and brought them back to the table. Then he got a plate and filled it with bacon, eggs, toast, butter and marmalade and a muffin. That was more than he usually ate for breakfast, but the buffet looked so appetizing that he didn't know what to choose or when to stop.

Charlene chatted about the trip so far and asked Billy how he'd slept.

"Like a baby. The drone of the engines put me to sleep quickly last night."

"Did your cabin mate sleep as well as you?"

Billy instinctively knew what Charlene was asking and he got a bit nervous. "I don't have a roommate."

"Bea and I are roommates, and I can tell you it is a bit crowded. She likes to go to bed early and I like to stay up late. You're lucky."

"I guess so. I thought I would have a roommate, but I'm not complaining."

Charlene switched the conversation to the weather and how she heard it would be changing. She said one of the deck hands was saying they would be experiencing some rough weather before the evening. Then she asked, "Do you get seasick?"

"I don't know," said Billy. "I didn't get sick when we came from Germany the first time, but I was very young then and I don't remember having any bad weather. How about you?"

"This is my third crossing. We had some rough seas the last time I crossed and I didn't get seasick. I don't think I will. Bea, on the other hand, gets sick if there is the slightest weather. I feel sorry for her. It must be terribly unpleasant."

Billy finished his breakfast and got a second cup of coffee. Charlene refilled her cup. They sat and talked and when Billy was finished he told Charlene that he was headed back to his cabin. She said that her cabin was down the same corridor, beyond where he was bunked. They walked the corridor until Billy got to his cabin. Charlene went on but he noticed that she glanced at the number on his door.

Charlene was a tall girl, probably five-nine. She had long blonde hair, blue eyes and a nice figure. She spoke well, was considerate and pleasant with everyone. She didn't appear to be stuck-up or snooty, and Billy was hoping that he could spend more time with her on the voyage across the ocean.

Charlene entered her cabin as Bea was brushing her teeth. "How's the weather on deck?" Bea asked.

"It's not bad yet, but we'll have some choppy seas today. You might want to go to breakfast now while it isn't too rough."

"I might. All I want is some coffee and toast. My stomach is already a bit edgy. Did you see that boy, Billy, this morning?"

"We had breakfast together. I'll put some money down that I'll be in his bunk before the day is out. So if I don't come back when you think I should, you'll know where I am. I didn't fall overboard."

"He seems a little naïve. I'll bet he's still a virgin. You might have more luck with some of the older guys. I think Billy is too young."

"He's probably eighteen or nineteen. That's not too young. If he hasn't had sex yet, it's about time he did."

"I think you're overestimating his age. In any case, I'm guessing he's inexperienced. Be careful; he can be hurt. I'm going to breakfast." Bea opened the cabin door and disappeared into the corridor.

Chapter Eleven

By mid morning, the weather was turning gray and the seas had increased. The *Queen Mary*, being so large, easily moved through the swells with little trouble. It was not comfortable being on deck, although Billy preferred being topside rather than in his cabin. He ate lunch with several of his original tablemates and made several more friends. In the afternoon, he took a little nap and paced the promenade deck several times for exercise.

On the second time around, a young lady who was also walking on the deck spoke to him.

"If you slow up a bit, I'd like to walk with you."

"I'd like to walk with you, too. My name is Billy."

"I'm Katherine, with a K. My friends call me Kate."

"May I call you Kate?"

"Please."

After a moment of silence, Kate asked, "Did you hurt your foot? I noticed that you have a limp."

"I was born with one leg shorter than the other. It's no big problem. I wear a shoe that helps a bit, but I still limp. I guess I always will."

"I just thought you might have stubbed your toe or twisted an ankle."

"No, I've always had a limp. I forget that I limp except when I have to dance or walk down the aisle by myself. Then I become self-conscious."

Kate looked dainty and sweet in a white dress with a knitted white shawl over her shoulders. Billy pegged her as one of the rich children who travel in first class. She stayed away from the rail as much as possible to avoid the wind and any spray.

"I haven't seen you in the dining room. Don't you eat?"

"I eat in the third-class dining room, below deck. It's not as elegant as first class or even tourist class, but the food is good."

"Why do you travel third class when you could go first class?"

"Money. My family is sending me to Europe to visit a cousin, and my aunt and uncle. It's considerably cheaper to go third class. Also there are a lot of students and young people close to my age who travel third class."

"That must be nice, speaking with people your age. I have to sit with my parents and other adults. They talk about such dull things: the stock market, world news, that crazy Hitler and President Roosevelt. I don't have anything to say and it's no fun. Maybe one evening I can eat with you."

"I'll bet we could do that. We can't eat in tourist or first class since we didn't pay for that privilege, but you can eat with us. Just make sure your parents know where you are so they don't make a big scene and send a search party after you."

"Oh! I can't go anywhere unless my parents know where I'm going."

"How old are you?" Billy asked.

"I will be sixteen in September. How about you?"

"I turned sixteen in May."

"I can't believe you are only sixteen. You look at least eighteen. I thought you were in college."

"It's because I'm tall and have a dark beard. Or it will be dark when it grows in completely. Maybe after I shave I'll look younger.

"Don't shave. You look swell they way you are. Very mature."

"Look, Kate, tonight it might be a bit rough at sea. Suppose we meet up here on the promenade deck tomorrow at five-thirty and I'll take you to supper with me and introduce you to some of my friends. Maybe your dad would like to meet me so he will know you are safe. I'll be here at this spot at five-thirty tomorrow."

"That will make my father happy. He will not understand why I would rather eat in third class."

"Oh, by the way. We're much less formal in third class. You don't have to dress up. In fact, dress down."

"Thanks for telling me. I'll see what I have that is less formal."

Billy said goodbye to Kate and headed below deck. It was almost time for supper and it seemed wise to eat before the weather got worse. Billy had some chicken and vegetables at the buffet and retired to his room.

The seas were increasing ever so slowly. When he lay down he could feel the rise and fall of the ship and a slight rocking from side to side. So far, he hadn't experienced any nausea. About seven there was a gentle knock at his cabin door. He opened it to find Charlene leaning casually against the wall.

"I missed you at supper," she said.

"I ate early. I wanted to rest a bit."

"Are you feeling seasick?"

"No, are you."

"Not yet. I hope that I never get seasick again. Are you going to invite me in?" she asked."

"Please. Please come in."

There were a few minutes of discomfort with neither knowing what they should say. Billy had the feeling that Charlene had practiced what she would say to get him to allow her to come in, but after that she was at a loss for words. Billy offered her a chair by the table and he prepared to sit on the lower bunk.

Just as Billy turned around to sit, Charlene put her hand behind his head, pulled his face toward hers and kissed him on the mouth. Shocked, he blurted, "If you want to kiss me, all you had to do…" She kissed him again. She pushed him into the bunk and climbed on top of him, pressing her breasts against him and holding his arms.

"Wait a minute. Stop. I'm not ready for this," he managed to say.

"Don't you want to make love to me?" she asked.

"Maybe…No…I don't know. I'm surprised, that's all. I don't know what I want."

"Then maybe I'll come back when you do," she spat at him as she climbed off him and moved toward the door. "And maybe I won't come back," she managed to say just before she slammed the door.

Chapter Twelve

Billy was left in a terrible state the rest of the evening. He alternately wondered why he was so stupid to refuse to make love to a beautiful girl. Then he was proud of himself for standing up to her. His next thought was that he was stupid. He decided to be glad that he didn't give in. Then he realized that he really didn't say no but rather that she surprised him. He decided he would have sex when he was ready, then changed his mind several times again. As the evening wore on he considered his last position as foolish. He didn't know what he should have done, but what he did just didn't seem very smart. He smashed the pillow five or six times and buried his head in it, putting the pillow from the upper bunk over his head. It took a while before he fell asleep.

The next morning was still gray and the seas quite rough. By noon there was light overhead, breaking through the clouds intermittently. By three, the seas had calmed down considerably and the sun was visible. Billy ate his meals by himself and stayed in his room. At five he walked the promenade deck and at five-twenty he met Kate and her father, Mr. Whitney. Mr. Whitney asked Billy some questions about where they ate and were any unsavory characters in third class.

"Mr. Whitney, the people in third class are there because they don't have as much money as the people in first class. I will personally guarantee that Kate will feel welcome and safe, and I'll return her to her cabin after we stroll once around the promenade deck."

"If I have your word that you will see to her safety, then she may eat dinner with you. Why she would want to, however, is beyond me."

"She would want to do that because she will be eating with people who are interested in the things she is interested in and can talk about," Billy said, using his most diplomatic tone of voice. "Believe me; I would rather travel in third class than first class even if I had the money. It's more fun and I don't have to dress for meals."

"I don't understand that, but if you say so. Kate, we'll stop by your cabin after dinner."

"That's fine, Father."

Billy led Kate below deck to the dining room and was pleased to see a few of his friends. Dave, Michael and Joseph were at the table for eight. Dave stood up and gestured for them to come over to sit with them. Billy was pleased that Kate was being warmly welcomed. She was dressed in slacks and a blouse and even though they were appropriate for the occasion, it was obvious that her clothes were elegant. Billy introduced Kate to everyone and told her that they would be eating buffet style. "Good. For once, I'll get to choose the food and the amount I want."

Dinner went well and Billy didn't have to encourage Kate to talk. She was a delightful conversationalist, asking everyone questions and showing quite a bit of naiveté as she did so. The boys were surprised with her lack of understanding of how most of the world lives but found her delightful, nevertheless. Billy just had to watch and listen as she made a hit with the dinner group. Charles joined them near the end of the meal and protested that Kate and Billy were leaving too soon.

"On my behalf and that of our little group," Dave began, "I hope you will grace our table again sometime. We enjoyed having you. And you don't need an invitation."

Goodnights were spoken before Billy and Kate made their way up several decks, to the promenade deck, then walked a full revolution. Billy conveyed to Kate how nice it was to have her for dinner and assured her that she was a big hit with Michael, Dave and Joseph. Even Charles wanted her to stay longer.

"Kate, maybe I'll see you tomorrow. In any case, it was a wonderful evening and I was glad that you accepted my invitation."

"It was my pleasure and if I don't get too much static from my father, maybe I'll do it again. It is much too stuffy in first class…although I like my cabin."

Billy followed Kate to her cabin and said goodnight as she extended her hand.

Chapter Thirteen

The fourth day out was good sailing and the crew were predicting they would make Le Havre sometime early in the morning of the sixth day. Billy was walking on the promenade deck shortly after breakfast, as was half the ship, when he felt an arm slip into his. He turned to find Charlene hanging onto him.

"I'm sorry I was so rude and pushy the other day. I need to apologize to you."

"No, you don't. I just wasn't ready." Billy hesitated, then said, "You took me by surprise. I…I wasn't ready…to tell you…I've never had sex before. I didn't want to tell you that. I didn't know how to behave and I guess I was a bit scared."

"Are you scared of me, now?"

"Up here on deck, of course not." He hesitated then continued. "I've been thinking about it and I would like to have sex with you. I know this is not a big romance…and it won't last, it will only be a fling…but I'm ready to try. You may have to give me a few pointers."

"Tell me when."

"Let's finish this lap around the deck and give me a few minutes to tidy up the room. Then I'll wait for you in my cabin."

Billy knew that he wouldn't be scared this time, as he'd thought about almost nothing else since Charlene had come on to him when she was last in his cabin. When she knocked on the door, he had the room presentable and had brushed his teeth. She locked the door and without embarrassment began undressing. He did the same.

She stood naked in the soft light coming from the porthole. Billy didn't know how beautiful anyone could be, presenting herself like that to him. He stepped forward, aroused and ready to make love for the first time. A moment later, they were in his bunk wrapped in each other's arms.

It was almost lunchtime when the two thought it was time to take a break. The truth was that their stomachs were dictating the need for some nourishment. Charlene left to go to her cabin to freshen up and told Billy that she would see him later in the dining room. Billy went to the dining room and waited. Charlene never came.

He returned to his cabin and lay on the bed, reading his novel. A tap on the door an hour later woke him from a catnap. Charlene charged in and announced that Bea wasn't feeling well and she had stayed with her for a while. She said that Bea's problem was more emotional than physical but didn't say more.

Charlene was not at all bashful stepping out of her clothes and standing naked in front of him. He had to admit that she was the most beautiful thing he had ever seen. Then she pulled back the covers and lay on the bed while Billy got undressed. They spent the afternoon in the bunk, getting up when it was time for supper. Charlene said that she wanted to check on her roommate. "I'll be back when I can get away," she whispered as she closed the door.

Near midnight, Charlene returned again. Billy was asleep but welcomed the knock on his door.

"I couldn't stay away," she whispered.

"I'm glad. I fell asleep but knew you would come. You realize that we have only one more day?"

"Yes, and I want to make the most of it.

And they did. They left the cabin only for meals. They made no attempt to fool anybody. They didn't care. At supper, on the fifth day out from New York, they were told they were getting near France and would be disembarking at about six in the morning.

After supper, Billy packed all his clothes, books and belongings. He decided to throw his journal away since he wasn't going to write about his experience with Charlene. He would just tell his parents that it fell overboard or he left it on the train. He was almost finished when Charlene arrived.

"I'm all packed and Bea is finishing up. I told her that I was spending the night with you."

"I'm glad. Maybe we'll get some sleep."

Both were so exhausted from their lovemaking that they did sleep. The bed was too small for both of them. Spooned, they managed to doze. They awakened when the engines stopped.

"Billy, let's say goodbye now as I don't know how much attention Bea will need. I may not be able to get away to kiss you goodbye. Besides, we don't know who will be watching us.

"It's better to say goodbye now. I'll always remember our time together."

"You were wonderful. I'll remember this crossing if I remember nothing else."

They kissed, longer than necessary but as was appropriate for the occasion. Then Charlene turned and quickly left the cabin.

Chapter Fourteen

After Charlene left, Billy felt empty. He went for breakfast and met Dave, who was having his second cup of coffee. Dave invited Billy to go with him as far as Paris and Billy said that he would appreciate having someone who was experienced to show him around. As they were lining up for Customs, Kate came over to Billy and Dave and told them that the dinner she had with them was the highlight of her entire trip. She kissed both of them on each cheek, French style, and returned to her parents.

They arrived in Paris shortly after noon and took a cab to the hotel near the *Gare de l'Est*. Billy changed some dollars into French francs, and he and Dave took a cab to Notre Dame. From there they walked past Le Louvre to the Place de la Concorde, the entire length of the Champs-Elysees, to the Arc de Triomphe. They crossed the river Seine and viewed the Eiffel Tower from below, not having time to ascend to the top. After a sandwich at a sidewalk café near the tower, they took a cab to Billy's hotel so that Dave could pick up his luggage. Then he left for his quarters.

As they walked the Champs-Elysees Dave asked Billy a few questions. "I hope you don't mind me asking, but did you sleep with Charlene?"

"Yes," said Billy. "The first time she came on to me I said 'no.' She scared me. I should say she took me by surprise. I thought I chased her away for good. She apologized and this time I wasn't taken by surprise. I wanted to sleep with her."

"I could tell that she was going to be in someone's bed during the crossing. Those girls are kept under fairly tight wraps. With Bea being seasick, Charlene had more freedom."

"Dave, that was my first sexual experience, and I liked it. I may never get an opportunity like that again."

"I'm sure you'll have many opportunities in the future. That was the first of many. May I give you a little advice?'

"Sure, what's on your mind?"

"I hope you don't mind me changing the subject but I need to tell you what I believe. Living in Germany is dangerous these days. The Nazis have no concern for human life. Americans are fair game. Don't let anyone, besides your relatives, know that you are American. Speak with your cousin and agree to one story. Decide where you will tell everyone that you live. It could be a nearby town or a section of Saarbrucken. You are staying with your cousin while your parents are on holiday. Make up a story like that. Just don't let on that you're American."

"Dave, I appreciate your concern and I'll talk about these things with my aunt and uncle. I'm sure they will tell me what I need to do to remain safe and not get in trouble with the Nazis."

"Please do, Billy. That's my concern. I don't have anything more to say."

After Dave picked up his luggage at Billy's room and took a cab to where he was staying, Billy had a chance to think about Dave's advice. He considered it wise advice even thought he thought Dave was a bit too cautious. That was probably because he was Jewish. Anyway, Billy was determined to be careful and keep his citizenship secret.

Billy thought about what Dave said about Charlene planning to sleep with him, probably the first evening on the ship. He was surprised that Dave was that astute and could tell what Charlene's intentions were. He was definitely a reader of people.

He went to bed that evening pleased that Dave took the time to show him the beautiful city of Paris. He thought that maybe he would leave a day early on his way home to see a few of the places that he missed. Sacre Coeur, the Place de la Bastille and the Latin Quarter were all on his list.

Chapter Fifteen

The train ride from Paris to Saarbrucken was pleasant. The train was delayed at the border while two German soldiers with machine guns entered the carriage with an equal number of Customs agents. A customs agent examined passports while the other checked luggage. When they got to Billy's compartment, they found an old woman sitting across from him and a mother with a baby near the aisle. He checked their papers and luggage first. The Customs agent looked at Billy's passport and asked him, in German, where he was born. He told the agent, in German, that he was born in Saarbrucken. After a cursory examination of his knapsack and duffel bag, the agents and soldiers moved on to the next compartment.

Frederick, the father, Ursula and young Frederick met Billy at the station. His aunt made a big fuss over him, about how much he'd grown and what a handsome young man he was. She called him Wilhelm, a name that sounded strange to him. Frederick shook his hand and asked about the train ride and the trip across the ocean. Young Frederick took his duffel bag with his left hand and shook Billy's right hand with enthusiasm. The smile on his face told Billy that he was welcome. Billy noticed the resemblance to his cousin, as did Frederick, but it was his mother who said, "You two almost look like brothers."

The Schmidt family lived in a brick house set on a small lot and quiet street with many trees and shrubs. It had a modern kitchen with a dining room on the other side of the pass-through counter. There was a nook in the kitchen for breakfast. The living room was generous; above it were three bedrooms reached by a circular staircase. It was a comfortable house, fit for the chief operating officer of a German company. The yard in the front was minuscule and the area in the back of the house wasn't much bigger. It was not for people who liked to garden.

They had a fine supper back at their house, and Wilhelm found that he was having a little trouble speaking German. Since he'd learned English, he had a tendency to put the verb in the middle of the sentence, instead of at the end, as the Germans do. Once when he suggested to his uncle that he be called Billy, his uncle said that it would be wiser to be Wilhelm for a month. Since their last letter inviting Billy, the authorities were paying closer attention, making more frequent visits and asking more questions than previously. "An American might be in some danger if it was found out by the wrong person or persons," was his uncle's explanation.

"So you are Wilhelm, and you are my nephew from the other side of Saarbrucken, just like it was before you left," said Frederick.

"I'll be Wilhelm and will keep my passport hidden. I'll tell people that my parents are on holiday and I'm living with my aunt and uncle for a few weeks. My ability to speak German will come back in a few days. Then I'll sound just like Frederick."

"You even look like me," Frederick commented. "At least the way I looked a few years ago. There is a strong family resemblance, you know. People will believe we are brothers."

"Why don't you take Wilhelm for a walk around the neighborhood while we do the dishes? Then I'm sure he will want to get to bed early," said Ursula. "Tomorrow you can tell me all about your trip and I want to hear about your sister and your parents. Go for a walk now."

Frederick and Wilhelm walked and talked and got caught up on the news. Wilhelm decided not to say anything about Charlene, since he wasn't sure how he felt about it and didn't feel he should talk about the experience just yet. Nor did he know how Frederick would handle the information. His conscience was bothering him a bit, although he couldn't say that he was all that sorry. Maybe time would heal his mixed feelings and give him some perspective on what had happened. He hadn't planned on having sex on his trip across the ocean but now that he had, he wasn't all that upset. Somehow, he felt older than his sixteen years just because of this incident. He knew that he wanted Charlene and enjoyed the experience but didn't expect it and was unprepared for the intimacy. Yet he concluded that he wouldn't regret this brief encounter even if his conscience told him he shouldn't have done it.

"Frederick, what about the youth rallies? I've heard bad things about them." He changed the subject so he wouldn't have to talk about Charlene.

"The Nazis want all the youth of the country to attend. All they do is rant against the Jews and the gypsies and praise the Aryan race. Then they sing patriotic songs and stir up the young people to hate those who are different. At every opportunity they get everyone throwing out their arms and shouting 'Heil Hitler.' And they play military music over the loudspeakers so loud as to wake up the dead. I try to avoid going to the rallies."

"How can you avoid them? Aren't you required to attend?"

"Yes, but my father sometimes insists that I work overtime on nights we have rallies. Sometimes I'm out of town on business. This new regime forced us to make ball bearings in addition to making gears, giving me a good excuse to work overtime to meet the quota."

"I don't like that I have to keep my American citizenship a secret. I feel somehow like I'm a traitor."

"Look at it this way, Wilhelm. You would get me and my parents in a lot of trouble if the authorities were to find out. If America were to get in the war, they would look at us as sympathizers. I know it must hurt you to deny being American, but do it for us, so we don't get in trouble."

"I will, Frederick. I would feel awful if they hurt you because of me."

Frederick told Wilhelm some of the things that he planned for his cousin while he was on holiday. A weekend trip to Trier was planned, and the next to last week of the holiday they would hike in a forest about fifty kilometers from Saarbrucken. They would ride bikes to the forest and stay in a pension with other hikers. Frederick would have two full weeks that he could do with as he pleased. Several days at the swimming pool were on the calendar. Various friends would accompany them to the movies or to a party.

"I see that you still have your limp."

"Yes. I'll always have the limp. It's much less when I have the proper shoe for that foot. But, yes, I've learned to live with it. It doesn't hinder me in any way, so I guess I'm lucky."

Back at Frederick's house, Wilhelm yawned and stretched, ready for sleep. He was taken to his room and within minutes was dreaming of his time with Charlene.

Chapter Sixteen

The days sped by and Wilhelm enjoyed his time with Frederick, who was supposed to be on holiday. Nevertheless, he was sometimes called back to the factory for several hours. Since Frederick had finished the German equivalent of high school, he had worked in his father's factory and postponed going to the university. He confessed to Wilhelm that he would probably be forced to join the military, a prospect that did not please him at all. His father was using the excuse that he was needed at the factory in order to make the change to manufacturing ball bearings. Frederick, the father, even faked a heart attack and turned the factory over to Frederick to convince the Nazis that his son was needed. So far it was working.

Wilhelm had use of one of the two bikes that belonged to Frederick and so was able to travel when he wanted. He found a small park not far from the house where he liked to go to read his western novel when Frederick was called in to work. He covered his book with brown paper so the English title wouldn't be seen. He found a café that served tea and *Kuchen* and Wilhelm often found it difficult to resist the temptation. The cakes were all so inviting, smothered in icing.

One evening, Frederick and Wilhelm drove their bikes to his girlfriend Inga's parent's home. There Wilhelm met Elizabeth. She was about the same age as Wilhelm and very pretty. Her hair was red and her cheeks and nose were peppered with freckles. She could have passed for an Irish colleen. She seemed so innocent. Wilhelm thought that was probably because he no longer was. Would she be able to see that he had lost his innocence? They walked in their neighborhood and stopped for some tea and *Kuchen* at a small restaurant nearby. Wilhelm told Elizabeth and Inga that he lived in Burback, a neighborhood on the western side of town where his parents once owned a home and where he grew up. He said that his parents were on holiday and he was visiting his cousin during the time they were away. They easily accepted his lie.

Wilhelm felt uncomfortable telling the lie, even though he knew it was necessary. It didn't mean anything to Elizabeth but was important to keep his aunt and uncle out of trouble. He just didn't feel right denying his allegiance to his new country.

These days passed quickly with bike riding and swimming in the day and visits with Inga and Elizabeth during the evening. Frederick was promised two weeks for holiday without interruption. The two young men planned in earnest what they would need for their hiking and how much it would cost. Staying in a youth hostel would save them a lot of money; food would be their only real expense.

They enjoyed the first week of his vacation around Saarbrucken and on Monday, August 1, they put their gear on their bikes and pedaled the fifty kilometers north to the forest and the hostel. The first evening they met many young men like themselves, and the conversation flowed around questions of which trail would be best to take. Frederick had hiked one of the trails and was inclined to take a different one. Wilhelm didn't care which trail they took. There were several young female hikers, but they were obviously attached.

On Tuesday they put lunch in their knapsack and took plenty of water. They would start on the blue trail. The trees were sparse, making the views panoramic. They talked it over and decided it would be better to start out slowly and increase the difficulty as the week went on. It was a glorious day. The temperature was cool in the morning and the air clear. Both Frederick and Wilhelm enjoyed the trail.

"I think we were wise to begin with the easiest trail our first day," said Frederick.

"We get to know what shape we're in and what our capabilities are."

"I don't think we'll have any difficulty, although I understand some of the trails are difficult."

"I look forward to the challenge," Wilhelm said.

It was a good trail to begin their hiking. About fifteen kilometers long, gentle hills but nothing too steep and low bushes set back from the trail made it ideal. It was the trail with the best views.

The following day, they chose the yellow trail and found it to be a bit more strenuous. "Now this is hiking," said Wilhelm. They found themselves breathing hard and being forced to stop to get their breath. The hills were steeper, the trail was eighteen kilometers in length, and there were some spectacular overlooks spaced far apart.

"Look at this view," said Frederick. "It was worth the long, uphill climb."

"It also gives us a reason to take a water break. I'm sweating and my heart is pumping."

"We're ahead of schedule. Let's take a good break." The two cousins talked freely to each other throughout their hike and Wilhelm was anxious to hear his cousin's thoughts about his liaison with Charlene.

"Coming over on the boat, I met a young woman."

"How old was she? You said a young woman so I'm guessing she was twenty or older."

"I think she was twenty. She came on to me in my cabin and I acted stupid and she left. I was angry with myself. Several days later she apologized and we spent a lot of time in my cabin…in bed." Wilhelm paused. "It was wonderful. I feel a bit guilty."

"I wouldn't feel too bad. Is the relationship over or will you be seeing her again?"

"It's over."

"Then don't let it bother you, get on with your life and count it as an experience you had when you were sixteen."

He told Wilhelm how close he and Inga had come to almost ending their relationship because it was starting to become sexual. Now they had decided to avoid times and places that would get them in trouble.

"That doesn't make it easy," said Frederick. "It just means that we will be able to continue our relationship. I really love her and hope to marry her someday. I'm afraid that I'll get her pregnant and then all my plans will have to be discarded."

"You know, I didn't even think about that when I was having fun with Charlene. Now I wish she didn't know as much as she does about me."

"Did you exchange addresses?"

"No."

"I suspect you'll never hear from her again."

"I hope you're right."

"She was probably smart enough to know that she wouldn't get pregnant. In any case, pray that she doesn't."

"Speaking of prayer, why don't you go to church?"

"Our pastor has spoken out against the Nazis and now is missing. He is probably in a camp someplace or maybe he's dead. The Gestapo can be seen every week at Mass, not to worship but to observe, monitor the sermons and arrest anyone they think is against them. Times have changed, Wilhelm, and my parents would rather avoid Mass than be labeled as against the regime."

"I didn't know things were so bad."

"They are terrible for the average German but ten times worse for a Jew. Being Jewish is a crime in itself." He got up from the log they were sitting on and gazed off into the distance, his expression dark, as if he saw something evil out there. "Hitler is gathering up as many as he can and shipping them to work camps and executing those who are unfit for work. The country has gone to hell in just the last few years."

"Is it dangerous for me to admit that I'm an American?" asked Wilhelm.

"It is now. A year ago no one was paying attention. But now, they might put you in a camp. Being Catholic isn't a plus either, at least in our area, since many priests have spoken out against the Nazis. I should have told my parents that it wasn't safe for you to come, but I did want you to visit. Now I'm pleased that you came but still have my concerns about the wisdom of the trip. One reason we are hiking is because we can be away from the city and not be bothered by the Nazis."

"I'm glad I came. I don't like it, but I'll keep my American citizenship a secret."

Chapter Seventeen

By Wednesday Wilhelm and Frederick were feeling like brothers. They had no more secrets and trusted each other with all their hopes and dreams. They had known each other since they were children, and both had memories of happy family get-togethers. Now Frederick was doing work for a government he didn't support and strongly opposed; Wilhelm had a promising but as yet unplanned future ahead of him. They were both aware that they could be on opposite sides of this conflict.

Frederick would probably be forced into the military and Wilhelm might eventually join, fighting against his cousin. Yet on this day they were dear friends whom they could rely on and trust, so they agreed that they would enjoy this trip and cherish the memories for a lifetime. It was a day filled with spectacular vistas, beautiful weather and a friendship that neither young man had ever experienced before.

With a full canteen of water and after hydrating themselves before and after breakfast, they filled their knapsacks and started for the trailhead.

They were leaving early and assumed that they were the first team on the red trail. They were confident that they wouldn't have any difficulty since they prepared themselves with two easier hikes the two days before. With clear skies and comfortable temperatures they set out on the red trail.

"Keep me from falling backwards and I'll reach for that ledge," said Wilhelm.

"Use that bush on your left to get a grip. Good. You've made it. Now give me a hand."

They communicated like this all during the morning, both being good hikers. This trail was indeed difficult but also had the most spectacular views of the forest and hills. One part of the trail would take them into a deep, dark forest; a few minutes later it would open up to the bright morning sunshine. It also had some overlooks that allowed them to rest and enjoy the view of the valley below. Both cousins were running out of adjectives to describe their amazement at what they were seeing and witnessing. Fog shrouded the valleys while sunlight washed across the hills.

About mid-morning Wilhelm had the first sign that he might be having trouble breathing. He said nothing. Then at eleven he was certain and told his cousin that he might be feeling the first signs of asthma. "I'm beginning to experience a shortness of breath."

"What does that mean? I remember you used to have asthma when you were very young."

"I don't get asthma often, but it is usually when I'm exposed to pollen. Maybe I've had too much exposure these last few days."

"Will you be all right? Do you think you will be able to make it?"

"I think so. We're almost halfway to the trailhead, so it doesn't make sense to go back. Let's keep hiking."

"Let me know if you need a rest. We're ahead of schedule so we don't have to rush."

By noon he was in considerable distress. They decided they needed to take short but frequent breaks.

It was with great difficulty that they covered the next kilometers. About three in the afternoon, Wilhelm asked to take a rest. He told Frederick that he was experiencing severe difficulty breathing. They had already conquered the most difficult part of the trail and were now on a downward path of about three kilometers. Twenty minutes later, after they had gone almost two kilometers and were just a short distance from the trailhead, they were forced to stop again.

"Frederick," he said between breaths. "I'm unable to continue. I can hardly breathe and my legs are like rubber."

"Sit for a moment. I'll run ahead to the trailhead and get some help."

Just at that moment Frederick saw two hikers on the trail behind them. He waved to them and they waved back. He made the gesture of help that is used universally on the water, waving his extended arms up and down. The two hikers understood and ran toward them.

Frederick explained that his friend was having an asthma attack. Could they get help?

"Let's carry him. Make a seat with your hands," said the taller of the two. "Hans, take all the gear."

Frederick grabbed his own left wrist and the right wrist of the hiker, who did the same. Wilhelm sat between them while Hans carried all the knapsacks and water canteens. They moved the last kilometer quickly, switching positions several times. At the trailhead they rushed up to a man with a car. They asked him to drive them to the pension. He helped Wilhelm walk into the pension. When the man with the car found out how serious the attack was, he offered to drive Wilhelm wherever he needed to go. The manager of the pension recommended St. Elizabeth's Hospital in Trier as the nearest and probably the best. Frederick asked the manager to call his father in Saarbrucken and tell him where they were.

He told the manager that they would come back for the bikes and gear when they could.

The man with the car drove quickly but with respect for the mountainous roads. Wilhelm could feel his passageways closing. Frederick noticed that even though he was still and not exerting himself, his breathing was becoming more labored. The driver knew exactly where the hospital was and dropped the two young men at the emergency room. Frederick shouted a "thank you" at the driver as he assisted Wilhelm inside. A nurse saw the situation and provided a wheelchair. Moments later, Wilhelm was breathing pure oxygen. Some color returned. Wilhelm's uncle arrived about an hour later and was led to the cubicle where his nephew was receiving treatment. His breathing was still labored but he could talk with some difficulty.

"I've just spoken with the doctor and he believes it would be best if you were moved to Saarbrucken," said the elder Frederick. "The medicine you've been given will keep you comfortable for at least another hour. Let me make financial arrangements at the desk and we can be on our way."

Wilhelm whispered a heartfelt "thank you."

Wilhelm was admitted to St. Theresa's Caritas Clinic just before the dinner hour. In the car ride down from Trier, the two Fredericks spoke of what they should tell the authorities and the hospital so that they wouldn't know he was American.

"I don't think he should use his passport," said the elder Frederick.

"He can use mine. I won't need it and the picture is close enough that he would easily pass for me."

"I would prefer that they don't find out he's American. They might report that to the authorities. We could be in trouble. Let's just pass him off as you. That way he will get free hospital care."

"I agree. I'll stay out of sight as much as possible. Don't worry, Dad. It will work."

The name on the passport was Frederick Wilhelm Schmidt and the American passport said Wilhelm Frederick Schmidt. They would require some proof of identification and both thought the passport would be proof that Wilhelm was German. The only troubling aspect was that Wilhelm would be eighteen years old if he used that passport. They decided to chance the deception rather than use the American passport. After all, Wilhelm really did look eighteen.

Frederick and Ursula returned in the evening to fill out the paperwork. Frederick explained to the hospital that the boy was called Wilhelm to avoid confusion. even though his passport said Frederick Wilhelm. So they put Wilhelm on all the paperwork.

"Mr. and Mrs. Schmidt. This is irregular for us to put a false name on a hospital application."

"It is not false. We have always called him Wilhelm to distinguish him from Frederick," said Ursula. "If we put 'Frederick' on the application, that would be a false statement."

Ursula kept the administrator engaged until he saw the wisdom of her words and agreed to put Wilhelm on the application.

Then they visited Wilhelm, who was resting comfortably but still breathing with difficulty. Wilhelm tried to speak, but they told him it wasn't necessary. Frederick told him that the combination of a difficult trail and being so close to all that pollen was probably the reason for the attack. They remembered that Wilhelm had these attacks when he was small but thought they were over. He shook his head to indicate that it wasn't entirely true.

"I'll go to the desk to retrieve the passport," said Frederick.

"I'll go with you," said Ursula.

At the desk a cantankerous old nun refused to release the passport.

"The moment they release him, he'll be given the passport," she said with all the authority of an SS Officer.

Ursula spoke up, "You know young boys. They have other things on their mind. I prefer to take the passport with me. It will be safer."

"When he's released. Those are the rules and they aren't about to be changed for you or anyone. The passport will be given to him when he's released. Good Evening." With that last pronouncement, she got up and walked away from the desk, nodding to the soldier standing by the door to watch the desk.

Chapter Eighteen

Wilhelm stayed in the hospital for the next three days and on Monday, August 7, the doctor told him he could be released if he did nothing strenuous.

"Sister, could you call my parents and tell them I can be released," he asked the nurse.

A man dressed in a long black leather coat, the kind worn by the Gestapo, pushed past the nurse and entered his room. Two soldiers accompanied him and stood at attention. He had a passport in his hand and started asking Wilhelm questions.

"Name?"

"Frederick Wilhelm Schmidt."

"And where do you live?"

"Here in Saarbrucken...69 Turnerstrasse."

"Why does it say Wilhelm on all your paperwork?"

"Because my father and I have the same name and they always called me Wilhelm to avoid confusion," he lied.

"And why are you not in the military?"

Wilhelm was at a loss for words. He didn't know how he should answer. Finally he thought of a plausible answer.

"I have these attacks of asthma. They keep me from strenuous activity and I shouldn't go anyplace where there is pollen. I have always been exempt from outdoor activities," he lied. "I also have a limp because one leg is shorter than the other."

"The military has plenty of use for clerks and people to do the accounting and organizing. I'm certain that we can find a place for you and keep you out of the forest. You are eighteen and you should be in the military now. I'll see to it."

The man in the black leather coat turned around abruptly and with a click of his heels, departed. Wilhelm got up moments later and made his way to the nurse's station.

"Please, may I use the phone?"

"Tell me the number and I'll dial it," said the lady at the desk.

When Aunt Ursula answered, he told her what was happening. "I'll tell your uncle. When he comes to the hospital to pick you up, I'm sure he will straighten it all out." Wilhelm hung up.

It was only a half hour later when two soldiers entered Wilhelm's room. One had only one stripe on his arm and the other, three stripes.

"Get dressed. You're coming with us."

"I haven't been released yet."

"By the time you are dressed you will be. Hurry! We'll be right outside the door."

Wilhelm dressed slowly, stalling until his uncle would arrive. He could only stall so long, as getting dressed was a routine procedure. He was putting on his hiking boots when the soldiers came in and handed him papers that said he was released. Frederick's passport was among them. When he could find nothing else to do he tried to stall. "Could you please tell me where I'm going?"

"You'll find out soon enough," the soldier with the three strips laughed.

"I would like to leave word for my parents."

"You can write to them," he sneered.

With a soldier on each side of him, holding his arm firmly, they escorted him to the elevator. They rode down to the main floor and lobby in silence and led him to a waiting brown car. The soldiers, one on each side of him, held the door for him to sit in the back seat.

When his uncle got to the room, it was empty. He asked about his nephew at the nurse's station and was told that he had been released and had left moments ago. "I'm surprised you didn't see him. He left with two soldiers."

Chapter Ninteen

By five that afternoon, Wilhelm was sitting in the mess hall of the Karlsruhe Kaserne, dressed in basic camp uniform and drinking a cup of coffee. He had been assigned a bunk, had been through a physical, was issued a uniform, underwear, boots and socks. He was awaiting the camp doctor. The doctor was meeting with the medic who provided the physical. The physician examined Wilhelm and told his training officer that he was to have two days' rest before beginning training. He also said that he would reexamine the soldier after the two days' rest to see if he was fit for training

"What has been done to eliminate your limp?" the doctor asked.

"The left shoe was made a centimeter higher. That eliminates most of the limp. I'll never get rid of it completely, but that seems to be a good workable height."

"I'll have boots made with those specifications. We can't have you walking like you're a cripple."

It was the following day that Wilhelm received new boots with the left boot raised a centimeter. They were comfortable and eliminated much of his limp.

Getting out of training didn't make Wilhelm popular with his fellow recruits. They thought he was getting special treatment and they didn't like it. He looked healthy enough in spite of that little limp. They figured that if they had to march and run, he should also. Wilhelm asked to do some office work while he was recuperating as he thought his fellow soldiers would see he was not avoiding work. He knew that most soldiers would hate to do office work. The *feldwebel*, the equivalent of sergeant, was pleased to get some help and had Wilhelm do some filing. He completed the work in a short time and asked for more work.

"Can you type?" asked the *feldwebel*.

"Yes…I'm out of practice, but it will come back," said Wilhelm.

"Good. I have some papers that need to be sorted and typed on a master form. Do you think you can do that?"

"Let's see what needs to be done."

Wilhelm worked in the office for two days before going back to the infirmary. The doctor who held the rank of major said that he could begin training but slowly. For that reason, he requested that the *oberfeldwebel*, the master sergeant in charge of training, come to his office.

"This young recruit can't be pushed too hard. If you do that you will harm him and possibly incapacitate him. I'd be forced to send him home and he would be no good to the Fatherland. He cannot take training in the woods or be outdoors when pollen is falling and the count is high. He's a healthy young man only if he's free from asthma."

"He's useless," said the *oberfeldwebel*. "What can I do with him?"

"There is plenty of need for people in the office. Just because I'm not able to go into the field, am I useless?"

"You have skills. You're a doctor."

"This man has skills too, and you need to find out what they are and use them. Maybe he would be a good cook or work with the quartermasters. Find out what he can do and assign him to that group. Not everyone has to shoot a rifle to be a good soldier."

"Yes, Herr Doctor," he said as he clicked his heels, abruptly turned and indicated to the doctor by his actions that he didn't approve.

Wilhelm went through a light workout that afternoon. He was feeling better but was still not up to his former self before the asthma attack. He was worried about his aunt and uncle and his cousin not knowing where he was and also what they would tell his parents and sister. Each day he pushed himself a bit more, and soon the *oberfeldwebel* was pleased with what he saw. He concluded that this young recruit was not a slacker and maybe he had some talents that could be used. The *feldwebel* in the office asked him if the new recruit would be returning for duty any time in the near future.

"Why? Is he causing any trouble?"

"Hell, no! He's the best help I've had since we set up this Kaserne. He knows how to organize, he can type and he learns fast. The doctor asked me if he was any good and I told him that he's a real help to the office. When his training is finished, let me have a crack at him if he can't go out in the field."

"Well, maybe we've found a use for him," said the *oberfeldwebel*.

Wilhelm did the tasks assigned to him but worried that somehow they would find out he was American. That would be a problem, as his relatives would be accused of deceiving the authorities. He might even be accused of being a spy. Perhaps they might believe that Wilhelm was brought to Germany to spy on the Nazis. He worried that somehow they would find out he was not a German citizen. Wilhelm made sure he didn't write anything since cursive writing was so different and his penmanship was abominable. If he had to write, he would print.

Now he was thankful that he'd learned to type when Greta was learning. What a stroke of luck that was.

One of the first things Wilhelm attempted to procure was a map of the area. If he was to escape to France he would need to know where he was going and, for that matter, where he was located presently. Not having lived in Germany since he was a child, he didn't know the geography as well as he should.

It was in mid-September when the recruits finished their basic training. The new soldiers were assigned to a Kaserne where they would be needed. New recruits would soon be arriving. *Feldwebel* Erik Buckholz requested that *Obersoldat* (private first class) Schmidt be assigned to him. The orders were cut. Not having to spend his day outdoors suited him, as did the fact that he didn't have to go through any more of the training than he already had. He did practice with a rifle and took several hikes, with the warning that he shouldn't overdo any exercise for now. He would certainly avoid the outdoors on days when the pollen count was high. He was satisfied that he achieved the rank of *obersoldat*, which is the rank given a soldier when he completes basic training. *Too bad it had to be in the German Army,* he thought.

One day, in the mess hall, he inadvertently switched his knife to his right hand when cutting his meat, as Americans do when they eat. At school he would often eat like the other students.

"Schmidt, are you American?" asked the soldier sitting across from him.

"No, why?" His face flushed noticeably.

"You're eating like an American, switching your knife and fork."

Thinking quickly, he grabbed his left wrist. "Today I sprained my wrist and am trying to avoid using it. By tomorrow it should be better." The color subsided a bit and the soldier who asked the question didn't appear to notice.

The soldier dropped the subject and Wilhelm realized that he almost got caught. He was glad his companion accepted the explanation and didn't pursue the subject. In the future, he would definitely have to avoid behavior that could betray his identity.

One of the first things he had to do was get a letter to Uncle Frederick and Aunt Ursula. He didn't know if all mail was censored or not, but he had to let them know where he was, that he was safe and recovered from his asthma attack. He wanted his parents to know this as well. He wrote a letter one evening and addressed it but didn't put it in the mailbox in the barracks. He kept it in his shirt pocket, unsealed. He also told his aunt and uncle in the letter to censor anything that would get him in trouble as he thought that incoming mail might also be read.

"Will I need my passport in the future?" he asked *Feldwebel* Buckholz.

"No, we know all we need to know. I would send it home," said the *feldwebel*.

He put the passport in the envelope with his letter, sealed it and asked *Feldwebel* Buckholz how he should mail it. "Take the letter to the mail room and look for a bag marked POST. Drop it in that pouch. The other bag marked BERLIN goes to headquarters. Take this envelope and place it in that pouch. It should go out this afternoon." He handed Wilhelm a large envelope.

Wilhelm walked to the mailroom, looking around. He couldn't see the man in charge. Wilhelm called and when no one answered, he found the mail pouch destined for headquarters and the one with letters from the soldiers to their families and friends. He added his letter to the second pouch and buried it among the other letters. Just then a soldier with stripes of a sergeant came in and Wilhelm introduced himself and told him that Buckholz wanted this envelope to go out in today's mail to headquarters.

The two men spoke for a few minutes and Wilhelm got the impression that he and Buckholz were good friends. If so, it would be easier getting his letters out. Wilhelm told the sergeant that if he could help in any way, he would be glad to do so. He felt that the more friends he had, the easier life in the German Army would be.

He might need a friend or two in order to get into France.

Chapter Twenty

Each evening when Wilhelm returned to his bunk, he thought of how he could escape from this camp. He had a lot of questions about swimming. *If I swim across the Rhein into France, I'll have to swim against the current. It's a strong current, I was told, and that will whisk me north, deeper inside Germany. I would need to go south to Rastatt if I needed to swim to France.*

He found a map of Germany folded in one of the drawers in the office and verified that it was a good distance. *Might the water be too cold since it's now late September? How would I get my clothes and boots across? The only thing I'm certain of is my ability to swim. All the other problems…well, I'll just have to figure a way to solve them.*

If I escaped from the Kaserne, perhaps I would be able to find a boat. And if so, would it have oars that I could use? I might even be shot trying to steal property belonging to someone living on the river. Then again, I might be arrested and my identity exposed, bringing harm to my relatives.

How will I get out of the Kaserne? They line up each morning and everyone is accounted for. I would have to leave in the night when everyone is asleep. In the evening, someone missing from his bunk would draw attention, and the whole camp would be put on alert. The soldier would be found. If he was absent from the office during the day, his superior would immediately want to know where he was.

Wilhelm found a map of the camp and was overwhelmed with the size of it. He studied it carefully. It was obvious that some places would be off limits such as the shooting range, but he could move to some of the remote sites only if he was part of an exercise and under the supervision of a superior. Nor would it be easy to climb over the fence, each one topped with barbed wire. It also appeared that there may have been electrical current alerting authorities to anyone trying to enter. That would also prevent anyone from leaving.

While all these obstacles seemed daunting, Wilhelm had no intention of giving up. He considered that with time he would be trusted and might have more opportunities to get into France. He was safe for the time being and was certain that eventually an opportunity would present itself.

Chapter Twenty-One

"Schmidt, the *Oberst* wants to see you in his office," a soldier from the post office announced late one afternoon.

I hope I didn't screw up, was Wilhelm's thought. *He has no reason to call me to his office unless I messed up.*

"Schmidt, you've been here since August and haven't had a day off. I don't pay much attention to those details but *Feldwebel* Buckholz told me you need some time in Karlsruhe. I have a two-day pass for you. You will not be expected to do anything except visit a few of the points of interest." The colonel smiled, insinuating that his listener would know what he meant.

"That's great. I could use a day off and I'd really like to see the city."

"I understand that four other soldiers will be going. Be ready at 0800 at the front gate. A truck will pick you up there and drop you off at the *Hauptbanhof.* At 1700 hours the truck will return the following day. Wear civilian clothes."

"Yes, Sir. Where can I get a map of the city?"

"They have one in the post office. They also have condoms there. You'll need them. The sergeant will show you where the 'red light' district is, although you'll have no trouble finding it. He'll also give you a list of some of the hotels in the area."

Wilhelm couldn't believe his good fortune. *I've been trying to find a way to leave the camp and they hand it to me on a silver platter. I'll have no trouble getting away from the other soldiers. I'll just tell them I want to visit the museum or library. They'll rush to get away from me. Then I'll take the train to Rastatt and look for a way to cross the river there.*

He was so excited he could hardly get to sleep. Finally, his brain exhausted all the possibilities and he drifted off.

The drive into town was pleasant even if the only view was over the tailgate since the truck was covered with canvas. The other soldiers had also labored for months without time off, and the doctor suggested young men needed time to blow off a little steam. Finally someone listened.

The truck stopped in front of the railroad station and everyone headed toward the area where the "ladies of the evening" would congregate. Wilhelm told everyone he wanted to go to the museum first. They ditched him as fast as they could.

Wilhelm pretended to walk toward the museum, but when his companions were out of sight, headed for the ticket counter inside the station. A train was leaving for Rastatt in thirty-five minutes. *Perfect.* He spent the time getting timetables from Rastatt to Karlsruhe and asked at the information booth if he could have a city map of Rastatt. The elderly lady at the booth found one for him.

The trip to Rastatt was only twenty minutes. Wilhelm studied his map and realized that he needed to know where he could eat. He was planning on being in France by the evening or first thing in the morning.

He stopped at the information booth in Rastatt to get information about hotels and restaurants.

"You're new in town. I don't remember seeing you before," she said as she handed him the map. Her speaking to him interrupted his thoughts.

"I am new. Where would you suggest I visit?"

"Any number of places. Most are listed on the map. How long will you be in town?"

Wilhelm saw that she was a pretty girl, about twenty, with brown hair and a pleasant personality.

"I'll be here today and tomorrow. Where would you suggest I eat supper?"

"The Hotel Amkulturplatz has a nice restaurant that is not too expensive. We can look at the menu together if you meet me there at six this evening. You can see the hotel on your right from the entrance to the station."

"I can't promise you but I'd like to have dinner with you. I will try to return to the railroad station this evening." *It's always good to have a backup plan and this young lady would definitely be someone who would make a delightful dinner partner.*

"Then, we may meet at six. I would like that."

Wilhelm left the railroad station and headed west toward the Rhein River. He'd walked about two kilometers before he saw the north bridge. He walked down to the ferry, which was securely docked. Due to the tensions between the two countries, no service was available. Wilhelm also saw tanks securely blocking the entrance to the bridge on the French side.

Following the information on his map, he chose a road that took him to a dirt road. He would have to swim across the river someplace near this spot or else he would end up in Germany instead of France. The dirt road took him to the river. It looked like a place where a fisherman could put in a boat. He threw a stick into the river.

"Look at the speed of the current," he almost shouted as he searched for another stick. So many things passed through his mind, now that he was here. *There is no way that anyone, even a good swimmer, could swim across that river without being swept down river five or ten kilometers. Look at all the boats carrying cargo. It would be difficult to stay out of their way. I wonder just how cold the water is.*

Wilhelm found a flat rock at the water's edge and sat on it while he removed his shoes and socks. Then he placed both feet in the rushing water. He could not believe how frigid the water was. *Five minutes in this water and one would be frozen like an icicle.* He deliberately kept his feet in the water while he watched the hands on his watch. After three minutes, he removed his feet, armed with the knowledge that he would be unable to swim across the Rhein. *After all, this water was probably snow yesterday, coming as it does from the Alps. Why didn't I realize that?*

Wilhelm walked back toward the bridge and found a café. He ordered a cup of coffee and wurst in a bun. It looked like a hotdog he could get back home. As he sat in the café he considered that his only chance to get to France would be by rowboat. He studied his map and realized that he would have to find a boat in the area he just left to about one kilometer to the north. Otherwise, he would end up in Germany and be shot as a spy.

The afternoon walk in the sunshine was pleasant but yielded little by way of results. He found no boat and after a short distance saw the German tanks guarding an entrance route into Germany. French tanks were located on the other side of the border. Wilhelm's heart was crushed. He might never get this opportunity again. He knew it was impossible to reach his goal. Discouraged, he began the long walk back to Rastatt.

Chapter Twenty-Two

Wilhelm looked forward to meeting the lady in the railroad station but was experiencing a feeling that maybe he should be cautious. *What if she suspects that I might not be a German? Or maybe she'll think I'm a deserter. She was very forward when I first met her. Be careful.*

"Hello," he greeted her as she approached the hotel from the direction of the station.

"Hello. Waiting long?"

"No, about five minutes. Please tell me your name."

"I'm Inga. Inga Hoffmann." She extended her hand.

"I'm Dieter Brosche. Shall we go in?"

The two were ushered by an older waiter to a table where they could see the street. Wilhelm told the waiter to put everything on one tab.

"I can't let you do that. We don't even know each other."

"Maybe we will before the meal is over."

"If that happens, I'll provide the accommodations for the night. I don't live far from here. That would make a delightful end to a long day."

"It most certainly would." *She was direct and knew what she wanted.*

The two talked about their work. Inga claimed her job was boring except for the occasional interesting character she would meet. Wilhelm spoke of his work in an office and of the sameness of his job. He didn't tell Inga that he was a soldier, although he suspected she understood that he was. They both ate the special of soup and wiener schnitzel with potatoes.

"You haven't booked a hotel room yet, have you?" she asked.

"No, I thought I might be taking the train, after we ate."

"Stay with me. I don't have much company and I could use a friend tonight."

"I would like that. Traveling alone can be lonely, and you're wonderful company."

When they finished the meal and paid the bill, they walked the four blocks to her apartment, where she led the way up two flights of stairs. The apartment was small but neat and clean. Inga opened a cabinet and took out two wine glasses and a bottle of Mosel wine from the refrigerator. She poured the wine and toasted their friendship.

By nine, they were in bed together and asleep by midnight. It was about six in the morning when Wilhelm heard Inga talking quietly on the telephone in the kitchen. He left the bed and moved toward the voice.

"I don't know if he's a soldier but he has to be the right age." There was a pause. "I wouldn't call you if I didn't think he ran away from his unit." Another pause. "Look, you owe me, if he's running, and I think he is." After another pause, she continued. "He's wearing a brown jacket and he has a limp. It's not bad but it is noticeable. He'll be taking the train somewhere. His name is Dieter Brosche."

Wilhelm was already in his clothes and was putting on his shoes when Inga tiptoed back into the bedroom.

"You slept with me so you could make some money by turning me in.

Just so you know, I'm not away from my unit. I'm on a two-day pass." He was out the door without waiting for a response.

The *Bahnhof* was not busy at this early hour, but a train to Karlsruhe was not scheduled to depart for another forty minutes. Wilhelm wondered what train would be leaving next. He looked at the gates and saw a train due to arrive in five minutes on Track 2. He went to the ticket counter and bought a ticket to Offenburg. As he was walking away from the counter, he saw two men in black leather coats and hats enter the main waiting area. Wilhelm continued his pace away from them and entered the rest room. He got a paper towel, took off his coat and waited for them to announce that a train had arrived on Track 2.

Wilhelm boarded that train and moved as far to the rear as possible. He sat by a window and saw the two Gestapo agents near the first car. One agent went forward to speak with the driver while the other boarded the train. Wilhelm headed for the nearest bathroom. On the paper towel from the station he wrote, "out of order" and put it on the jam, holding it from the inside. He closed and locked the door and waited. It may have been only two minutes but it seemed like an hour. When the train was again moving, he felt safe to come out.

Forty minutes later, he arrived in Offenburg and discovered he would have to wait an hour to take a train to Karlsruhe. He found a park near the station and sat there watching the pigeons and admiring the fall turning of the leaves. He felt safe for the first time since waking up.

It was near noon when the train arrived at the *Hauptbanhof* in Karlsruhe. With his jacket over his arm, he headed for the men's room. He did not see any men in black coats and hats but felt the need to be cautious. After a five minute delay and a thorough search of the waiting area, Wilhelm headed for the southernmost door. Once outside, he surveyed the area in front of the station.

Sitting on the cement flower boxes were two men dressed in leather. That was the spot where the truck would return. Wilhelm made sure he kept a person between him and the agents and he kept his jacket folded over his arm. He needed to get out of there but was afraid his limp would betray him.

He saw an old lady walking past the two agents. She was relying heavily on her cane and her walking was labored. When she came by where he was sitting he joined her by supporting her arm. "May I walk with you?"

"I'm walking slowly. Are you sure you want to walk that slowly?"

"I'd consider it a favor. Those two men back there are looking for a young man with a limp. When I walk this slowly the limp is not noticeable. So I'm grateful to you."

They walked several streets before Wilhelm said goodbye and thanked the nice woman. He crossed the street and headed for the *Schloss*. He wanted to be able to tell others that he visited the landmark attraction. He spent the afternoon enjoying the sights and sounds of Karlsruhe.

At four thirty, he was standing with a crowd of people across from the railroad station, observing the two Gestapo agents. His goal was to reach the travel office directly across from the station since he knew that is where the truck from the post would park. A sign reserved that spot for military vehicles. He could sit inside studying travel brochures and wait for his fellow soldiers. When one of the agents went inside, Wilhelm joined a group of people and hid among them until he reached the travel shop. Inside he felt safe and sat at a table to look at brochures and observe the activity across the street.

When the soldiers arrived, they waited near where the agents were sitting. They were checked out thoroughly by the Gestapo. When the truck pulled up, it blocked the view of the agents and allowed Wilhelm to cross the street and climb in the back of the truck with the other soldiers.

"Well, Schmidt, how was the museum?"

Wilhelm didn't mind the kidding one bit.

Chapter Twenty-Three

The next morning the two Gestapo agents asked to see *Oberstleutnant* Karl Dengel.

"Colonel, we have reason to believe that you have a missing soldier. Is that correct?"

"I am not aware of any soldier being away without leave. Who is this missing soldier?"

"His name is Dieter Brosche. He's a soldier who was seen in Rastatt, but we lost him."

"What has he done?"

"We don't think he returned to his unit."

Dengel reached for the morning report and told the two agents that no one was missing, "You have been misinformed. Can you tell me anything else that might be useful?

"This soldier has a limp."

Dengel immediately knew he was referring to Schmidt but trusted this soldier without question. Besides, he didn't want to lose the soldier who made him look good with his superiors. Schmidt would have an explanation, he was certain. "I'm sorry, Gentlemen. I don't believe that I can help you. Leave your name and telephone number with my secretary and I'll notify you if anything turns up."

There was nothing more for them to do but leave since they were speaking with the top officer on the post.

Fifteen minutes later, Schmidt was standing in front of Dengel. "Schmidt, two Gestapo officers were inquiring about you. They said you had given them the slip in Rastatt and were missing from your unit. Is that true?"

"Yes. The young lady with whom I spent the night turned me in for the money. I gave her a phony name. She just presumed I was AWOL. I had too much to see and didn't want to spend the day being interrogated, so I hid from them."

"How come you were in Rastatt?"

"I always wanted to visit that city. I thought I could see Rastatt one day and Karlsruhe the next. I didn't plan on sleeping with the young lady, but an opportunity presented itself and I was happy to take advantage of it. If I may ask a question, Sir, how did you know it was me?"

"They said the soldier had a limp. Since no one was missing, I had no information to give them. We don't have a soldier with a limp, do we?"

"I don't think so. I've never seen anyone limping."

Chapter Twenty-Four

Fall turned into winter and the German Army continued to mobilize. Each two months a new group of recruits reported, and the paperwork never seemed to end. In April of 1939, the day after Easter, a young recruit by the name of Hans Kohler, who looked frail and weak, was assigned to work with Wilhelm. He was frightened just being in the army and could do only a portion of the physical requirements. The doctor again intervened and suggested he be assigned to the office. Wilhelm tried to help him adjust to army life.

The first week in May, *Feldwebel* Buckholz called Schmidt into his office. He asked him to have a seat at his desk.

"Schmidt, I'm being reassigned to Berlin. Do you think you could keep the office running until they get a replacement?"

"If you tell me what I need to know. Maybe we can make a list of all the duties and I'll tell you which ones I need to learn," said Wilhelm.

"I'll be glad to show you. It will be two weeks before I have to leave. If

I have to stay longer than two weeks, they will subtract those days from my furlough home. Will two weeks be enough?"

"I believe I should be able to learn everything by then."

"While I'm still here, you better start training that young recruit. He's a sorry ass specimen of a German soldier. Let's hope that he can type," Buckholz said out of the side of his mouth.

"I wasn't much good when I first came here, but I learned. I appreciate all that you taught me. Maybe he will, too."

"For your sake, I hope he does. There is too much work for one person, but he doesn't look like he's worth a damn. His ass is yours, Schmidt. Good luck."

Buckholz left in the middle of May and a week later Wilhelm became *Gefreiter* Schmidt, or corporal. The new recruit didn't complete basic training and so remained a *soldat*, a private. Wilhelm tried to put *Soldat* Hans Kohler at ease. He gave him some easy filing to do, some extremely light typing and had him do small errands. He could tell that Kohler was eager to please and wasn't at all lazy…only nervous.

"Kohler, what were you doing before you were called to report for duty?"

"I…I had enrolled to take classes at the U…U…University in Frankfurt."

Wilhelm nodded. Kohler stuttered when he was nervous, so he'd just have to get him over his nerves.

"What kind of classes? What were you studying for?"

"The classes were basic but I had thoughts that I would like to be a History professor."

"I'm sorry that your studies were interrupted, but we'll do our best to make you a useful member of the office. I need someone who is smart to assist me and I think you'll work out just fine."

"Thank you, *Gefreiter* Schmidt."

"Kohler, call me Schmidt. You don't have to give me a title. When we're alone you can call me Wilhelm and I'll call you Hans. But only when we're alone."

After Wilhelm and Hans had formed a bond, the two managed to handle all the office work without too much difficulty. Wilhelm found that Kohler was smart and typed reasonably well, once he got over his nervousness. "Hans, this will be a good assignment for you. You won't have to sleep in a ditch or fire a rifle. I'll do what I can to teach you the system. Together we can avoid mistakes and make ourselves useful to our superiors. They like it when we make them look good."

The two soldiers got along well. Wilhelm ran a tight office, aware that being punctual and giving commands would impress his superiors. Kohler was a worker who made few mistakes when he typed, a rarity in the military. Wilhelm saw to it that everything went out on time. He was also able to get letters out and found that most incoming mail was not read. But then you could never be sure when a batch would be inspected.

The commanding officer, *Oberstleutnant* (lieutenant colonel) Karl Dengel, visited Wilhelm weekly. He took a liking to the young soldier. After all, Wilhelm made him look good with all the reports looking so neat and being on time. No one liked to do the paperwork even though doing it properly was the key to making points with his superiors. He was determined to make everyone look good. That became his key to being safe.

When the *oberstleutnant* visited, he told Wilhelm that he hadn't asked for a replacement for *Feldwebel* Buckholz. He told Wilhelm that he thought he was better than the office manager he had in Berlin.

"I believe you can take over all these office duties," Dengel began. "It looks to me that you are already better at this job than Buckholz was. Do you need anything?"

"Now that you've asked me, I do need something."

105

"And what is that?"

"*Soldat* Kohler needs to be promoted to *obersoldat*. Kohler does almost all the typing and really pays attention to detail. He's deserving of that promotion."

"If you think he deserves it, I'll put in the paper work. Don't tell him, just in case they don't agree with us."

Chapter Twenty-Five

When Wilhelm next visited the post office, the *feldwebel* whom he got to know well, was in a talkative mood.

"Schmidt, where did you get your accent?"

"In Saarbrucken, where I was born."

"You sound like my cousin, who now lives in Toronto."

"No one ever told me I had an accent. I've always sounded like this."

"No, your accent is different. It's not from here. I'll call you 'Toronto' because that's what you sound like to me."

"Just call me Schmidt like you always do. I'm not Toronto." Wilhelm didn't want anyone pointing out that he had an accent. Someone might just recognize it as American and he would be in a lot of trouble. Perturbed he said, "Call me Schmidt." With that remark, he turned on his heels and left.

Two weeks later the papers came through and Kohler was promoted to *obersoldat* and Wilhelm was made an *obergefreiter*, senior lance corporal.

Kohler had a big smile on his face when the *oberstleutnant* handed him his stripe. When they were alone in the office, Kohler told Wilhelm how he appreciated being taught. "I can't thank you enough for helping me survive these first few months. I was afraid when I came here that they would see how frail I was and take me out and shoot me, like they do the Jews and the sickly."

"I was doing what was expected of me and I needed the help. Besides, you could type," explained Wilhelm.

"Now I feel I have some value around here, even if I can't shoot a rifle."

"Kohler, I'll try to make you more valuable, so maybe they'll let you have my job."

"What would you do then?" asked Kohler.

"They would move me someplace else. The army is mobilizing. The next country we conquer will probably be France."

"We'll invade France?" He blinked rapidly and wrung his hands.

"I think so. Do you speak French?"

"Some. I've had two years of French in school."

"That will definitely help. If we're assigned to France it will be as occupiers not as infantry soldiers. We could do worse. When the fighting breaks out, we could be sent to the eastern front." Wilhelm stopped and gazed at the map on the wall. "Possibly Russia. I'd rather be sent to France."

Kohler nodded his head in agreement.

"Tell me, Kohler. What did you mean when you said they would take you out and shoot you like they do the Jews and sickly? Do they really do that?"

"I have a friend who worked in Dachau. He says they have no use for anyone who can't work. When those who are sick arrive at the camp they are separated and taken to the crematorium. They are gassed or shot and their bodies are burned. Jews are especially targeted for harsh punishment. Every morning prisoners must line up outdoors, with barely enough clothes on and some, barefoot. Even when the weather is freezing or snowing, they may be forced to stand for a half hour or more. They don't like the gypsies, either. It's sick what they're doing. If you say anything about it you might be sent to the camp. They call them work camps but they're death camps."

"Thank you, Kohler. I didn't know it was that bad."

"You must have heard them ranting about the Jews and homosexuals at the youth rallies. They blame the Jews for everything. Now they're rounding them up and sending them to the camps for extermination. Men, women and children. It doesn't matter the age. They're all enemies of the state."

"I'm sure the authorities wouldn't want to hear us talk like this. We'll just have to keep these thoughts to ourselves."

Both men went back to work, but the news that death camps were operating to eliminate undesirables left them disturbed. Both these sensitive, intelligent men found it impossible to fathom how one human could perpetrate these atrocious acts on another human. It was against everything they had been taught from birth. Yet it was happening.

One of the jobs that Wilhelm gave Kohler was to get the mail to the post office and the pouch for headquarters to *Oberstleutnant* Dengel. This allowed him to avoid the *feldwebel* in the post office. When the mail pouch was brought into the office, Wilhelm could find something for Kohler to do so that Wilhelm could add a letter that wouldn't be censored. He seldom used this ploy except when he didn't want anyone to read his mail.

With summer came a new set of recruits—and more paperwork. Wilhelm sat down with Kohler one morning in July and asked him about his workload. Hans said that he was doing more and working much harder than when he first came.

"I don't mind the work as it makes me feel useful," Hans began, "but sometimes there is just too much and we have to work overtime. We could definitely use more help."

"I'm going to request another body in the office to take some of the jobs you've been doing. Since we are inducting more men into this army, the size of each recruiting class has gotten larger. Jobs that used to take an hour now require two," said Wilhelm.

That afternoon he called the *feldwebel* who was the *obersleutnant's* secretary.

"This is Ober*gefreiter* Schmidt. I need to see the *Oberstleutnant*. At his convenience."

"How about the last hour of work this afternoon? 1600 hours."

"I'll be there."

At four in the afternoon, Wilhelm waited outside the office for about five minutes. This gave him the opportunity to talk with the secretary and to observe how he did things. Finally, he was invited in to see *Oberstleutnant* Dengel.

"How is everything going in the office?"

"Fine, sir."

"And how is Kohler working out?

"Fine, sir. That's why I'm here. We've been increasing our recruits every new class, and the paperwork grows with each class. Last fall two of us could handle the office and even have a few minutes to relax. Now we work past five o'clock almost every night."

"We haven't increased your responsibilities, have we?"

"No. We have the same number of jobs but with the increase in recruits it takes twice as long to do the work as it did last year. Kohler has turned out to be extremely valuable. His typing is more than adequate and he's very capable at catching errors. I don't want our work to slip as it would be a bad reflection on me. Then it becomes a bad reflection on you. Sir, we need another man."

"Schmidt, you've worked out well and have made a good recruit out of Kohler. I can see where your workload has increased, but do you really think you need another person?"

"We cannot sustain this pace. I need another man or the quality will suffer. I wouldn't ask if we could do it ourselves."

"All right. We'll find a man for you. I'll ask the *oberfeldwebel* to pick out a good recruit to work with you, preferably one with a good education."

"Thank you, *Oberstleutnant*."

"Oh…Schmidt. I do appreciate what a good job you're doing running the office. My fellow officers ask me how I found you and I just laugh and tell them that they wouldn't believe how I recruited you."

Wilhelm left and couldn't help but laugh to himself. *The oberstleutnant would be absolutely furious if he knew the soldier he held in such high regard was really the enemy. That must never be known.*

Chapter Twenty-Six

The new man was assigned to the office upon completion of his basic training. He was promoted to obersoldat, as was customary. He had a year at the university and was smart but thought he shouldn't be working in an office. He wanted to be a soldier, shoot his rifle, kill the enemy and save Germany from the Jews and gypsies. He considered the jobs that he was asked to do as menial. In addition, he was lazy. Wilhelm sent him off on a mail run and called Hans to his desk.

"What do you think, Hans?"

"He's not going to work out. His attitude is poor. Can we get someone else?"

"I'll ask the *oberstleutnant* if we can go through the personnel files of all the new recruits. There is a lot of information that might be useful if he will let us see the files. Then we'll talk with the *Oberfeldwebel* and get his opinion about the two or three we select. Maybe we can even observe them while they're training."

"Problem is we may have to put up with him until we get the new man," said Hans.

"If we get any work out of him, I'll be happy."

Wilhelm got permission to review the personnel files of each of the new recruits. He wanted those who graduated from school but preferred somebody with at least a year in the university. He found seven who looked as if they might fit the bill. He found out that five of the seven had typing skills. He asked the training *feldwebel* if he had any feeling for the five that they named. He said they were all good men, except one who was a complainer. With the field narrowed down to four, Wilhelm visited *Oberfeldwebel* Hecht and asked him for his opinion. He knew the sergeant was judging them for infantry soldier material, making his needs and Wilhelm's different. He'd sent them a soldier who was gung-ho when they needed a civilian who was organized. The four recruits that were discussed were acceptable in the eyes of Hecht. None of these four had any major disqualifications.

Step three was for Hans and Wilhelm to evaluate independently those four, without them knowing they were being observed. They would take time to watch them on the training field and would get to know them after hours in the barracks. After a week, the two men had a meeting.

"Who is your first choice, Hans?"

"Gustav Sauer seems to be the best of the bunch."

"I agree. He's my first choice also. We don't have to go any further, but if you don't mind I'd like to know how you ranked the other three."

Hans showed Wilhelm the ranking he had for all four and Wilhelm showed him his rankings. They were identical. When Wilhelm went back to see the *oberstleutnant*, he was agreeable to making a change in assignment. He said he would transfer the new man out and send Gustav Sauer to the office. Wilhelm told his commanding officer that he was quite certain this man would work out and everyone would be happy. He also told him that Sauer was the first choice of both Kohler and himself. While he was there, he added, "It's time for Kohler to be promoted to *gefreiter.*"

"I believe it is. Don't say anything until we're sure the promotion will go through. I'm often not sure what criteria they use to determine if a man should be promoted."

"I'll wait for you to tell me."

It happened that Gustav Sauer was happy to be in the office and not sent to duty at a concentration camp in the east. He was eager to learn and he recognized that Hans Kohler could teach him a lot. The three of them got along well. Soon, for the first time in several months, they were finished with their day's work by 1700 hours.

One night while the men were drinking beer at the local *Gasthaus*, it hit Wilhelm that he had been in the army for an entire year. He, Hans and Gustav had become good friends. Even though Wilhelm was younger than his subordinates, the passport that had got him into trouble said he was nineteen. Because he was tall, had a dark complexion and acted mature, his false age was accepted. Here he was, a corporal in the German Army, in charge of records and the office. In addition, he had two people who reported to him. Not bad for a year in the German Army.

I feel safe now. Still, I would rather be home than have any success as a German soldier. I want to escape but don't know how. I can't even drive a car and have no reason to ask anyone to drive me. I have to escape. I can't be part of this killing machine.

Several weeks after his conversation with *Obersleutnant* Dengel, he and Hans were called into Dengel's office and both were promoted, Wilhelm to *feldwebel* (sergeant) and Kohler to *gefreiter.* That evening the two were given permission to visit the local *Gasthaus* and they drank several beers together.

Lying in bed that night, feeling slightly tipsy, Wilhelm considered that he was on the verge of making a momentous decision. His conscience bothered him that he was doing so well in the German Army. *He didn't want to be a part of this terrible evil regime, a choice that he didn't make. If he were to renounce it and tell his superiors that he was an imposter, he would be put into prison, sent to a death camp or shot on the spot. He would have to double his efforts to find a way into France. He'd learn to drive so he would increase his chances to escape and do what he could to foul up the war effort.*

The next morning Wilhelm had a new thought. *He would continue to advance in the German Army so that he would be in a position to do some real harm to their evil behavior. For now, he would continue to be a cog in the gear, a small player in a big game. But the time would come when he would be in a position to do some good, only if he was trusted. He decided he would consider these ideas for awhile.*

Chapter Twenty-Seven

The fall of 1939 brought another class of recruits, this time almost twice as many as the previous class. More barracks had to be built to house them. On September 1, Germany attacked Poland and, several days later, Czechoslovakia. Every able man was being pressed into service for the Fatherland. One officer offered the statement that this was the start of the Second World War. Wilhelm believed he was correct but didn't add any comments to the officer's remark.

The mess hall was overcrowded and had to be enlarged. There were numerous gripes about the mess hall and the food. Wilhelm heard the gripes of his two employees as well as those of the other soldiers and decided to call a meeting with Hans and Gustav.

"I want you to find out what the gripes are concerning the mess hall. Listen to the men, talk to the cooks in the kitchen and those that serve in the hall. We'll all listen to the men. Gustav, you talk to the servers and Hans, talk with the cooks. I would like to know what must be done to improve the situation and then present a plan to the colonel. And I don't want people to know what we're doing."

"How will this help us?" asked Hans.

"If we can create good will and solve problems, our value will increase, and they'll think twice about sending us to the front. We'll be too valuable to them back here."

"That makes sense, but who ever said the army made sense?" said Gustav.

"It wasn't me," Wilhelm said.

It took about a week to compile all they'd learned. *If you want to know what a problem is, ask the people closest to the problem.* Isn't that what Mr. McCann had taught him? He'd promised that he would always remember that bit of advice.

The men complained about the way the food was being cooked. Good meat was cooked to death and often burned. All vegetables were overcooked and pasta, rice and potatoes were boiled until they were indistinguishable from mush. Wilhelm was getting powerful evidence that it wasn't the food, just the way it was prepared. The cooks were not trained, simply assigned to that detail; few had any previous experience. They hated their superior who, they said, behaved like he thought he was a general. The serving crew was ordered about by the chefs, who were called that only because they cooked the food. In addition to not knowing how to cook, they took all the abuse of the soldiers for serving such terrible food. They got absolutely no respect and had a sergeant for a boss who was afraid to stick up for those who worked under him.

The three young men gathered many suggestions. It was obvious to them that the present system was not working. They needed someone who knew what he was doing. They agreed that the first step would be to find out what talent was available. A questionnaire was devised that could be given to each recruit, asking him about his background. They were looking for chefs, restaurant owners, and waiters or anyone with a background in food handling. They also asked the recruits about their interests and hobbies. They asked on the questionnaire for each to list his favorite meal

They were surprised with how many had food service backgrounds. They even found one man who had owned a fancy restaurant in Frankfurt and supervised several chefs. On single sheets of paper spread before them on the desk was all the talent they needed. Rather than choose who should do what, they considered that the person chosen to be the boss should make the other choices. They decided that it was their job to recommend who the boss should be, then give him the information to select the right men to work under his guidance.

Wilhelm, Hans and Gustav got to know the recruit who owned the restaurant. The story, told by one of his friends, was that he'd suggested that a certain German officer leave his restaurant because he was drunk and attempting to fondle the waitress, his wife. The officer left but within days the restaurant owner found himself in a soldier's uniform. He was twenty-five years old, had a child and a wife and had to leave the restaurant in his wife's hands. Hans, Gustav and Wilhelm all liked the recruit and thought he would be perfect to head up the project.

Wilhelm called up the *oberstleutnant* and asked for a meeting. He was told that he could come to his office immediately. The colonel said that it would have to be a quick meeting as he had a lot on his mind. Wilhelm was at his office within five minutes and launched into his reason for the visit.

"Sir, one of the biggest complaints is the terrible situation in the mess hall."

"Yes, I know. Feeding the recruits is one of my biggest headaches. In fact, the meeting I have this morning is to see what can be done to solve the problems in the mess hall," the colonel admitted.

"Good. We have a suggestion. Get someone to run the mess hall who knows what he's doing."

"Great idea, but who would we get?"

"Remember when we did that little survey about interests and hobbies and something about each soldier's background? We found out that we have many recruits who have food-service experience. One man owned a restaurant and would be perfect for being in charge and choosing those who would do a good job."

"You've been doing some good work. Where did you get these ideas?"

"It wasn't just me but Kohler and Sauer who agreed the mess hall needed fixing. After all, we have to eat the same food. It's prepared as bad as the men say it is," said Wilhelm.

"Then what do you suggest?"

"Bring in the restaurant owner. His name is Conrad Becker. He's a few years older than most of the men. Tell him that he will be promoted to *gefreiter* and he needs to start planning who will do the cooking, serving and cleaning. We have a lot of information that will assist him. We have background information on many who have done this work before. He'll know whom to choose. By the time these recruits are graduated we'll have a whole new mess crew, so we can release those working in the kitchen for more stimulating duties."

"Schmidt, I appreciate your initiative. Will you get Becker started?"

"I'd be glad to. Kohler and Sauer can help. But first, he must know that you support him."

"Yes, yes. He'll have my full support."

That evening at quitting time Becker came to the office. Wilhelm couldn't read the man to know if he was coming to complain or to say thanks. He said that he had just finished a meeting with the *oberstleutnant*. He was told that the ideas for a proper mess hall came from the office staff. Wilhelm waited in anticipation as to the outcome of that meeting. He couldn't tell if he was happy or angry.

"I want to say that I would be pleased to accept that assignment. My whole life is food, and eating that slop that they feed us is sickening. What do you have in mind?"

Wilhelm told Becker that they had a list of some of the skills he would need. There were several cooks on the list and several more who had fairly extensive work in a restaurant. He would have to choose his own people. If he needed a specific skill, Hans and Gustav could search the questionnaires and find someone who might have those skills. He was told to choose carefully because it wasn't easy to replace a soldier. He would probably have to wait until the end of the next training session.

They also gave Conrad Becker a summary of the gripes from cooks, service people and recruits. He looked over the list and smiled. Then he said that these would definitely be his gripes as well.

"Let me study the list of people you think would be useful and I'll make a list of what I need," said Becker. "By the way, I'm grateful if this assignment will keep me here instead of sending me east. I may have antagonized an officer and am being punished by being recruited in the army. I would rather stay in this part of Germany since my home is near Frankfurt. Thanks."

It was the last week in October when the new class of recruits was promoted and given an assignment. All but two of the present mess crew transferred out. Most of them were happy to go. Recruits with food-service experience replaced them. Most were happy to be out of the kitchen. Even several of those doing the menial jobs of dish washer and serving were pleased not to be going to the eastern front. Conrad had chosen well.

The new recruits didn't know how fortunate they were. They took the good food and service for granted. But everyone associated with the mess hall was pleased to prepare and serve food the way it should be prepared and served. Griping about the food was a complaint of the past; even the officers would occasionally join the recruits in the mess.

Wilhelm overheard one of the officers talking to a *hauptmann*, (a captain). "I like to eat with the men, sometimes. The food's the same."

"The only difference that I can see is we get a few choice cuts of meat and an occasional bottle of beer, once in a while."

Wilhelm was forced to smile.

Chapter Twenty-Eight

By the first of January, 1940, Conrad Becker was promoted to *feldwebel*. Wilhelm was also promoted to *oberfeldwebel* (master sergeant) and Kohler became an ober*gefreiter* (senior lance corporal). Sauer was promoted to *gefreiter*, (corporal). *Oberstleutnant* Dengel was extremely pleased with the improvement at the Kaserne. He moved the responsibility for handling mail to Wilhelm and liked to visit the office frequently. Often he would ask if Wilhelm had any suggestions for improvement; he listened and usually supported his ideas.

Wilhelm hated to meet the *feldwebel* in the post office who insisted that he had an accent and called him "Toronto." He thought someone with more experience and rank just might recognize his accent as a New York accent. He was secretly pleased to have this new responsibility since it caused the *feldwebel* to be moved to another Kaserne.

Wilhelm felt the need to know how to drive. He asked Hans to teach him. His plan was to drive to France and have the French get him to safety. He told Dengel that he needed to know how to drive to get the mail to the post when his men were otherwise occupied and for various other emergencies that might come up. Dengel thought it was a good idea.

After quitting time and before mess, Hans would take a car from the motor pool and pick Wilhelm up at the office. Behind the motor pool was a large field for marching. It was there Wilhelm learned to drive. Shifting smoothly was the biggest obstacle. His coordination between foot and hand was not always accurate and the car jerked more than would be acceptable. They usually practiced for about a half hour. Within a week, Wilhelm had improved considerably. He liked the fact that nobody was around to see his mistakes or to get hurt if he did not drive as straight as he should. Hans would sometimes place cones so Wilhelm could parallel park. He learned quickly, and by the end of the month, he drove solo into town to deliver the mail to the post office.

Uncle Frederick and Aunt Ursula continued to correspond weekly, as would any good parents. They occasionally made mention of Aunt Hilda and Uncle Otto and Wilhelm appreciated the news. There was mention that Frederick was drafted into the army and had completed basic training at a Kaserne near Kaiserslautern. Cousin Greta was mentioned as having entered her third year at the university this past September. They were most careful to keep the letter full of news and not give away any information.

When Wilhelm was in Karlsruhe he decided to take the long way back by way of Rastatt to the Kaserne. South of Rastatt, according to the map, was a bridge that crossed over into France. At the town of Iffezheim he took a right, going northwest toward France. In four kilometers he saw the bridge in the distance. He stopped the car and parked it behind some bushes, then made his way through those same bushes to get a better look at the bridge. He was glad he'd grabbed the binoculars from the glove compartment.

Only two soldiers guarded the bridge. He could see no barrier on the German side but there was a barrier on the French. *It might be possible to drive slowly toward the bridge, as if he had a message for the two guards, then at the last moment speed toward the French side. When the French saw what was happening, they would raise the iron barrier. In any case, the German soldiers would be afraid to shoot, thereby causing an international incident.* As he observed the bridge, he didn't see anyone on the French side. Even after a half hour no soldier was observed.

Without someone to lift the barrier, he wasn't sure this plan would work.

Wilhelm felt safe at the Kaserne. He was a sergeant in charge of administration. He was not at all pleased with all the saber rattling by the Nazis. That war was on the way with France was certain. Only the day and hour were uncertain. Some thought Germany would attack England next while others thought France would most certainly be the next target. Through the cold winter months in Karlsruhe, Wilhelm and his crew kept the office humming efficiently. All reports and correspondence were sent out on time. He frequently visited Sergeant Conrad Becker in the mess to keep informed. He always made himself available to the *oberstleutnant*.

One afternoon, near quitting time, he was invited into Dengel's office. "Have some schnapps with me, Wilhelm." That was the first time Dengel had used his Christian name.

"I don't usually drink, Sir. Just an occasional beer."

"Well, this is a celebration and you might drink a bit to my success." Dengel poured a generous glass for himself and about two fingers for Wilhelm. It was obvious that Dengel was already a bit tipsy.

"If you insist, Sir," said Wilhelm.

"Keep this quiet for a while, Wilhelm, but I'm being promoted to *oberst* (colonel). It may be several months, but my superior has a position in Berlin that should soon become vacant. If it does I may be able to bring you as my assistant, although that is not certain."

"I'm very pleased for you, Sir. You deserve the promotion."

"I'm telling you about this because you have made me look good in the eyes of my superiors. They really don't care what kind of soldiers we turn out as long as the paperwork is on time and looks good." He laughed at what he considered a clever remark.

"Sir, that's my job."

"Yes, but you do it very well. And you trained Kohler and Sauer well and straightened out the problems with the mess hall. Other posts are experiencing these problems and haven't solved them. We have. That's why I'm being promoted." He was now slurring his words. "Look, Wilhelm, I'll ask for you to be my assistant, but that may not happen. If it doesn't, just keep me in mind and if you ever need help or my assistance, I'll be glad to give it."

"Sir, that isn't necessary, but I'm certain we will keep in touch. I appreciate all that you have done for me while I was here."

Wilhelm noticed that Dengel was getting extremely sloppy. This was not his first drink. Wilhelm drank about a fourth of his glass and recognized that it was a good time to take his leave.

"Sir, I'm needed back at the office. I like my job here and hope that I can stay in this area of Germany, as it is near my family. Please don't go to any trouble to bring me to Berlin as I'm happy here."

"I'll keep that in mind, Schmidt. I can't say that I blame you. There is too much politics in Berlin"

"I'll keep this information about your promotion quiet. If I can ever be of assistance to you, please call."

"I'm pleased that you like your position here and I won't be too eager to bring you to Berlin if you would rather stay here."

"I would rather stay here. But I appreciate that you were thinking of me." Wilhelm rose from his chair. "Congratulations again and thank you."

On the walk back to his office, his mind wrestled with this news. *He wouldn't want to go to Berlin with Dengel. Being in the office of an oberst would require that they get him secret or top secret clearance and that would require somebody looking into his background. Scrutiny of his past was in nobody's best interest and might even endanger his aunt and uncle and possibly his cousin. He would also be in danger. Maybe he could find something that would keep him away from Berlin and all the politics. He would keep his eyes and ears open for something to turn up in the next few months. He wouldn't be averse to a position in France after Germany occupied it as he knew they would. For now, all he had to do was wait and see what would happen.*

Chapter Twenty-Nine

In March of 1940, Finland signed a treaty with the Soviets. A few days later bombs were dropped by the *Luftwaffe* on the British submarine base called Scarpa Flow. Then in April the Germans invaded Denmark and Norway. On May 10, the Germans invaded Belgium, Luxembourg and the Netherlands, completely bypassing France. Several days later, they began their drive toward Paris, launching their attack from Belgium. They completely avoided the Maginot Line with its concrete tank defenses.

Wilhelm's blood was boiling, yet he had to ignore his feelings and go on with his job. He sensed that Hans and Conrad were upset by the news, not only because it might mean trouble for them but also because they thought Germany was evil. Yet no one dared voice what he felt and believed.

Wilhelm got a cryptic letter on Wednesday, May 15, from his aunt and uncle writing as his mother and father. He read the letter many times before he figured out the code. It was Friday evening when the formula was recognized. The first word in the first paragraph was significant, then the second word in the second paragraph and so on. The letter was well written and would not arouse the immediate suspicion of any censor. In his bunk that evening he reread the message that they wrote: NOW GET OUT THROUGH FRANCE WHILE STILL POSSIBLE.

On Monday, May 20, he tried to figure out what he could do. *His thoughts kept returning to the bridge at Iffezheim. The bridge was the key. If he could drive to the bridge he would hold up an envelope that would surely get the attention of the guards. They might even put down their rifles, although that would probably not happen. They would not be suspicious of a German car coming to speak with them. Then he would floor the accelerator and drive over the Rhein. With a little bit of luck, he might not be killed.*

Wilhelm started going through the files looking for a company near the border with whom they did business. He would visit it on some pretext or other. Finally Wilhelm found a printing company that provided them with forms, located in the town of Rastatt. He looked at his supply of forms and found that he had plenty. He decided to take one form and lose all copies of it in a file cabinet. Then he filled out a requisition to buy that one form at the printing shop in Rastatt. He made a phone call to the company and they said that it would be three days before the form could be printed as they were backed up. Wilhelm told them to print a reasonable supply of one thousand and to call him when they were ready.

The next step was to take the requisition to the *oberstleutnant*. "Sir, I've ordered forms that we need. They will call when the forms are ready."

"Send someone for the forms, Schmidt. You don't need to go."

"I'm afraid, Sir, that I do. They have made mistakes on this form in the past and we don't have enough to get us by if they make the mistake again. I want to look at them before I accept them."

"I can see where it's best if you go. We wouldn't want another bad batch. Tell them at the car pool that you're doing a job for me."

He got a call from Greiser Druck, the printing company, on Thursday, May 23, telling him that the forms were ready to be picked up. Wilhelm said he would be there in the morning. Friday morning he called and informed the *oberstleutnant* that the forms were in and he would get a car from the motor pool. Receiving permission, he told Kohler he would be back late in the morning. He then left for the motor pool.

Driving by himself was a delightful change for Wilhelm. The trees and flowers were all in bloom and for the first time since he was inducted into the German Army, he was elated with the possibility of escaping. Somehow the air seemed cleaner and clearer and he felt free. He would get his forms first, find out what information he could about the present situation and where the German Army was in France. Then he would drive to Iffezheim to execute his dash to freedom.

Wilhelm drove into Rastatt and found Greiser Druck at 22 Karlsruherstrasse. He looked over the forms and approved them. One of the printers, an older man with graying hair, asked Wilhelm if he would be taking those to France.

Thinking that the man knew what Wilhelm was planning, he said, "What do you mean, taking them to France?"

"Germany invaded France several weeks ago and all day yesterday and today our troops have been crossing the Rhein and pouring into Seitz. They are also crossing at Iffezheim. They received no resistance so far. You might be going to France next."

"We have been busy and we don't get much news. We hear less than you do."

"I would think the military would know before we did," the man said. "It's all over the radio."

Wilhelm was shocked. *His chance of escaping was frustrated. It might take a few days or even weeks for Germany to consolidate the country, but it was probably too late to use France as an escape route. The area around Rastatt on both sides of the river would be filled with soldiers.*

After leaving the printing company, Wilhelm drove the car past the bridge spanning the Rhein at Rastatt. As he suspected, a checkpoint had been established where papers were being looked at. It would be impossible to cross now without the proper authority and papers to back that up.

Reluctantly, he continued driving. He would have to consider another plan that had a greater chance of success.

Chapter Thirty

Dengel was promoted the last day in May and three days later Paris was bombed. On May 31, a Friday, *Oberst* Dengel completed his last day at the Karlsruhe Kaserne. He stopped by Wilhelm's office and closed the door to the office.

"Wilhelm, I know the man who is taking my place here at the Kaserne. He will arrive here Sunday, June 9. I don't like him. He'll have everyone 'Heil Hitlering' the first day on the job. You're not going to like him either and, what is more important, he will dislike you."

"Are you certain that he will be that bad? Maybe he's changed."

"He's changed all right. He's gotten worse since I've first worked with him. Here is my number in Berlin. Call me and tell me I'm wrong…that he's a pussycat. In the meantime, I'll look for someone who will need and appreciate your services. I have someone in mind. I'll contact him when I get to Berlin. He would appreciate you."

The two men shook hands and Dengel once more thanked Wilhelm for making him look good. He promised he would try to find a good position for him.

Monday morning, barely after 0800 hours, *Oberstleutnant* Heinrich Vedder walked across the compound straight toward the administration office. When he entered he clicked his heels and shouted, "Heil Hitler."

Kohler, getting a file from the lowest file cabinet was kneeling on the floor. He had his back to the commanding officer. Nor was he in a position to return the salute. He actually thought someone was being funny and so continued his task.

"What is your name, soldier?"

Kohler turned and raised himself slowly, his face turning beet red as he came to the realization that this was the new *oberstleutnant*.

"*Obergefreiter* Kohler, Sir."

"And who is your superior?"

Wilhelm spoke up and said, "I am, Sir."

"I'm speaking to the *obergefreiter*. When I want to speak with you, I will address you."

This first meeting said it all. There was no compromise with this maniac. Nor would there be any chance to make improvement, offer ideas or run the office as it had been run in the past. When the *oberstleutnant* came into Wilhelm's office, he began a one-way conversation. He told him what he wanted done, how it would be done and when. Wilhelm could do nothing but listen and nod that he understood. He made up his mind to call Dengel as soon as possible.

When *Oberstleutnant* Vedder was finished, he stuck out his arm in his 'Heil Hitler' salute, clicked his heels even before Wilhelm was able to return the salute, and was gone. Wilhelm reached for the phone to call *Oberst* Dengel.

"Wilhelm, how nice to receive a call from you," Dengel began. "How are you getting along with your new commanding officer?" This comment was dripping with sarcasm.

"Sir, can you get me out of here? The man is unbalanced. I'll go just about anywhere."

"Wilhelm, you speak some French, *n'est pas?*"

"*Oui. Je parle francais bien,*" answered Wilhelm.

"Good. I have a friend who is a major. He was a college professor and doesn't know a damn thing about forms, requisitions and doing things the way the military wants things done. He's a good man but ignorant with regard to things military. Would you help him?"

"I'd be glad to. When and where."

"He's being put in charge of a post near Audincourt near the Swiss border. The town is Faymont, and it is his responsibility to guard the French border to make sure no one passes into Switzerland."

"Will I be walking in the woods or will I be working indoors?"

"You'll be his secretary, in charge of the office. When I told him about you this morning, he asked me to see if you were available."

"I'm ready to go the moment you can cut the orders. What's the major's name?"

"Major Fritz Decker. He's a nice man who has been a university professor. He has had very little understanding of the military. You will be good for him and I know you will like him. Help him do a good job in France."

"I will," said Wilhelm and he meant it. "I'll wait for orders to move out. See what you can do for Kohler and Sauer. In a few days, Vedder will be ready to get rid of them and replace them with his own men."

"I'll call you as soon as this can be arranged. It's a lot easier getting things done when you're an *oberst*. You will hear from me soon. By the way…don't let the orders scare you. It will appear that you are being sent to the front. In a day or two new orders will be cut and you'll be sent to France. It will work out, you'll see. *Auf Weiderherren.*"

"Auf Weiderherren und Danke Schön."

It was late that afternoon when *Oberstleutnant* Vedder called Schmidt into the office and told him to pack, that he was being assigned to an infantry unit in Stuttgart and would be assigned from there to the front. Vedder didn't know what was meant by the front but assumed it was in the east. Wilhelm was certain that Dengel made this assignment sound like a demotion. Vedder was happy to get rid of this young *oberfeldwebel*, so he could appoint his own master sergeant. Wilhelm accepted the orders, turned on his heels and left the office without saying a word.

Wilhelm said goodbye to Kohler and Sauer and told them that Dengel was trying to find a place for each of them. He shook hands with his fellow soldiers moments before a car pulled up to drive him to Stuttgart. He threw his duffel in the back with a box of forms that he would need in his new job. He climbed in next to the *gefreiter* who was to be his driver.

The drive to Stuttgart was only an hour, even being delayed behind the horse-drawn wagons on the back roads. Wilhelm felt instant freedom and began a conversation with the *gefreiter*. It didn't take but a few minutes to find out that he despised the new commanding officer and thought that Schmidt was lucky to be transferred, even if it was to the front. Wilhelm didn't tell him that he was being assigned to a desk job in France near the Swiss border.

Wilhelm stayed a day at the Stuttgart Kaserne. He reported to the commanding officer, who was an *oberleutenant*. He was told to make himself comfortable. The officer told Wilhelm that new orders were being processed and he was to remain in Stuttgart until new orders arrived. Before the day ended, new orders came over the wire ordering Schmidt to proceed to France.

Oberst Dengel was doing what he said he would do and was doing it efficiently.

"*Feldwebel* Schmidt." A young *gefreiter* called to him from a truck.

"I'm your driver to Faymont. Grab your gear and let's go."

The driver drove to Strasbourg, then south to Mulhouse and the barracks at Faymont. They stopped a farmer on the road to ask where the barracks were. The farmer understood Wilhelm's French but refused to speak with him. He responded by pointing in the direction he should go.

It was late in the day when they arrived and the driver was determined to return to Stuttgart. There didn't appear to be anyone to tell Wilhelm where to go, what to do, when and where to eat and sleep. So he looked around, found a soldier who seemed to be free and asked him for the information he needed. He found a room that was not in the barracks and decided to make it his. He headed for the mess hall and found several soldiers having supper. He joined them. After dinner, he headed for his room to sleep. Later that evening, the major arrived, but it was not until the next day that Wilhelm met his superior.

Chapter Thirty-One

The compound was carved out of a pine forest, surrounded by a fence with barbed wire on the top. The trees had been cut down another fifty feet past the fence to provide security to the post. It had just been built, so everything looked shiny and new. The main office where Wilhelm would be working occupied the north end of the post and was near the gate that allowed vehicles to come and go. If the gate was open, which it usually was, the soldier stationed there would raise or lower a steel bar to allow a vehicle to enter or exit. A soldier would always remain on alert in the guardhouse.

The building on the west side of the compound had sleeping quarters for as many as twenty. These were for officers, sergeants and visitors. These private rooms were small, with a bed, sink, closet and a small desk and chair. They were austere but adequate. Halfway down the hall was also a bathroom with toilets, showers and sinks.

Barracks were provided for soldiers under the rank of sergeant. This large building was able to hold forty soldiers comfortably but could accommodate fifty if needed. Wilhelm suspected that this post would never billet that many soldiers unless it was required to guard a larger area. It too had an adequate tiled bathroom.

The mess hall was the next building south of the barracks. A small room attached to the mess hall was used only by officers and visitors. Food was placed on a long serving table and the soldiers filled their plates, then chose where they would sit. Each of the six tables in the mess hall would seat ten.

A warehouse occupied the south side of the compound. All these buildings, with the exception of the warehouse, were on the west side of the compound; the east side was reserved for equipment, vehicles and a shop to repair whatever needed service. All in all, it looked like any other German army post. The only difference was the size. This post was relatively small.

The next morning as Wilhelm approached the office, Major Fritz Decker was emptying boxes and placing the contents on the floor. He was of medium height, overweight, with graying hair. He looked like the college professor he had been instead of an officer in the German Army. His office consisted of a desk and chair and one chair for a visitor. Wilhelm introduced himself and Major Decker came from behind the desk to shake his hand.

"I've heard good things about you from *Oberst* Dengel. He says that you really made him look good. Can you do that for me?" Decker returned to his desk chair and sat.

"I'm young but know how to handle paperwork the way the military wants it done. I'll do whatever I can."

"Good. Good. Would you know by any chance how to get some furniture here?"

"Yes. I'll requisition it. I'll need your signature, two trucks, drivers and four men. While I'm at it, I'll get furniture for the entire barracks. How many men will we have here?"

While the two men estimated their needs, Wilhelm suggested that they take a walk around the barracks and see what else they could use. He suggested that they make it look like the major was giving orders as to what he wanted and Wilhelm was taking notes. Then when furniture and provisions arrived, the major would be credited with the results.

"Dengel was right. You do know how to make me look good. We're going to get along fine, Wilhelm."

"Major, call me Schmidt and I'll call you Major. Addressing me as Wilhelm will sound like we're good friends, and we can't have that now, can we?"

"No, I guess we can't," the major agreed. Then… "Let's take a walk around the grounds and see what we need to requisition."

By noon they had compiled an extensive list of furniture and supplies. Wilhelm found a miserable typewriter in one of the trucks. He rescued the requisition forms he brought from Karlsruhe and began to fill out requests for furniture, supplies and equipment. It was fairly late in the day when the task was finished. He decided to leave early the next morning. He called the supply depot in Freiburg and told them what he needed by way of furniture and asked the quartermaster there to have it ready by ten in the morning. He would bring the requisitions and four men to help load the two trucks. He understood that those working at the supply depot would like that he was bringing help since they wouldn't have to do all the heavy lifting.

He rushed to the barracks and picked out four healthy-looking soldiers who would be happy to use their muscles to get needed furniture, bedding and office supplies. A ride in the country was a bonus. He couldn't choose the drivers, as they had already been assigned to a specific truck.

Wilhelm sat in the first truck with a driver who liked to talk about Heilbronn, where he lived. When he finished talking about a subject, Wilhelm could get him on to another subject with just one question. By the time they got to Freiburg, he knew all about the soldier's family, his girlfriend, his love life and why he joined the army.

And the loquacious soldier thought that *Feldwebel* Schmidt was a great conversationalist.

The furniture was ready when they arrived, and Wilhelm got the soldiers started to load beds, office furniture, tables, book cases, file cabinets, chairs and lockers in the back of the trucks. He retrieved the requisition forms and compared them with the list given him at the depot. He went over the list to make sure nothing was forgotten. He also asked the quartermaster about a typewriter. "Choose what you want from the warehouse," came the terse reply.

He found one that looked like it hadn't been used. He was pleased with this find.

They ate lunch at the mess and started back early in the afternoon. Wilhelm rode with another driver so he would get to know as many as possible. He also didn't want to hear the same stories again from the first soldier. He found this second soldier was easy to be with but not as talkative as his previous driver.

It took several days to get everything where it belonged. They had anticipated they would have to prepare for fifty soldiers, even though forty would be the actual number. They procured more than they presently needed, knowing a few more might be assigned to their post. These other items were stored in the warehouse. Wilhelm, being the only *feldwebel* presently on the staff, was responsible for seeing that every piece of furniture was properly located. He also made mental notes of the good workers and which ones had to be watched. Then there were those who took initiative and did what needed to be done and those who waited to be told what to do. Wilhelm was learning whom he could count on. By the end of the week, on Saturday, June 15, the task of locating all the equipment and furniture for the compound was complete.

So much had happened in one short week. Wilhelm wondered if he made the right choice taking this assignment but eventually concluded that the decision wasn't his to make.

Sunday, Major Decker told Wilhelm what a great job he did. "I wouldn't have known where to begin or how to accomplish all that you did."

"That's why you have men who work for you, Sir. I had to learn when I first came into the army, but, as you know, I'm prone to asthma attacks if I'm subject to pollen. Dengel put me in an office, and a good man taught me what I needed to know. My mind seems to run along these lines, so I learned fast and got promoted. Let me take care of these small things."

"I was told about your asthma. We'll try to keep you indoors. I'm glad you know your way around the paperwork and I'm counting on you, Wilhelm…I mean Schmidt, to keep me out of trouble."

"I'll do my best. I've put together a list of some of the things we need to do to get the unit running. I'll leave the list with you and maybe you can tell me which ones you want to do first, second and so forth. Then we'll get on it. I'm going to spend the weekend getting the office organized, unless I'm needed."

"Take whatever time you need. And thanks."

"Oh, Major,…if I may be so bold as to make a suggestion. Sometime in the next few days it would be wise to visit the checkpoints and get a thorough understanding of the terrain and the situation. I would like to visit them also. I'm certain it will help us to make better decisions when changes need to be made."

"Good idea, Schmidt. Set it up for us when the new *hauptmann* (captain) arrives."

Chapter Thirty-Two

Wilhelm learned that a *hauptmann* would soon be assigned to assist Major Decker. At the moment, the only officer was the major; Wilhelm was the only non-commissioned officer. He told the major that other *feldwebels* were needed. One would be in charge of the mess, another the warehouse. He also told the major that a *feldwebel* was needed to be in charge of the patrolling duty and one for all the equipment. They looked at several of those with the rank of *gefreiter* and found four who had held the rank for over a year and were up for promotion. The major liked the idea that he would promote from within the post. It was easier than having someone brought in from outside. It would boost morale. It allowed the major to promote four to the rank of *feldwebel* and four from *obersoldat* to *gefreiter.*

Once the right men were promoted, Wilhelm set about telling them what he expected of them. He was the *oberfeldwebel* (sergeant major) even though he held the title of *feldwebel*. Yet all these details of running the barracks fell to him. He knew that the faster he could get the new *feldwebel* in each area performing up to par, the less work he would have and he'd be able to concentrate on his job.

It was the fifth of July when Wilhelm realized that he missed the American holiday and his anniversary of becoming an American citizen. He couldn't believe that the day came and went without his realization that it was an important day for him. When he did comprehend his oversight, he felt bad and had a severe case of homesickness. His mother, father and sister occupied his thoughts and the images in his head.

As he lay in bed that night, the memory of his first big league baseball game was on his mind.

He was eight and it was the Fourth of July weekend. His father took him to see the Brooklyn Dodgers play the Cincinnati Reds at Ebbets Field. They sat on the first base side, and a foul line-drive headed toward them. His father caught it cleanly in his right hand, without a bobble. Billy was bursting with pride as all the people applauded. His father took a bow, presented the ball to Billy and took his seat. No one could have been more proud of their father than Billy was. It was a moment he would never forget and the baseball had since that moment occupied the place of honor on Billy's chest of drawers. He could see it sitting where he placed it just days before he left for Europe.

Wilhelm heard but had trouble assimilating all the news taking place in Europe. Norway surrendered to Germany in June of 1940, Hitler and Mussolini met in Munich, France signed an armistice with Germany, U-boats were having success in the Atlantic sinking allied shipping, the Soviets occupied the Baltic States and German planes and rockets continued to bomb Britain. He knew that the assignment of this barracks was to patrol the border between France and Switzerland and control the three checkpoints that led into Switzerland. There were twenty-two kilometers to patrol. No one had permission to cross into Switzerland.

Anyone who tried was to be arrested and would most likely be shot. Anyone trying to escape from France was to be shot.

The orders from the high command were clear.

Hauptmann Horst Schlayer arrived on the fifth of August, a Monday. He was a tall, good-looking captain. He was dressed impeccably and exuded an air of arrogance. He entered the office with a click of his heels and a loud "Heil Hitler."

"Do you wish to see the Major, *Hauptmann?*" Wilhelm asked as he came to attention.

"Yes, please."

Wilhelm went into the major's office and announced that a *hauptmann* was reporting for duty. Major Decker told Wilhelm to show him in.

"Heil Hitler," Schlayer roared when he reached the door.

"Come in, *Hauptmann*, and close the door. First of all you need not use the 'Heil Hitler' greetings while at this barracks. We are all patriotic Germans here and we profess our loyalty by doing a good job. The duty we have is to prevent anyone from crossing the border into Switzerland. That's a twenty-four-hour-a-day job, covers twenty-two kilometers of border and involves every man we have on the base. We are understaffed and do not need to antagonize our soldiers with unnecessary ritual and commands."

"We always used that greeting in Nurnberg and..."

"Schlayer, I don't give a damn what you did in Nurnberg. Here the greeting is not necessary and is not used. Understood?"

"*Yawohl.*"

Wilhelm was pleased to hear the major assert himself and not let this arrogant young officer walk all over him.

"Now, sit down and we'll talk about what is necessary," said Decker. "We are manning three checkpoints twenty-four hours a day. So far, we have not had to turn back anyone from the border. One of the first things we need to do is find out where our weak spots are. There are mountains that may not be passable and we need to know which ones so that we don't have to worry about sending patrols there. We also need to know the neighbors who have land that borders the mountains and the borders themselves."

"Do you have a good map of the area to be patrolled?" Schlayer asked.

"Yes, but it's not good enough. You'll have to check out the entire length of the border yourself. Bring a couple of men with you for protection and get to know the area well. Then visit the farms in the area. Get to know the people and their capabilities. One or more of the farmers may have ties to the Resistance. I'm counting on you to handle the security aspects of this job."

"I can handle it. Is it possible to be assigned quarters? Then, possibly, I might receive a brief tour of the barracks?"

"Yes, I'll get *Feldwebel* Schmidt to take you around. He's been doing everything until recently. I'm sure he's pleased that you're here."

Wilhelm was asked to take *Hauptmann* Schlayer to his quarters and give him a tour of the compound. Schlayer was humbled after his meeting with Decker and knew that he had a lot of work ahead of him and needed the cooperation of people like Schmidt.

This is not going to be easy getting this post in shape, Schlayer thought. *This is a lazy post because the major is lazy. The sergeant is too young. I'm the only one who is trained to be a soldier. It may take a little time, but there will be changes made.*

It was several hours later when Schmidt showed Schlayer his newly furnished office. Schlayer was impressed. It was next to the major's. Wilhelm had positioned his desk between the two offices in the larger office. Behind Wilhelm were file cabinets and in front of him was a bench for visitors and enough folding chairs for a meeting. One of the other sergeants had a desk just off the mess hall. It had a window so the *feldwebel* could see what was happening even when he was in the office. The other sergeant had his quarters in one of the barracks. An office was built for him. Work areas were built for the *feldwebel* in charge of the garage and warehouse."

"I can't help but notice that you have a limp," Schlayer began. "From a war injury?"

"No. One of my legs was longer than the other from birth. Those doing the recruiting didn't consider it an impediment."

"How are you able to march?"

"I have not been required to march. I work in the office. Because of asthma, I'm forced to avoid the woods and the outdoors on certain days. Other than those minor problems, I'm a fit soldier."

"I didn't know that the German Army would allow men with these impediments to serve."

"Sometimes they're only impediments if we let them be." Wilhelm increased his speed a bit to put a few steps' distance between him and the *Hauptmann*. He wanted him to know the discussion was over.

As Schmidt showed Schlayer around the compound, he noticed that none of the sergeants had the new insignia on their uniforms.

"*Feldwebel* Bauer. Why haven't you sewn the new insignia on your uniform? How will anyone know you are a *feldwebel?*"

"I don't think I have the skills to sew on the insignia. I've never sewn anything."

"I can see where that can be a problem. Do me a favor. Get the uniforms that need sewing, have the new *feldwebels* and *gefreiters* pin the insignia where they belong and I'll see that they get sewed."

This will give me a good excuse to go into town, since I'm one of the few people who speak French, he was thinking. *Eventually I might meet those who can help me escape from the army.*

When this chore was taken care of, the captain and Schmidt continued their tour. Near the end of the afternoon, after Schlayer had received a thorough briefing, Wilhelm sat down with Major Decker.

"It might be wise if we make some effort to enlist the good will of the villagers. We can command them to obey us as their conquerors or maybe use a different approach. We can show that we are only occupying their country for a while and are not trying to make their life miserable."

"The latter would be my choice, Schmidt. What do you propose?"

"That we tell the soldiers what we expect of them, that we buy goods in the shops in the village and we treat the villagers with respect."

"I agree. Put together some ideas for me to present to the men and we'll have a meeting this week."

"I will. Also may I suggest that we use the services of the tailor in town to sew on the insignia for any soldier who receives a promotion or needs to have new insignia? He might farm the work out to one of the village women but, in any case, it will create some good will. We can take the money out of petty cash; it won't be expensive. Let's see how this first visit goes."

"That's a good idea. Who will you get to do this?" asked Decker.

"I would like to do it, Sir. I am less threatening since I'm not an officer. Having a limp might even get me some sympathy. Besides myself, I don't know who can speak French. Until I find out, it is probably best that I be the messenger. It will give me a chance to find out which people in town we can trust and who might cause some trouble. I might even find out whom we can't trust. Not everyone is pleased with our presence. Getting the insignia sewn is a first step. We can't have German soldiers wearing insignia that looks like they were sewn by an amateur, now can we?"

"Thank you, Schmidt. I appreciate that you think of these things."

"Sir, few officers would see the importance of keeping the good will of the villagers. I'm pleased you do. I'll do the best I can."

Chapter Thirty-Three

Wilhelm drove into town with a backseat filled with uniforms. On the main street in Faymont stood the shops that provided the villagers with most of the services they needed. Here was the butcher, the baker, the wine shop, the grocer, the cheese shop and the tailor. Wilhelm stopped his car in front of a shop with the one word *TAILLEUR* above the door.

In his best French, he asked if the gentleman standing behind the counter was the tailor. The tailor nodded and asked if he could help. It was obvious that he wasn't pleased to be visited by a German soldier, even if he wasn't an officer and had a limp. Wilhelm told him that he had a car full of uniforms that needed insignia sewed on them.

The tailor remained silent, forcing Wilhelm to make his request.

"Would you be so kind as to sew insignia on them? They are all pinned where they need to be sewed."

The tailor didn't know yet whether he was being commanded to sew the insignia or if his services were being requested. He feared the former and wasn't at all sure he would be compensated.

"How much would you charge for each item?" asked Wilhelm.

"Bring a uniform in and I will look at it," said the tailor. His attitude said that he wasn't happy with the German soldier standing in front of him but less uncomfortable now that he knew he would be paid.

Wilhelm brought several of the uniforms into the shop and placed them on the counter. While the tailor was determining what he should charge, Wilhelm had a chance to observe him. He was middle-aged, short, thin, with black hair, and sporting a neatly trimmed goatee. His trousers had a sharp crease which Wilhelm suspected was sewn. First impressions were that this man knew more than he let on and that his diminutive size was misleading.

"I would charge five francs for the larger insignia and three for the small ones."

"That would be acceptable. Would you accept Deutschmarks?"

"Yes, but I would add the fee the bank would charge to exchange."

"That's only fair. We will have many uniforms this month, but I presume it will be much less in the future."

"That's fine. Any business is welcome."

"When will they be ready?"

"In several days I'll have them all ready. Come back Wednesday."

There was a slight change in his attitude, which Wilhelm believed was caused by the prospect of more business.

"I'll be here Wednesday afternoon. Would you be upset if I brought more work with me?"

"No, more work is always welcome."

"Then thank you. I'll see you Wednesday."

Wilhelm was sensitive to the tailor wanting work and yet didn't want to appear as cooperating with the enemy. Surely sewing on some patches would not be misunderstood.

When Wilhelm left the shop, he didn't go immediately to his vehicle but rather visited the wine shop across the street. He could feel the eyes of all the villagers observing him even though he couldn't see them. He would be remembered because of his limp. He kept his eyes straight ahead, aware that he was being watched. He chose a nice bottle of French red wine, which he paid for from his own money, and then visited the bakery next door and bought a loaf of white bread. The young lady behind the counter was extremely attractive. He could see the baker working in the back room, probably her father, watching him out of the corner of his eye. He looked none too pleased to be visited by a German soldier. His last stop was to the shop with the sign, *FROMAGE* across the front. He bought some cheese that had holes in it and he believed was Swiss. These items he also bought with his own money, even though he really didn't need the wine, cheese or bread. He just didn't want the tailor to be under suspicion because Wilhelm had visited his shop. Now four shops were visited, and when they compared notes it wouldn't seem unusual. He believed this would deflect suspicion that the tailor was cooperating with the enemy.

Wilhelm returned the following Wednesday to pick up the uniforms. Not only were they sewed but pressed as well, and on hangers. "These look great. If you wish, I'll return the hangers."

"That would be helpful. Hangers are not always easy to procure."

"We have some more troops arriving soon and, if you wish, I'll have more uniforms."

"That would be fine. I appreciate the business." There was definitely a different attitude in the tailor's voice from the first visit. This was as close to a thank you as he could expect.

"Do you do fitted shirts?" asked Wilhelm.

"Yes. That is my specialty."

"On my next visit I may bring a shirt with me."

He went from the tailor to the grocery store and bought two pears. Then he went to the cheese store and bought some Camembert cheese to go with the pears. It seemed to Wilhelm that this time his visit caused less of a stir. He hoped that soon most of the villagers would know that he meant them no harm. That was what he wished. He hoped to help them even if they were unaware of his intentions. Being able to speak good French proved an asset.

Wilhelm made it his business to visit the village once a week. He would visit the tailor even if he didn't have work for him. He felt sure that the tailor was one of the elders of the village and others listened to him. One day Wilhelm dropped the hint that he wanted to get some information to the mayor, whoever that might be.

"We don't have a mayor," said the tailor.

"How can I give information that might be helpful to the villagers?" asked Wilhelm.

"What kind of information?"

"Sometimes the Nazis want to do terrible things, like kill Jews. We have not been given orders to do that but only to guard the border. Who should I tell when evil things are about to take place so the villagers can be warned?"

"That would be a very dangerous thing for you to do."

"Only if my superiors knew."

"But you are a German."

"I wear the uniform of a German soldier. That is all I can tell you," said Wilhelm.

"Then tell me if you need to warn us and I will get the information to the proper people."

"*Monsieur Le Tailleur*, I knew you could be trusted. You know my life depends on you."

"I know it does. And, as you say, you know I can be trusted."

The two men parted, and for the first time since Wilhelm was inducted into the army, he felt as if he was doing something for his own country, even if they hadn't yet joined the war. To keep up appearances, he stopped and bought a loaf of dark bread, partially to keep suspicion away from the tailor but, more to the point, to see again the beautiful girl in the bakery.

Chapter Thirty-Four

"**S**chmidt, arrange for me to visit the border early next week. I want you to go with me." That was Major Decker's terse command on Thursday afternoon.

The following week, Major Decker and *Feldwebel* Schmidt drove to the border. At checkpoint #1 they spoke with the soldiers on duty. The major walked the trail with the two soldiers who would patrol the border. Wilhelm stayed with the other two, asking questions and getting their opinion as to how secure the border was in their section.

When Decker returned they drove to checkpoint #2 and repeated the inspection. Wilhelm wanted to avoid being in the woods and was most interested in what the men had to say. He wanted to know if they believed people in France could cross the border into Switzerland. The operation was repeated at checkpoint #3.

"Do you believe that anyone has crossed the border in your sector?" Wilhelm asked.

"No. We have a lot of border to guard, but these mountains are making our job easy. We still need to patrol but, in my opinion, one would have to be a mountain climber to get into Switzerland or would have to be invisible to walk past our checkpoint," commented one patrol leader. That opinion was shared by all the soldiers with whom Wilhelm spoke.

"Do you believe there is a passageway through these mountains?" asked Wilhelm.

"If there is, we haven't been able to find it. As long as we have men at the checkpoints and keep regular patrols, no one is going to cross here."

"We are fortunate with these rock formations. They keep the border secure and make our job easier," said another.

On the ride back to the barracks, Major Decker asked Wilhelm what he'd found out by talking to the men.

"The men don't believe anyone has crossed the border. They think the mountains are impossible to cross and, as long as they patrol, no one would attempt to cross."

"I can't help but agree with the men. Did you see those rock formations? Most rise up straight, and there doesn't seem to be a break in them, except where we have checkpoints. Nevertheless, I'm going to suggest to *Hauptmann* Schlayer that he check the formations from the French side just in case there is an easy way over those cliffs that we can't see from here. My opinion now, from what I've seen, is that the rock formations provide a natural barrier that is protecting the border from anyone who wishes to cross. That will be a huge help to us." Major Decker tapped his hand against the car door. "Huge."

"I believe you're right. The men who do the patrolling share that belief."

The two men continued to talk as Wilhelm drove back through town and to the barracks. When they had a moment late in the afternoon, they met with Schlayer and told him what they'd found.

"*Hauptmann*, both Schmidt and I visited the three checkpoints today.

Schmidt spoke with the men and I walked with the patrols. The borders appear to be secure, especially if we keep up the patrols as we have been. The rock formations are steep and provide a natural barrier to crossing. It would be smart for you to check out the formations on the French side to be certain that there are no easy passages through the formations. According to the men, anyone attempting to cross into Switzerland would have to be a mountain climber to get over those formations."

"I'll make that a priority. I will take a truckload of men and search the formations to see if there is a way across that we don't know about. Then we'll be able to relax a bit if we're certain that no one can cross. The patrols will give us added assurance."

"Fine, Schlayer. I'm sure you'll do a good job."

Chapter Thirty-Five

The summer was over and the children in the village were all back in school. Wilhelm was asked by Major Decker to set up times for small groups of about a dozen to meet with the major. He wanted to tell them how they were to conduct themselves on a visit into town.

"Gentlemen, until now the village of Faymont has been off limits to you. I'm going to allow soldiers to go into town, with certain restrictions. You are to conduct yourself like gentlemen; you will not fraternize or try to date any female; and you will avoid antagonizing the merchants."

He paused to allow his words to sink in. "Our task here is to protect the border, not to harass the French people. Consider going into town a privilege. If it is abused, it will be withdrawn. Understood?"

The soldiers all nodded or indicated they understood.

This meeting was repeated three times and the soldiers appeared to appreciate a chance to visit the village and buy fresh food and bread. They had no place else to buy items with their meager pay except the commissary, which sold only what was absolutely necessary—cigarettes, toiletries and stationery.

Wilhelm ate with the soldiers and played cards with them. He was promoted to *oberfeldwebel* the first of September, a position he'd held without the title since arriving in Faymont. Except for the sergeant major stripes on his arm, he was considered one of the men. He began to hear more and more grumbling from the soldiers that they had just come off patrol and were assigned again just eight hours later. He was told that one group of soldiers pulled a double, that is, two eight-hour patrols in a row.

He spoke with the *feldwebel* in charge of setting the schedule and was told that *Hauptmann* Schlayer was the one who would change the schedule. The *feldwebel* would draw up the schedule for a month and present it to the *hauptmann* for his approval.

"He's in charge of security. He told me that he is supposed to sign off on the schedule. I had already drawn up the schedule when *Hauptmann* Schlayer arrived. He changed it a week later. This month I drew up the schedule and asked for his signature. He kept it a day and made massive changes. The men gripe to me, but I can't do anything."

"Remember, when he asks, that I came to you to find out why there was so much griping about the schedule. Now, may I see the revision?"

Wilhelm looked at the schedule and saw many patrols that were scheduled without sufficient rest. He also saw that the patrol size was unnecessarily increased. It was obvious that he would have to go over the captain's head if he was to get this straightened out.

"May I have a copy of the revised schedule, and I would appreciate it if I could have a copy of the schedule before revision?"

When Major Decker came in, Wilhelm asked to see him. Wilhelm entered the office and closed the door.

"What is it, Schmidt?"

"The *hauptmann* has changed the schedule, assigning six men to each patrol instead of four. This is causing severe discontent among the men."

"Who said he could change the schedule?"

"He told the sergeant that since he was in charge of security he needed to see the patrol schedule. Then he revised it. It has been like this for about a month. The complaints are increasing. We can't keep this schedule for much longer."

"Do you have copies of both schedules?"

"Yes."

"Let me see the old and the revised schedule."

The two men looked at the schedules; it was soon obvious that the first schedule prepared by the *feldwebel* was better than the second. They discussed what changes needed to be made and how they would incorporate other duties into the time between patrols.

"I'll speak with *Hauptmann* Schlayer. You get with the *feldwebel* and have him revise the schedule with four men to each patrol. That will stretch us to the limit. Do we need to make any other changes?"

"I think it would be wise to have the patrols rotate so that they get to know all three border sites we have to guard. While we're at it, let's set up a schedule as to when the men can go into town, possibly only on their off days. That will limit the number annoying the villagers. And we have to listen to the villagers to make sure they aren't being bothered or harassed."

"Great ideas. When *Hauptmann* Schlayer arrives, send him in. You better disappear for a while. This might get loud."

Wilhelm did disappear and sat down with the sergeant in charge of the patrols. They discussed how the schedule could be improved. He liked Wilhelm's ideas about assigning them to all three sites and told Wilhelm that he would make up a new schedule and would let him see it before he released it.

"Do you think I'll have to clear it with *Hauptmann* Schlayer?"

"I don't think so, but let's wait for what the major has to say."

Hauptmann Schlayer walked past Wilhelm later that day and, without saying a word, closed the door to his office, obviously annoyed. When the major arrived, he called Wilhelm to his office.

"Schlayer will not review the schedule since the schedule doesn't pertain to security. Patrols will return to four men and the patrols will alternate between three posts."

"I'll tell the sergeant not to report to Schlayer and to bring any difficulties to my attention…with your permission?"

"Yes, that is the way it should work. If you have any questions, bring them to me."

"I will."

"I also like the idea of limiting the soldiers to visiting the village on their off days, only. If they have to go to the village at any other time, they will need permission from me or you, and I guess we can't bypass Schlayer. Let's see how he handles that minor limitation of power," said the major.

The next few weeks were relatively peaceful. There was some confusion finding the new checkpoints and several soldiers got lost, thus annoying those they were to relieve. By the third week, everyone knew their assignment and was relatively content. Wilhelm, when he had nothing to do, played with the numbers and worked out a schedule fair to everyone. Everyone had the same number of days to work before they got a day off, everyone had equal time at each of the shifts and everyone spent the same amount of time at each site. It was as fair as it could be made before Wilhelm presented his ideas to the *feldwebel* in charge of the patrols.

The *feldwebel* was extremely pleased with the plan and was certain it would be satisfactory to all the men. He also felt that the soldiers were enjoying being able to go into town occasionally and that the griping was confined to the food. Wilhelm thought that was a good sign but nevertheless decided to have a talk with the mess sergeant. He realized that it was no easy task running a compound, regardless of the size.

It was the mess sergeant who asked Wilhelm to help him assign the soldiers to kitchen duty. Together, they studied the new schedule and decided to give those on night patrol some kitchen duty to help them pass the time during the day. They also realized that night patrols required only two men at each post since they didn't have to patrol the border but only the checkpoint, freeing two men for working in the kitchen. Coordinating all the duties with the two sergeants meant that the task of keeping the border secure, using everyone to their full potential, and not wasting manpower, were all maximized.

Chapter Thirty-Six

Schlayer was like a caged cat, wanting to tear at anything that got near him. He found it difficult to sit at his desk for any length of time and he growled at anyone who tried to ask him a question. For two days he refused to speak to Schmidt, even to say hello. He answered Schmidt's greeting with a grunt. Nor would he speak with Major Decker. He kept his door closed and was civil to nobody.

Major Decker told Schmidt that he wanted to speak with Schlayer. Wilhelm passed along the message by using the intercom. "I'm busy at the moment." Nevertheless, he left his office and knocked on his superior's door.

"Come in, *Hauptmann.*"

The captain came in and stood at attention.

"Sit down, Schlayer."

"I'd rather stand."

"I said, sit down." There was no mistaking the tone with which that was spoken. Schlayer took a seat.

"Have you visited the three checkpoints and walked the border?"

"I visited the checkpoints."

"But you haven't walked the border."

Schlayer nodded and shifted his weight in the chair.

"I want you to walk the borders. You need to understand the security problems the borders can pose. Have you searched the cliffs from the French side?" Schlayer shook his head. "Have you visited the farms in the area?" He received the same response. "You have been remiss in your duty of seeing to the security of the borders we are to patrol. You have a lot of work to do. Do your job and let others do theirs. Now get out of here and tend to your business. If I have to speak to you again, it will be to dismiss you and recommend you be sent to the eastern front. Dismissed."

Schlayer didn't speak to Wilhelm for the next two weeks. He also spent most of his time away from the office. Wilhelm suspected that he was taking the major's command to walk the border and search for any passageway from the French side.

Major Decker called Wilhelm into his office one evening to ask how everything was going. Wilhelm told him that Schlayer was as mad as a rabid dog but that everyone else was pleased with the changes.

Schlayer singled out two soldiers who were not too popular with their fellow bunkmates and found extra duty for them. He did ask for Decker's permission. He used them to drive him wherever he wanted to go and excused them from guard duty when it suited his purpose. Since it seemed that he was doing what he was supposed to do, it appeared wise to not chastise him for using the help he needed. If he started to abuse his position, Major Decker would have to step in.

The two soldiers were *Obersoldat* (Private First Class) Herman Hess and *Obersoldat* Conrad Westphal. Schmidt wondered why these two men were chosen. Hess was tall and bold, left-handed and had a mean temper. He was always looking for a fight, certain that what he said was correct. He would come down hard on a fellow soldier who would challenge him. He expected everything he said to be believed as if he couldn't make a mistake. He usually prevailed because of his size and aggressiveness.

Conrad Westphal was more reasonable than Hess but always did what the taller man asked him to do. It was just difficult to say no to Hess. He made small attempts at asserting himself, but Hess did what he wanted and Westphal just tagged along as his "yes" man. Since *Hauptmann* Schlayer was using them as drivers, they had much more freedom from kitchen duty and from patrols and they had use of the vehicle assigned to Schlayer. The only person they answered to was the captain.

The young lady in the bakery didn't like it when these two came in. The tall one stared at her breasts and made crude remarks to the other. The shorter one bought a loaf of bread and some cookies. Most of the communication was by pointing. The young lady gave no indication that she understood any language but French. When he indicated that he was finished, the bakery lady wrote out the cost on a slip of paper and the shorter soldier paid her, anxious to leave before he was further embarrassed.

One evening they parked their vehicle down the street from the bakery and turned off the headlights. At quitting time, the young lady turned out the lights but didn't come out the front door. So they drove to the street that would allow them to see the back of the shop. Her bike was gone. They knew she couldn't have gone far, so they drove a short distance on one of the two roads that would take them out of town. When she didn't turn up on that one, they backtracked and tried the other road. They still didn't see her. Frustrated and annoyed, Hess turned on the car lights and drove back to the barracks.

"All I want to do is find out where she lives," said Hess.

"Why is that so important?"

"It is. That's all. I want to know where she lives."

The following evening they were again parked on the street with their lights off. They could see the beautiful girl with the long, dark hair moving about in the store. From their location they could see her partially when she was in the front of the store, but she was out of view when she was in the back. They didn't know whether the young girl was aware of their presence.

They couldn't see the girl go out the back door, run to the alleyway behind where their car was parked. She memorized the license plate before she returned to the bakery, wrote down the plate number and returned to her chores. She was gone just a little over a minute. Finally, when she turned the lights out, the soldiers drove to the corner. Hess got out and Westphal watched the front door. Hess went around the back and noticed that the bicycle wasn't there. He wondered if she could be inside, so he tried the back door. Locked. No light was on inside.

"Where the hell is she?

"She must have known we were watching her," said Westphal.

"If it's the last thing I do, I'm going to find out where she lives," Hess mumbled as they drove back to the Kaserne.

The day after this incident the young lady and her father rode their bicycles to the barracks and requested to see the commanding officer. They waited while a soldier went inside to find out how he should proceed. Obviously, not many French civilians came to visit the barracks. The soldier who had greeted them returned with another soldier, who introduced himself as *Oberfeldwebel* Wilhelm Schmidt, the soldier they'd seen in town, the one with the limp.

The civilian and his daughter noticed that the tall soldier spoke excellent French. He escorted them to the main building directly ahead of them. They waited for a few minutes and were then ushered in to see the commanding officer, Major Fritz Decker, according to the nameplate on his desk.

"How may I help you?" inquired the major in perfect French.

"I am Jacques LeVoie and this is my daughter, Annette. We own the bakery in town. Several of your soldiers have been stalking my daughter and even went so far as to attempt to enter the shop after hours," Jacques began. After an uncomfortable pause he continued. "Do you have children, Major?"

"Yes...two."

"Is one a girl?"

"Yes."

"Then you would understand my anger if something were to happen to my daughter. And the anger would extend beyond me to this entire village. Annette grew up in this village and is known and loved by everyone. Your soldiers would find themselves hated and in danger because of the action of these two. We are simple country people who make bread for our fellow villagers. We don't want to make trouble...but your men will not harm my daughter." He banged his fist on the major's desk.

Annette reached into the pocket on her dress and showed the major the license number of the vehicle the men were driving. She told the major that she could identify both of the soldiers, if necessary. "It is the taller of the two, the left-handed one, who is causing most of the trouble. He has a very foul mouth and is most offensive."

"I can assure you this matter will be handled," the major began. "And the fact that you didn't take matters into your own hands was the correct way to handle the situation."

"I'm going to trust you, Major. I do not want these two to bother her."

"We want a good relationship with the villagers. We are here in the spirit of brotherhood." He tapped an impatient finger on the edge of his desk. "I will personally guarantee her safety." Major Decker extended his hand to the baker. "Schmidt, please escort our visitors to the gate."

The baker and his daughter were escorted to the gate, where they got on their bicycles and pedaled home.

Wilhelm overheard the conversation between the major and the villagers and recognized the dark-haired young lady. When he heard that two soldiers were stalking her, he knew immediately who they were. Hess and Westphal were the only two who had access to a vehicle, supposedly doing tasks ordered by *Hauptmann* Schlayer.

Major Decker beckoned to Wilhelm. "Schmidt, get those two men in here immediately."

In short order, Hess and Westphal stood at attention in the major's office. Westphal's legs trembled.

"It has been brought to my attention that you have been harassing one of our villagers. Hess, what do you have to say?"

"We were only trying to talk with the lady in the bakery. We weren't doing anything."

"You were doing more than looking. It seems, Hess, that you have a filthy mouth and say things that are insulting. Westphal, you're no better, doing what Hess tells you to do. Both of you were stalking that young lady, and it will stop."

"We meant no harm. We just wanted to see what she was doing. She's a pretty girl and we don't see many of those," Hess explained.

"I don't believe for a moment that your only motive was to get a glimpse of the bakery girl. You even tried to open the door."

"That was only to make sure she didn't need our help."

"If I hear or find out that one of you was observing, stalking, or speaking with that young lady, you will be stripped of your rank and sent to where the fighting is the heaviest. And that goes for visiting the bakery.

It is out of bounds to you. Do you understand?"

Both soldiers said they did and were dismissed.

"Schmidt," Decker yelled when the two were gone. "When Schlayer returns, ask him to come in here."

"Yes, Sir."

Late that afternoon after Schlayer returned from whatever he was doing in the field, he was invited into Decker's office and the door was closed.

"*Hauptmann*, two men under your command have been stalking the baker's daughter. They are supposed to be your drivers. If you can't control them and if they insist on further harassing a villager, they will be shipped out of here and you with them. Do I make myself clear?"

"Yes, Sir."

"*Hauptmann* Schlayer, this is twice that I've had to reprimand you within the month. There will not be a third time. Understood?"

"Yes, Sir."

"Dismissed."

Chapter Thirty-Seven

Conrad Westphal was concerned about the threat made by the major. He didn't want to lose his rank, what little he had, and he sure as hell didn't want to be sent to the front, where he could lose everything and be miserable doing it. He understood that it was his life he was contemplating. Guarding the checkpoints and patrol duty were fine with him.

He made a resolution not to have anything to do with that beautiful girl in the bakery. Herman Hess, on the other hand, acted as if he thought the major's threats were a joke.

"That's what he has to say. He knows that we Germans are in charge and that France has surrendered. To the victor belong the spoils. He knows how soldiers will behave, and if I'm not the one to screw that young lady, it will be another soldier. I'll let it rest for a bit and then we'll see what the situation is." Hess smirked as he slicked back his hair with his left hand.

Westphal decided he would distance himself from Hess as much as possible. The problem was that *Hauptmann* Schlayer would frequently request the two of them. Recently, however, Hess was volunteering to drive at night, and he didn't invite Westphal along. That was fine with Westphal. He did wonder what Hess was planning; his thoughts were not reassuring. At least he wouldn't be implicated.

It was near the end of the month of September and the moon was full. He and Hess were driving through town shortly before six o'clock. Hess drove past the bakery then turned the vehicle around and parked across the street from the shop.

"Get out of here," said Westphal. "Put the car in gear and drive. I don't want to have anything to do with that girl."

Hess ignored Westphal and lit a cigarette. "Her old father died and now she lives alone outside of town."

"How do you know that?"

"I heard that the old man who owned the bakery died. I assumed that was the man who spoke with the major. One day I got lucky and followed her home."

Westphal found out that he got the information from a soldier just assigned to the post. He was in a different company and was in the hospital after breaking his leg. That's when the baker passed away. Hess was bragging to the soldier that he was stalking her and was watching her house.

Hess could not keep quiet about his plans. He told Westphal that he would put a move on her one evening when she was alone. "After several weeks of living by herself she'll enjoy my company."

It was no use telling him he was deceiving himself. Hess was obsessed and wasn't interested in listening to anyone.

"Leave me out of this," Westphal said emphatically. "Don't invite me to go with you if you are having anything to do with that girl. The whole village would despise you if you harm her in any way."

"Don't worry. I want her all to myself," he said. Then he saw that the woman in the bakery was the older woman who worked there. He put the car in gear and headed back to the barracks.

Westphal watched Hess over the next few weeks and could tell that the soldier was getting weird. He considered going to the major and telling him what he knew, but the major might consider the flimsy evidence as insignificant. Thoughts refused to leave him alone. *He sure didn't want to get on the wrong side of Hess. Maybe if he had just a little bit more evidence he could talk to the major. That way it wouldn't look like he was trying to kiss the major's ass. It didn't look as if Hauptmann Schlayer had any control over Hess or, for that matter, didn't even know where he was most of the time. Hess just signed out the vehicle when he wanted it.*

One night late in October, Hess was on duty at ten but signed out at nine. Westphal just happened to be passing by and, after Hess left, looked at the log, noting the time he'd signed out was 2145 hours. *That gave him forty-five minutes that wouldn't be accounted for. No one would pay attention to Hess's movements, especially during the evening and night shifts. Had he waited too long?*

When he saw Hess the next day, his instincts told him that nothing had happened. Westphal was glad of that. *Maybe he would get enough nerve to tell the major.*

The following evening was the last day of October, and Wilhelm thought of how they'd celebrated Halloween evening in the states. He kept his thoughts about home to himself and retired early. After a little reading he fell asleep. About midnight, he was awakened by a loud knock on his door. One of the soldiers told him that he was wanted in Major Decker's office, immediately. Bleary eyed, he put on a pair of trousers and put his shirt half on, buttoning as he walked across the compound toward Decker's office.

Major Decker was sitting behind his desk and *Hauptmann* Schlayer was sitting in the chair on the other side of the desk. Decker pointed to the empty chair by the wall and Wilhelm brought it over to the desk and sat in it.

"Gentlemen. It seems we have an incident," he began. "I was just informed that *Obersoldat* Hess is unaccounted for. He was scheduled for night duty at checkpoint #2 but never showed up. Then I was informed that he traded places with *Obersoldat* Steinbrink and was supposed to show up for duty at checkpoint #2 at 2000 hours. He never showed up at that time. The soldier whom he was to replace finally started the walk back to the barracks and found the car Hess was supposed to be driving. It was located a short distance from the checkpoint. The keys were still in the car and it looked like a scuffle had taken place in the bushes near the car. That's about all we have. *Hauptmann* Schlayer, can you explain what might have happened?"

"I don't have the slightest idea what happened. I thought he was on night duty this week. Possibly *Obersoldat* Westphal knows something we don't know. They were friends."

"Schmidt, send for Westphal. I asked for a guard to wait outside. Have him get Westphal."

The three men looked at the situation from as many sides as they were able. *Hauptmann* Schlayer was not able to admit that Hess was not an ideal soldier who didn't always follow the rules. The captain insisted that he always followed his orders and that he had no trouble with his behavior. He also thought that he was only being a soldier when he parked his car near the bakery to observe the pretty girl, or bought bread on his day off. Schlayer wouldn't admit that Hess was stalking her.

When Westphal came, hair messed and eyes still resisting the light, he stood at attention as best he could. Major Decker told Schmidt to get the chair from his desk and Wilhelm gestured for Westphal to take the one he was sitting in.

"*Obersoldat* Hess is missing. You and he have been working together for *Hauptmann* Schlayer and probably know more about him than any other soldier here. What can you tell us about Hess?"

The open-ended question left Westphal speechless. Westphal started to speak and stopped, began again and started to stammer. "He was…he was on duty. He was stalking the girl from the bakery. Hess had no intention of obeying your command to stay away from the young lady who works in the bakery," he said, looking directly at the major. "He found out that her father died and he's been watching her house. He signs out fifteen minutes before he's on duty, but he leaves forty-five minutes before he has to leave. He parked in front of the bakery last week to see who was there. He's still stalking her. I told him that I didn't want to have anything to do with harassing this young lady. I asked him to leave me out."

"Why didn't you report this to *Hauptmann* Schlayer or me?" said Decker.

"I wanted to. Then I thought that the evidence I had was too weak. Besides, Hess would make life miserable for me if I told anyone what he was planning. He's got one mean temper. He frequently took the car to the checkpoint early but signed a later time. I think he would go to the farmhouse where she lived. He was planning something. Yesterday, he left at 1700 hours but he signed 1745. I knew his intentions were not good. I should have told somebody."

"Go back to bed. We'll probably have some more questions in the morning," said Decker.

The three continued their discussion. Decker wanted to know if Schlayer still thought Hess was a good soldier, just following orders. There was a lot of sarcasm in the major's question. Schlayer wasn't required to answer. Decker said he wanted to know if Hess went to visit the girl in her home. Surely, she couldn't overpower him. Maybe she had a gun or a knife. Perhaps there was someone living with her. The suppositions were endless about where Hess was after he left the barracks and how his car got to the checkpoint. What was the meaning of the scuffle in the bushes near the car? Was someone waiting for him there? Did the locals take care of Hess before he could create an incident? Was he doing some illegal smuggling? Where was he or his body? The questions were endless. Finally the three men decided to get some sleep and to continue the investigation in the morning.

Chapter Thirty-Eight

The first day in November used to be All Saints Day. The Nazis made it known that they opposed religious holidays like this. While they couldn't eliminate these practices throughout the country, they could in the military. Therefore, Friday, November 1, was just another day. Right after mess, Decker called a meeting with Schlayer, Schmidt and the four sergeants who ran the barracks.

The major brought everyone up-to-date on what they already knew. Since the information was going to get out, if it hadn't already, the sergeants were to tell their men what was known and to solicit from them any possible information they might have. They were then dismissed. It was determined that Schlayer and Schmidt should go first to the checkpoint and examine that site. Later, Schlayer was going to speak with the young lady who works at the bakery, at her home. He told the major that he wanted to search the house.

"I think we need to do that, but please request permission. Bring several soldiers with you and search the grounds for any indication that the vehicle Hess was driving was there. You may want to check at the bakery as to her schedule so she will be at the farmhouse when you arrive."

Wilhelm went with Schlayer. As they drove through town, they saw the young lady in the bakery waiting on customers. The checkpoint, five kilometers from town, displayed a new marker where the car was found. They got out and looked carefully at the area where it appeared a scuffle had taken place. Wilhelm's thought was that it was made to look like a scuffle had taken place. Wilhelm came to that conclusion when he closely examined the footsteps. They seemed to be all made from the same boots. Yet he decided not to voice his opinion.

Schlayer, after a cursory examination of the bushes, believed that someone had accosted Hess as he stopped the car to pee in the bushes, or possibly had hailed him down. Wilhelm suspected that someone had killed the soldier because he was about to attack the girl, but he kept that thought to himself.

They remained at the site and the checkpoint until almost noon, when they returned to the barracks. Wilhelm begged off going to the young girl's farmhouse, citing that he had too many chores to do, having missed a half-day of work. After lunch, he took the major's vehicle and a shirt and drove to the tailor. Since only the tailor was in the shop he told him that a crime had been committed and they were going to question the young girl in the bakery. He left the shirt with the tailor and asked him to fit it for him. The tailor thanked Wilhelm and immediately after Wilhelm left the shop, headed for the bakery to tell Annette LaVoie, the young lady in question. She had already left for the day and her replacement was there. As the tailor left the bakery, he saw the captain with several soldiers headed south, out of town. He closed his eyes and uttered a silent prayer that she would be prepared for this visit and the search that was inevitable.

Chapter Thirty-Nine

Hauptmann Schlayer was on his best behavior when he visited the farmhouse. He questioned the young lady and repeated the questions while he searched the house, looking for any discrepancy in her story. He asked the soldiers with him to search the barn and the grounds.

Schlayer started in the cellar and questioned her about the shotgun found there. "Do you shoot?"

"No. I don't remember the gun being fired for several years."

Schlayer picked up the shotgun, sniffed it and replaced it on the floor. He climbed the stairs to the living room and looked at the kitchen and living quarters, opened the closet door, looked in the cabinets under the sink and counters and asked to go upstairs. Annette nodded.

After searching the bedrooms he asked about the door to the attic. "Where does that go?"

"To the attic."

"May I?" He opened the door and climbed the stairs. He went only half way. "Why the cot?"

"In case we have company. We haven't had any recently."

"You always say 'we.' Who is 'the we'?"

"My father and I. I'm not used to his being deceased. I guess it will take me a while before I adjust to that."

"When did you learn to drive a car?"

"I don't know how to drive. I've never even sat in the driver's seat of an automobile. We never had a car and I would have been too young to learn to drive. I don't know why you asked that question," she said indignantly.

"I had my reason," he said over his shoulder as he led the way down the stairs. "Thank you for answering my questions and for your cooperation."

Schlayer asked about a radio and she said that she had one at the store for music. He told her that it was against the rules to have a radio and he would send someone to the bakery in the morning to pick it up. He then abruptly left.

After evening mess, Decker wanted to hear what the two men had discovered. *Hauptmann* Schlayer was in his glory, acting as if he knew what he was doing. He did most of the talking.

"Someone attacked Hess when he stopped the car. Perhaps he was doing something illegal or, more likely, he wanted to use the bushes to urinate. That's where he was attacked. It was quite simple to determine that a scuffle took place."

"You don't think he was doing something that he shouldn't be doing?" asked the major.

"I think he surprised someone or several people in the bushes and they silenced him and took him away. Why would he drive there, leave the keys in the car and not return?"

"Did you visit the bakery lady?" asked Decker.

"Yes, she lives alone now that her father has died. We didn't find any

176

tracks or any indication that the car was there. I personally searched the house from cellar to attic and saw no indication of anything suspicious. The men I brought with me searched the grounds, the barn and the work shed."

"So you believe she is innocent?" asked Decker.

"I didn't say that. I just didn't find any indication of Hess having been there, and merchants in town told me she was baking bread when they arrived at their shops. She said she arrived at her usual time of four in the morning. She didn't appear to be tired, and she answered all my questions without making me suspicious."

"Schmidt, what are your thoughts on what happened?" asked Decker.

"It looked like a fight had taken place near where the car was found. The car was not involved at all."

"Well, Schlayer. Stay on the case until it is solved. Keep me informed." With a nod of the head, he dismissed them.

Several days went by without any new evidence. Wilhelm went back to town to pick up the shirt he had fitted. The tailor told Wilhelm that the information he gave him would have been helpful but that it arrived too late.

"I believe that you are trying to help us and we appreciate that. But you don't know what information is helpful and what is not," said the tailor.

"Monsieur Girard, I will have to trust someone and it might as well be you. As I've said previously, anything you tell me will not get back to the Germans. You need to know that I am not a German. I am an American who was forced into the German Army. I assumed the identity of my cousin to get medical help. Now I'm in a position of authority and I hear just about everything that's going on. What is it that you need to know?"

"That is marvelous. I knew you could be trusted. We need to know if they suspect the girl from the bakery. Do they suspect that she had anything to do with the loss of that soldier or if they suspect her of any other activity."

"I can tell you that she is not a suspect now, but *Hauptmann* Schlayer will be looking to find somebody he can accuse. Nothing would please him more than to find her guilty of something. He's trying to catch her in a lie. I'll let you know as soon as I hear anything."

Wilhelm tried on his fitted shirt and told the tailor that it was perfect. He would wear it and maybe he could get more business for the tailor. He also explained that it would give him an excuse for coming into town. After he paid the tailor, he stopped off at the wine store and bought a bottle of wine. He thought that he and the major might enjoy it.

Chapter Forty

Wilhelm had changed into the fitted shirt as soon as he returned to the barracks. Major Decker noticed Wilhelm's fitted shirt within minutes after he returned and invited Wilhelm into his office. Wilhelm handed the bottle of wine to Major Decker.

"Thank you. Why do I deserve this?"

"I saw it in town and I know you like good wine. Besides, I was trying to make a few points with the locals."

Decker looked at the wine for a moment and put it in his desk drawer. "I'm interested in having my shirts fitted like the one you're wearing. It really looks nice. Besides, I can't have my secretary looking better dressed than the boss."

"The tailor will do it if you pin the shirt to tell him how much to take in. Try one shirt and if you like it, he can do several from the same pattern. The man knows his business," said Wilhelm.

"I'll pin a shirt up tonight and maybe you can take it to him tomorrow."

"That will be no problem."

"Will it be possible to have them all done in the next week or so?"

"I'm sure the tailor can do them fast. First, he needs one shirt that is pinned."

"Wilhelm, I want to take some time off and visit my family in Berlin. The big guys in Berlin also want to talk with me. It's possible I may have another assignment. I will be traveling to Berlin at mid-month and will be gone for two weeks."

"I hope you will remain here. I don't know how I would fare working for *Hauptmann* Schlayer."

"That's what I wanted to talk with you about. Schlayer is unbalanced, a loose cannon. I never know what he is going to do. Try to keep him from doing something really stupid, like starting a war or killing villagers. If you can't stop him, slow him down and keep a record of his stupidity."

"I'll do the best I can. But he does outrank me and I don't want to be demoted or shipped off to another outfit. With you gone, Schlayer will be in total control and as we know, he does like to throw his weight around and cause trouble. When are you leaving?"

"Probably Monday, the eighteenth. I should be gone for two weeks, so I'll return on the second or third of December. Keep good records and maybe I can have *Hauptmann* Schlayer shipped out of here. That would get rid of my biggest headache."

"Do you want to tell Schlayer that you're going to Berlin?"

"No. I'll tell him a day or so before I leave. I'll make it sound like an emergency. Let's keep it quiet for now. Wilhelm, at quitting time will you share a glass of wine with me?"

"Certainly."

The afternoon continued with Schlayer making the most noise and making believe he was trying to solve a crime. He interviewed a lot of soldiers but didn't learn anything new. He made it look as though he was attentive to his responsibilities.

At five o'clock Wilhelm knocked on the major's door. The two shared a glass of the wine that Wilhelm had bought.

"I'm not looking forward to this visit to Berlin," said the major.

"It will give you a chance to spend time with your wife and kids."

"That's the good part. It will be nice being home for the evenings. Like when I was a professor. Why they want me to come to Berlin has me confused."

"Maybe they have a promotion planned?"

"That's possible. But I don't want to be promoted if it means leaving my post here. I like it here, where I'm not in the fighting or in charge of an extermination camp. I couldn't do that. I'm happy here in France, guarding the border."

"You'll have a chance to see *Oberst* Dengel and renew your acquaintance."

"Yes, I'm looking forward to that visit. I don't believe Dengel would stand for them sending me to the eastern front or to a concentration camp. He knows I haven't got the stomach for all that 'Heil Hitler' stuff. I'll fight for my country but I won't kill innocent people."

"Maybe that's why we get along so well. I feel the same way," said Wilhelm. "And when you see the *oberst* tell him thanks for allowing me to work with Major Fritz Decker."

"I will, but I'm afraid I have to thank him for sending you." The major lifted his glass. "Prosit." Wilhelm echoed the toast.

Wilhelm refused a second glass of wine, telling the major that he would have trouble going to mess if he did so. The major understood.

Wilhelm was now accepted in town and didn't have to go to all the shops just to prove that he meant no harm. They didn't like his presence but also knew that he was not there to harm them. Most felt that he was one of the few personable Germans who would not cause any trouble.

Speaking French also helped. Wilhelm was pleased that he was perceived in that fashion. Having earned the respect and confidence of Major Decker allowed him to move freely. This could only happen because he got the reports in on time and accurately, causing the major to receive a word of praise from Berlin that he and Schmidt were doing a great job.

The shirts were completed to the satisfaction of the major, allowing Decker to pack and prepare for his trip to Berlin. On Saturday, November sixteenth, the major called Schlayer and Schmidt into his office to tell them he was going to Berlin at the command of his superiors. He also said that he would be spending a week at home. Both men wished him a safe trip. Decker told Schlayer his date for returning was a little vague but that he was in charge for the time he was away. He said that he hoped everything would run as smoothly for him as it was presently running. Then he asked Schlayer what was new with the investigation.

"I think we are close to a breakthrough," said Schlayer.

"How so? What do you have?" asked Decker.

"It is my opinion that the girl from the bakery is behind the loss of Hess and that she isn't as innocent as she looks. She may not have harmed Hess, but I'm certain she is somehow involved."

"Do you have any evidence?" asked the major.

"Not yet. But we visited most of the farms in the area, and her farm is the closest to the border. I don't have any proof but I'll get it."

"Look, Schlayer. Because her farm is nearest the border is not evidence that she murdered a soldier. Two men got in trouble for harassing the villagers. Hess was one of them. The baker and his daughter were trying to avoid trouble, unless you interpret their visit some other way. We are not here to prove to the French that we are in charge. We are here to guard the border. That is your primary task and that is what you will be doing the next two weeks. Understood"

"Yes, Sir. I think you will be pleased with my command."

"I hope so. Now I'd like to complete some work before I leave on Monday."

When Wilhelm went to town on Saturday he made his usual visit to the tailor.

"Anything new?" asked the tailor as he hung a jacket on a hanger.

"*Hauptmann* Schlayer is now in charge of the barracks, that's all."

"Should we be aware of anything?" The tailor walked to the window and glanced out at the shops on the main street.

"You need to know that Schlayer is unbalanced and there is no telling what he might do. Oh, yes. He suspects the bakery girl of somehow being implicated in Hess's disappearance. He has no proof, just a hunch."

"Does she have to do anything?"

"Keep to her schedule and give him no cause for suspicion." Wilhelm got up and walked to the door. "I'll let you know if I hear anything."

Wilhelm spent some time in town, buying a few items for his own comfort and a few items of food. Back at the barracks he sat down with the major. "I have a bad feeling about Schlayer."

"That's why you need to keep a record of what he does. Then when I return I'll be able to take disciplinary action. My problem is that someone with rank is a friend of his and might be protecting him. He acts as if he's immune from discipline and can do whatever he damn well pleases. Keep records, Schmidt. That's our only hope."

Chapter Forty-One

Major Decker asked Wilhelm to drive him to the airport at Belfort, where a military airplane was scheduled to fly him to Berlin. The trip was pleasant enough even with some patches of fog. Wilhelm left himself enough time so he wouldn't have to rush. By the time they arrived at the airport, the sun had burned off most of the fog and the day looked as if it would be cold, but pleasant.

"Keep a good diary, Wilhelm. If he's as unbalanced as we think he is, I'll find a way to get rid of him. I would love to find out who is protecting him, making him think he's immune from discipline. With a long list of facts to prove his aberrations, we might be able to get him sent to the eastern front."

Shortly after a small military plane landed and taxied toward the terminal, the major said goodbye to Wilhelm and walked through the airport doors to the waiting plane. The pilot didn't turn off the propellers, so that as soon as the major pulled the door closed, the plane taxied to the end of the runway.

Wilhelm slowly drove back to the barracks, which were only thirty kilometers from the airport. He was in no rush and didn't look forward to spending the next two weeks with Schlayer in command. When he arrived at the barracks there appeared to be much more activity than was usual for this time of day. Wilhelm considered that the soldiers were just trying to impress the new commander.

Something isn't right. I can feel it but don't know what I'm experiencing.

Finally, his curiosity got the best of him and he decided to check for himself. He walked to the mess hall and found a few soldiers drinking coffee. He got a cup and sat down with them.

"What's going on?" asked Wilhelm.

"Some of the men are being sent on an assignment to watch a farmhouse. That's going to leave the border patrol duty short, so we're going to be eight hours on and eight hours off," said one of the soldiers. It was obvious that he was annoyed, bordering on furious.

"When did you find out about this?"

"About an hour ago. As soon as the major left the Kaserne, we were assembled. This assignment will involve everyone."

"Do you know which farmhouse it is?"

"No, only that it is near checkpoint #2."

"Do you know when this is supposed to begin?"

"No. *Hauptmann* Schlayer said he wanted to begin at sundown. I think he's dreaming. We can't organize that fast. He wants twenty-four hour coverage at two places and wants extras to observe when the subject is traveling. We're supposed to get a fuller briefing just before we start the surveillance."

"Look, I'll see what I can do, but it seems that *Hauptmann* Schlayer is in charge." Wilhelm got up from his seat, took his mug and told the soldiers that he would try.

Wilhelm didn't need to see Schlayer. In fact, if he did, Schlayer might have him do something that would keep him from going into town. Schlayer could forbid him to use a vehicle or maybe confine him to the post for a day or two on some flimsy excuse. It was best that Wilhelm use his freedom now, before it was taken away.

He went to his room, picked up a shirt that needed fitting and looked about for Schlayer. He saw the vehicle he used to take Decker to the airport parked next to the office but still didn't see the *hauptmann*. He waited another minute and was rewarded with the sight of him walking briskly from the barracks to the mess hall. Once the officer was safely inside the mess hall, Wilhelm made his move, shirt in hand.

He drove the car to the front gate and only slowed down enough to allow the guard to open the iron bar. He raced into town and stopped in front of the tailor shop. The tailor was just finishing up with a customer and noticed Wilhelm's apprehension. He quickly ushered the customer to the door and asked Wilhelm what was going on.

"We have a problem. At least I think we do. They are going to put twenty-four hour surveillance on a person who lives in a farmhouse near checkpoint #2. That's the checkpoint southeast of here."

"That is a problem. We have to notify her immediately, and I will have to alert others, as lives will be in danger. You have no idea how much this means to us. You may have saved many lives. We are deeply indebted to you. Let me tell you what the situation is that you are protecting."

"Thank you. I would like to know."

"The bakery girl's farm has a cave on her property that continues through a seam in the rock formations. This allows her and a Canadian airman to smuggle Jewish children and airmen into Switzerland. The airman will have to stay in Switzerland for awhile if they plan twenty-four-hour surveillance."

"They are planning twenty-four-hour surveillance. It would be best if he wasn't there." Then, without hesitation Wilhelm said, "Could you get a letter to my parents in the States? Would that be possible?"

"Yes. Here, write it on this paper and put the address on this envelope," said the tailor as he found the paper and envelope under the counter. "Take off your shirt and make believe you are trying on a new shirt. The letter will be mailed from Bern in Switzerland so that it will not fall into German hands. Don't tell them the name of this town. I'll be back in a few minutes. Write quickly. Wait for me."

Wilhelm didn't have time to compose a nice, warm and informative letter but only to let his parents know that he was safe. He began writing the second the tailor left the store.

November 20, 1940

Dear Mom, Dad and Greta,

I'm alive and well in the German Army and have advanced to the rank of sergeant. I am staying away from the woods and my asthma has not flared up since I first arrived. I have a desk job in an office near the Swiss border. I try to tell the Resistance what they need to know to avoid being caught. I suspect that since we are near the border people are being smuggled across to freedom, and I believe I am helping in this work.

I love you and look forward to seeing you soon. Greta, I miss you.

Keep this letter, as it might be useful to prove that I am an American and am working to defeat the Germans.

Your loving son,

Billy

Wilhelm was addressing the envelope when the tailor returned. "I was able to pass on the information to the proper authorities and to the bakery girl," he breathlessly told him. "I know that you had some idea of what we were doing. Now you know how important the information you gave us affects our operation. In any case, this new development arrived just in time. You may have saved many lives."

"What you are doing is dangerous."

"We have been smuggling Jewish children into Switzerland to keep them away from the Bosch. We also rescue airmen if we can reach them before the Germans do. Then we smuggle them into Switzerland so they can fight again. Your information is a critical part of our operation."

"Tell me about the girl from the bakery."

"She lives close to the border. She and her father were asked to take the children across the border. When her father died, her life became more difficult. The airman was recovering from an injury, but he's strong enough. Together they do the smuggling. The Germans don't know about the airman. It is the airman who killed the soldier when he tried to rape her."

"Thank you for this information. Just knowing that the Germans will be watching her and her house is important for her to know. It will also allow us to get the airman away until this is all over. We will stop the operation until you tell us it is safe. You will tell us when it's over?"

"Yes, but until then I'll keep a good distance between us. They will probably have soldiers posing as civilians spying on the people in town. Most especially the bakery. They'll probably even observe Sunday Mass. I don't want to be seen in town if I can help it."

Wilhelm sealed the letter and gave it to the tailor. "This means so much to me to let my parents know I am safe. I haven't been able to do that."

"I will assure you it will be posted in Switzerland. Thank you, *Monsieur Le Yankee*."

"And thank you, Monsieur Girard."

Wilhelm returned to the barracks with his shirt draped over his arm. He went to his room, returned the shirt to the locker and returned to his desk. He didn't meet Schlayer until about an hour later.

"Where have you been?" demanded Schlayer.

"I took the major to the airport."

"Oh, yes. I forgot. We have an operation going that will involve most of the men. We are about to put surveillance on our primary suspect. We've got proof that the girl from the bakery is involved."

"Proof? Good! What kind of proof? What is she involved in?"

"We found a board that was hidden in the woods and was probably used as a bridge over the stream. We also found footprints. Small footprints like those made by children."

"So you think children are smuggling stuff across the border?" asked Wilhelm sarcastically.

"No. We think someone is smuggling children into Switzerland. Jewish children. We can't allow that, and we intend to find the person or persons who are doing it."

Wilhelm turned away from Schlayer, sat down at his desk and busied himself with paperwork. Schlayer, having nothing more to say, returned to his office. Throughout the day various soldiers reported to Schlayer that the transportation, tents, blinds and other equipment were ready. After it was dark, two units left by truck to be secreted into place.

The next morning one of the men, a *gefreiter*, told Schlayer about the evening before. He said that two units were in place and that they were able to get to a site where they could see the house without being seen. Both were in the woods to the west of the farmhouse. One slightly north and the other south. They told Schlayer that no one entered or left the house until the young lady pedaled her bike toward town at 0345. The only other activity was that the lights went off at 2015 and came back on at 0315 *Hauptmann* Schlayer thanked the *gefreiter* and dismissed him.

Wilhelm tried to be at his desk when the various soldiers made their reports. He was able to overhear most of what was said. There was nothing to report, but the men did it with true German accuracy and precision. The first few days could be summarized with the sentence: she went to work, came home, did chores, ate, and went to bed.

There was no deviation, except on Sunday. She got up at seven, went to Mass before eight, returned home and remained inside all day, except for feeding the chickens and gathering eggs.

Chapter Forty-Two

Schlayer was becoming increasingly frustrated because his men had nothing to report. He called in a *gefreiter* and told him that he needed four men for special duty. They were to watch the young lady when she pedaled to work on her bicycle, and they were not to be seen. They would also find a spot to hide along the route to her home to watch her. He wanted to make certain she didn't stop anyplace.

In this desperate state of mind, he ordered another crew to dress up like Frenchmen and to station themselves in town to see if she visited any other stores while she was supposed to be at work. To all the villagers who were known to each other, the outsiders were obviously spying on someone and everyone could guess who. There were no young men in France. They were off fighting somewhere or were languishing in a concentration camp. The only young men were German. This crew tried to make it sound like they had a lot to report.

"The girl from the bakery was in the grocery store on Tuesday," reported one soldier dressed like a French civilian. "She had a package when she came out. She took it to her bakery."

"She was in the cheese shop on Wednesday," reported another the following day "and she also had a package when she came out."

"She was in the butcher shop on Thursday and came out with a package. The package was wrapped in white paper. I believe she was buying groceries she could take home on her bike."

"I don't need for you to interpret what she was buying. All you need to do is tell me what you saw. I'll decide what it means," Schlayer barked at the soldier.

On Saturday morning, Schlayer asked Schmidt to get two volunteers to go with him to the farmhouse they were watching. He also asked Schmidt to reserve the car for the afternoon. After the mid-day mess, he left the compound with those two soldiers. When he returned he was carrying a shotgun that looked very old. In his right hand were two buckshot shells. "Take this out and see if it will shoot. I'd be careful not to put my face too close to the stock. Who knows when it was last fired? For all I know, it might blow up." He gave him the two shells.

"Well, did you get your proof?" asked Wilhelm.

"Not yet. She's a clever one. But she'll make a mistake," said Schlayer.

"It's a woman you suspect?" asked Wilhelm.

"Yes. She's the woman who runs the bakery now that her father has died. You know, the one who complained about Hess and Westphal."

"And you think she is smuggling children into Switzerland? It looks like she was trying to avoid trouble, not cause any."

"We'll see."

"Has the shotgun been used recently?" asked Wilhelm.

"No, the barrel is a bit rusty. I'm quite certain it hasn't been used in at least a year. I just wanted to have it so I'll have an excuse to go back and catch her in a lie."

"Has she lied to you?"

"Not that I can prove. I just know she's lying. Just like I know she speaks German but will not."

"So you know she speaks German?"

"No. I suspect that she does. She's just a bit too clever."

The driver, who was waiting to be dismissed, overheard this conversation. Wilhelm decided to ask him if he'd found anything. He responded that they searched the barn and the work shed and found nothing. He didn't volunteer anything more, knowing that his opinion would draw the wrath of Schlayer.

Wilhelm could see that the girl from the bakery was in danger because Schlayer wasn't about to be wrong or to give up. Even if nothing could be proven, Schlayer was determined to find her guilty.

He would have to be stopped somehow.

Chapter Forty-Three

Wilhelm kept a diary as he promised the major he would. He noted that the morale of the men became increasingly poorer each day. There were more disagreements and arguments. While there were no fights, that was due only to the harsh punishment that would follow. He attributed this to the fact that they were doing double duty. They resented all the effort to get one person who the soldiers thought was pretty and, as far as they could tell, lived a very quiet and admirable life. Most of the soldiers knew who she was from seeing her behind the counter at the bakery. They may never have spoken to her except for asking for a roll or a loaf of bread, but they knew who she was.

Some of the men, when the *hauptmann* was not nearby, even expressed the opinion that Schlayer was only doing it to get revenge because the bakery girl told the major that Hess and Westphal were stalking her.

The surveillance of the farmhouse went on over the weekend, the reports more of the same. Some of the soldiers complained to the captain that there was nothing to report and that they were wasting their time. Several said they thought it was too much for them to attend church just to spy on her. Privately they were angry that they had to be on duty every other eight-hour period and were required to do other duties in the kitchen and at the barracks guardhouse as well. And they especially didn't like standing out in the cold weather, especially at night. Tempers were ready to flare as the men grew more and more frustrated, and the number of hours they were on duty increased. Life had degraded into work and sleep.

Schlayer brought the shotgun back to the farmhouse on Monday. The soldiers thought that was the end of the surveillance, but it continued. As Schlayer listened to the reports the next day he could hear the frustration and rebellion that the men were experiencing. Finally yielding to the pressure coming from very tired and angry soldiers, he said he would call off the operation…for now. He suggested that the men be pulled out of hiding as soon as it was dark.

Wilhelm told Schlayer that he would like to go into town to buy some items but didn't want to interfere with the operation. Schlayer said it wouldn't be a problem since he was withdrawing the men in the village and would withdraw the others at sundown.

"*Hauptmann*, can I get you anything while I'm in town?"

"Yes, a bottle of the local wine and some cheese and bread," said Schlayer. "Here's twenty francs to cover the cost."

"Thanks. I'd be glad to. That might help you forget."

"I hope so."

The first stop was the tailor, who was pleased to hear the news. He said he would pass on the good news. He also told Wilhelm to consider a way to get Schlayer in trouble.

"It would be nice to get Schlayer out of the way. I don't think he is planning on giving up even though he cancelled the operation."

"I don't think so either," said Wilhelm. "I'll try to think of something."

Major Decker came back on the twenty-ninth of November. When he was leaving Berlin he put in a call to Wilhelm and told him his estimated time of arrival at the Belfort airport and asked him to be there. Schlayer was in the office listening to the conversation. He asked Wilhelm why the major asked him to pick him up.

"I presume it is because I drove him there and know how to locate the airport. I'm the major's personal aide and have been with him since he arrived on this post. Besides, it wouldn't be good for the acting commanding officer to leave the post when he was the only officer."

"I suppose you're right. I just wanted the chance to speak to the major about the surveillance operation before anyone else does."

"I'm certain the major will give you plenty of opportunity to explain why you initiated the operation," said Wilhelm, with a small amount of sarcasm in his voice. He was thinking that he would have plenty of time to explain what a fool thing he had done and how he'd violated the major's orders. In addition, Wilhelm had copious notes hidden under his mattress to back up his statements.

Wilhelm picked the major up and told him all that had happened. He said that the captain initiated the plan the moment the major was gone and he was in charge. "From what I can tell, the surveillance yielded nothing, yet the *hauptmann* is convinced the young lady is implicated in both Hess's disappearance and smuggling. He evidently found some children's footprints near the stream just south of checkpoint #2 and that is supposed to mean the bakery girl is the culprit. He's convinced that she speaks German although it would prove nothing if she did."

The major told Wilhelm that the reason he was called to Berlin was because he was being considered for a promotion and a transfer. He told the staff in Berlin that he had some unfinished work in France and now would not be a good time to transfer. He felt reasonably sure that he would remain at the barracks for the time being.

Once they arrived at the post, Wilhelm took the major's luggage and brought it to his quarters. When he returned to the office, Decker was sitting behind his desk and Schlayer was standing in front of it.

"Schmidt, please get in here and listen to this. I'm not sure I'm getting the truth. Now, *Hauptmann*, please start at the beginning. When did you initiate this operation?"

Schlayer hesitated, and now that Schmidt was there, was forced to tell the truth.

"A while after you left."

"Define 'a while,'" the major requested. Schlayer wasn't being allowed to get away with vague answers.

Schlayer didn't know how to answer. He knew the major would eventually find out that the minute the major left, the men were assembled and the surveillance was begun that night.

"Shortly after you left."

"*Hauptmann*. Must I pull the truth out of you? Did you begin the operation as soon as I left?"

"Yes."

"On what basis?"

"We found some footprints and a board that was used to cross the stream. The footprints were those of children."

"When did you find the board and discover the footprints?"

"The night before you left." Schlayer paused and then thought that he better tell the truth since it would most certainly be checked. "Maybe it was several days before you left."

"By several you mean two or three?"

"It was a week."

"And they led you to conclude that the young lady from the bakery was doing what?"

"Smuggling. Smuggling Jews into Switzerland."

There was a long pause, with the major still looking at Schlayer, waiting for the rest of the explanation.

"Jewish children. They were smuggling Jews into Switzerland."

"You could tell from the footprints that they were Jewish. You're amazing, *Hauptmann* Schlayer. Now tell me who was under surveillance, for how long, how many soldiers were involved and what did you find out?"

Schlayer tried to answer all the questions to the best of his ability, but even though the office was cool, the captain was sweating. The more he spoke, the worse it sounded. He was so convinced that he was right—that he felt justified in what he did.

"And after all this expenditure of time, money and effort, what did you find out?"

"Nothing as yet. But I'm convinced she is guilty, and one day I'll be able to prove it."

"*Hauptmann*, I'm not finished with you yet. I want to talk with some of those involved in the operation to confirm what you have told me. Nor am I certain that I want you to be my second in command. You could have presented your plan to me before I left the compound. But you had to wait until I left. It appears that you want to take all the credit but none of the blame for your actions. Return to your security duties and I'll have more to say to you later...when I'm not so angry."

The captain saluted and left the major's office for his own. He closed the door and locked it.

Chapter Forty-Four

There were several severe snow storms in the month of December, making work at the checkpoints cold and lonely. The soldiers knew that anyone attempting to cross the border would be leaving tracks. They believed that no one would attempt a crossing once the ground was covered with snow. Those patrolling were especially concerned and attentive at the start of a snowstorm when visibility was poor and the tracks would soon be covered.

The soldiers pulling guard duty were pleased to be back on their regular schedule. They considered that to be difficult enough. All expressed relief that the major was back. Schlayer was much more subdued, didn't swagger the way he previously did, and spent more time at the checkpoints.

"Schmidt, do you notice that Schlayer seems to be paying more attention to his duties? I think he might be trying to avoid me."

"I think you're right, Major."

Christmas came and went with little fanfare. A few bottles of local wine marked the holiday. There wasn't much to celebrate except that they weren't in the thick of the fighting. *Hauptmann* Schlayer, in an effort to appear tough, said that he was hoping to see some real action before long. Wilhelm prayed that his prayer would be answered.

The Monday after Christmas, Major Decker went to Audincourt for a minor procedure at the hospital: the removal of an ingrown toenail that had been giving him a lot of pain. Wilhelm drove him, promising he would return at 1100 hours. The weather had turned warm, and snow was melting rapidly, making the roads wet with runoff.

When Wilhelm returned to the post he found an officer talking with Schlayer. He had never seen him before. He was introduced as *Hauptmann* August Vogel, assistant commanding officer of a unit stationed outside of Belfort. He would be Schlayer's counterpart at that Kaserne.

Vogel was young, tall, blond and remarkably handsome. He exuded an arrogant air, most frequently found among elite officers of the SS who were stationed in Berlin. His confidence was palpable and his demeanor, haughty. His swagger eclipsed that of *Hauptmann* Schlayer's and seemed to say that he knew what he was doing.

"*Hauptmann* Vogel is going to dress up like an English flyer and visit our farmhouse," Schlayer began. "If nothing is going on, no harm will be done. If our bakery girl is smuggling Jews or airmen into Switzerland, then we'll know how she does it and who her contacts are. Vogel can overpower her when he has all the information or he can return and tell us what we need to know. That will be his choice."

"Does the major know about this operation?" asked Wilhelm.

"I haven't told him. It is a matter of security and that is my concern."

"Does he speak English?" The second Wilhelm asked the question he wished he hadn't.

Vogel immediately began to speak English. "I studied in London and joined the RAF shortly after graduation. I am an English pilot and have shot down many Messerschmitts."

Wilhelm understood his very good English but couldn't let on that he was fluent in the language. Schlayer would want to know where Wilhelm learned to speak American. "It sounds good to me," said Wilhelm, wishing to change the subject. "What will he wear?"

Schlayer told Vogel to get into the RAF uniform that was on the chair in his office. When he came out, Schmidt thought he really did look like a British pilot.

"We'll drop you off about a kilometer from the farm house. Walk on the path in the woods all the way to the barn, then head for the house. She should be home at twelve or shortly thereafter. You'll have to play it by ear, but she is a small woman and I don't think she'll give you any trouble. I wouldn't turn my back on her just in case she has a knife."

"I understand she is good looking?"

"She is," said Schlayer. "Don't let her beauty distract you. At least until you find out all you need to know." The latter remark was said with a knowing smile, as if they were sharing a private joke between them.

Wilhelm's brain was working overtime. He had to pick up the major at the hospital and could tell him about this operation then. But that would be too late. He could only hope that the young lady would recognize the imposter for what he was and refuse to assist him. If the airman were there, he might be forced to kill Vogel. He wished he could somehow get into town to warn them, but that didn't seem possible.

"I might be a day or so finding out this information," said Vogel. "Please alert your men at the guardhouses to be looking for a British airman coming from Switzerland, tomorrow or the day after. I'd like to make it so I can drink a glass of schnapps with you, Horst, to welcome in the New Year. But if not tomorrow, it will be the next day, New Years Day."

"Thank you, August. This young lady has been a thorn in our side for some time. While I can't prove it, I know what she's doing. Now you'll get the proof we need, and I'll be beholden," said Schlayer.

Vogel slapped him on the back and laughed. "I'm glad you thought of me for this assignment. Most of our security work is very boring. This should be interesting."

Wilhelm excused himself to pick up the major at the hospital. All he could do was pray that they would recognize the airman for what he was and that the operation would not be exposed. Wilhelm considered that he would be very careful with how he mentioned this to Decker. After all, the captain was only doing his duty. Maybe he should praise the captain for being so clever and suggest that at last he would have the proof that would vindicate him. Wilhelm finally decided to tell the major what Schlayer was doing and to keep his opinion to himself. Maybe that would be the best way. He thought about his best course of action as he drove to the hospital.

He had to sit in the waiting room about a quarter of an hour before Major Decker was released. His foot was heavily bandaged and he looked like he was in some pain. He was on crutches but appeared to handle them very well.

"Glad to see you, Wilhelm. You didn't bring along a bottle of wine, by any chance?"

"No. I'm afraid not. I should have thought to do so as I know the operation is painful." The major was unable to put on his right boot. He held the boot strings in his left hand as he manipulated the crutches.

Wilhelm suggested the major wait at the entrance while he got the car. Wilhelm took the boot and helped the major into the car. On the way home, Wilhelm casually brought up the subject of Schlayer's latest scheme.

"Well, finally, *Hauptmann* Schlayer might be getting the proof he wants," he began.

"Why? What's he doing now?"

"A friend of his from a post in Belfort is posing as a British flyer and is going to go to the farmhouse to find out what they are up to. He believes they are smuggling people across the border. He really looks British, speaks English and everything and has quite a story for this young lady. I wonder if we will finally learn something."

"That dumb idiot! He's incorrigible! I don't think he'll ever learn. He thinks these people are stupid, just as he thinks you and I are stupid. The only one who knows anything is Horst Schlayer."

"Don't you think it will work?"

"Of course not. If she's involved in some illegal activity, she'll see right through him. Besides they probably have a signal and a procedure that he won't be following. If she's not involved and is innocent, he might take advantage of her just because he failed to accomplish what he set out to do. In any case, it was ill conceived and he didn't clear it with me. The man is without discipline. I'll put an end to his dumb plan before it gets started."

"I think it may be too late. They were getting ready to leave as I was coming to the hospital. *Hauptmann* Vogel is probably at the farmhouse about now. He wanted to be there at noon when the young lady was expected from work."

"This is twice Schlayer has waited for me to leave to do something behind my back. My foot hurts or I'd kick him in the ass. He's going to pay for this even if he proves that she is smuggling. I don't like his underhanded ways."

Decker fumed and groused all the way to the barracks. The other car was gone when they returned to the office. The major told Schmidt to ask Schlayer to come into his office the second he returned.

Wilhelm told the major that he had some uniforms that he needed to pick up in town. The tailor sewed stripes and patches on them for several of the men who were promoted.

"It will be just as well if you don't hear what I have to say to Schlayer. Even if he proves that the bakery girl is guilty, I don't like his sneaky ways."

Wilhelm stopped at the tailor's shop and had to wait a few minutes until a customer left. He and the tailor spoke about Schlayer's latest scheme.

"Will the bakery girl recognize that she's dealing with an imposter?" asked Wilhelm.

"Instantly. We have a procedure, and this would be the first time it was not being followed. She would know he shouldn't be there, no matter how much like a British airman he appeared."

"Is there anything we can do to throw suspicion away from the girl?"

"Possibly. We'll plant some information in Switzerland that might confuse them, at least."

"That might buy us a little time. I wish there was more we could do."

"Maybe there is. Could you plant some jewelry on Schlayer?" asked the tailor.

"Yes, but not easily. He keeps one of his desk drawers locked…but not always. When he leaves the office for a few minutes he is sometimes careless, and that would allow me to get into his drawer."

"I have some jewelry given me by a Jew in payment for some work I did," said Monsieur Girard. "Two of the bracelets have Hebrew writing on them. One of them says *Shalom*. If they found these in Schlayer's desk…."

"I could hide them in the back of that drawer. I'll think of an excuse why we need to search everyone's desk. Something in our office will go missing. That might get him transferred."

"*Monsieur Le Yankee*, I like the way you think. Wait a moment."

Girard came back with a velvet cloth and four pieces of jewelry. As he said, two of the bracelets had Hebrew characters written on the back. The other two pieces were a ring and a necklace. Wilhelm looked at them, folded them in the cloth and put them in his pocket.

"I'll let you know how it works. Maybe you can find out what happened to that phony British airman?"

"I can tell you now that that phony airman will not be alive for his next meal. We now have to concentrate on shifting suspicion from the young lady."

"Schlayer seems to have it in for her. I hope he's discredited when they find the jewelry in his desk."

"You must be extremely careful. If they catch you and find out you are American, they will surely bring in the Gestapo and connect you to us. If they catch you, they will shoot you on the spot or hang you in the town square. You cannot be caught planting that jewelry. Please be careful," urged the tailor.

"I will. I can see how this could get a lot of us killed. I'll be careful," Wilhelm said as he shook the hand of the tailor. "I'll be careful."

Chapter Forty-Five

Wilhelm considered the things the tailor had warned him about on the ride home. He believed that the tailor was not exaggerating the problem. He didn't want to die.

Would it be possible for him to be smuggled into Switzerland? After all, he was an American citizen and was in the German Army by accident. He thought that by now enough time had passed that maybe his relatives would not be investigated. The Germans had enough problems to deal with besides the desertion of one soldier. He'd considered the possibility before, but it didn't seem possible. Now he knew that it would be wonderful if he could be free. If he was to fight, he wanted it to be against the Nazis. He concluded that he had a lot to consider before he could make a decision, yet he was defeating the Nazis and helping children and airmen to safety.

Several times Schlayer left his office that afternoon and Wilhelm made a hurried inspection of his desk. The top, right-hand drawer was locked. The next morning when Schlayer went to the bathroom, Wilhelm noticed that he had a magazine rolled up in his hand. He suspected it was a girlie magazine. This time he checked his desk and found the drawer open. It took him but a few seconds to put the jewelry in the back. He decided that it would be a good time to visit the mess hall to get a cup of coffee. Ten minutes later he returned to his desk. Schlayer was at his desk looking busy. Wilhelm suspected that he wasn't too happy being chastised over the Vogel incident and didn't know how that idea would work out. He wasn't speaking to anyone these days.

Wilhelm overheard him speak to the *feldwebel* who scheduled the patrols. "Expect a German officer to show up at one of the checkpoints. It will probably be Checkpoint #2. He may be dressed up like a British pilot and he'll be coming from the Swiss side. Bring him to me when he arrives."

Wilhelm was thinking that he had to find something that Major Decker would miss if it turned up lost. He decided to take a fountain pen that was always on Decker's desk. Wilhelm knew it was a gift from Decker's daughter. He would drop it in his briefcase and tell Decker after desks were searched that he must have done it inadvertently. He knew that Major Decker wouldn't blame him for a small, absentminded mistake, especially if incriminating evidence was found on the *hauptmann*.

All during the afternoon, a meeting of all the *feldwebels* was held in the mess hall. Wilhelm chaired the meeting, asking the sergeants to brainstorm ways to make the compound more efficient. It kept Wilhelm out of the office all afternoon. He stopped back at his desk at five and at that time snatched Major Decker's pen, dropping it into the briefcase that he brought to his quarters. He hid the pen in the bottom of a manila envelope holding a stack of old reports.

The next morning he could not have anticipated the reaction of Major Decker.

"Where is my fountain pen? That is a gift from my daughter and I want it. Schmidt, have you seen it?"

"No, Sir."

"Schlayer, get in here. Have you seen my fountain pen?"

"No. I haven't. You're talking about the gold pen?" asked Schlayer.

"Yes. I want it back. If we have to tear the camp apart, I want my pen."

Decker's reaction could not have been anticipated. It was like a little boy just had his candy taken away. Both Schmidt and Schlayer started to look through their personal belongings. Wilhelm started looking through the drawers of his desk and asked the major to observe him search his drawers.

"Sometimes we do things when we're busy that we can't remember," said Wilhelm.

"I hope it is a case of carelessness and not theft," said the major.

He took all the items out of a drawer and placed them on his desk. Then he put them back and removed the contents of another drawer.

"Schlayer, after we check Schmidt's desk, we'll check yours," said Decker.

Schmidt's side drawers were mostly files, forms and folders. The center drawer was filled with pencils, pens, paper clips and assorted office stuff. Decker looked over Wilhelm's shoulder and was satisfied that the pen was not among his office supplies. In Schlayer's office, the captain opened all the drawers except the upper right-hand drawer. The one that was locked.

"Schlayer, you're not going to open that drawer?"

"I wasn't going to open it. I keep personal things in there. I always keep it locked."

"Well, humor me and open it."

Schlayer did and Wilhelm saw, sandwiched between some papers, the girlie magazine that he suspected Schlayer was reading the day before.

Schlayer was embarrassed. The major was not about to cut him any slack.

"Let's see everything in that drawer," said Decker. Schlayer reached to the back and pulled the contents forward.

"What's this?" he inquired when he saw the cloth bundle. He put the cloth on the desktop and unrolled it, spilling the contents on the top of the desk.

"Very nice, Schlayer. Where did you get these?" He held up a very pretty necklace and a green ring that Wilhelm suspected might be an emerald.

"They're not mine. I don't know where they came from. I've never seen this jewelry before."

Decker continued examining the jewelry and saw the inscription on the bracelets. He didn't understand the meaning but was certain that the language was Hebrew.

"Wilhelm, put these on my desk. Post a guard outside Schlayer's quarters until we get to the bottom of this. Do you have anything to say, *Hauptmann* Schlayer?"

"All I can say is I've never seen that jewelry. I have no idea how it got in my drawer."

"As of now, you're confined to your quarters. You'll be given your meals and escorted to the bathroom. First, we will send a detail to your quarters to see if they can find my pen. Remain here. Schmidt, get two *gefreiters* and search his quarters."

Wilhelm went to the *feldwebel* in charge of patrols and told him to post a guard in front of *Hauptmann* Schlayer's quarters. The guard was to accompany him to the lavatory. He then went to the *feldwebel* in charge of the mess and told him that *Hauptmann* Schlayer would be confined to quarters and was to be fed at mess time.

He searched Schlayer's quarters with the help of two *gefreiters* and reported back to Decker that nothing further was found.

Returning to the office, Wilhelm told Decker that he thought the major needed to report the theft to higher authorities as Schlayer's behavior indicated that something more was going on. He excused himself to get his briefcase. When he opened it, he reached in the envelope and took out the major's pen.

"Major, here it is. Your pen. I must have inadvertently dropped it in my briefcase last night when I was in such a rush."

"Wilhelm, I'm glad you found it. Now I'll have to apologize to Schlayer," the major said as a stupid grin spread across his face.

"If we weren't looking for the pen we would never have found the jewelry. I think you need to call the Gestapo. There may be more to this than meets the eye, and it might explain why we lost one soldier and another has gone missing. I wouldn't worry about Schlayer. He has friends in high places anxious to assist him," said Wilhelm.

"This gives me a perfect excuse to get rid of him. I haven't liked him from the first day he walked in here. Whether he stole the necklace and bracelets and stuff or came by them legitimately is not my problem. I'll let someone else figure that out. I'd also like to know if that phony airman that Schlayer brought in to help him is involved in smuggling jewels into Switzerland. Maybe it is time to call the Gestapo."

Wilhelm was pleased with himself that they were able to implicate Schlayer in what looked like a plan to smuggle jewelry out of the country. It even appeared that the jewelry came from Jews. He never liked Schlayer and maybe now he would be moved or imprisoned or sent to the Russian front. Not because he stole some Jewish jewelry but because he disobeyed orders, acted behind Decker's back when he was away from the camp and just didn't give a damn about the soldiers, their feeling and their work. He was a sorry excuse for a German officer.

As Wilhelm lay in his bunk waiting for sleep to set him free, he thought of what it would be like to be smuggled into Switzerland and be returned to his parents and his sister. *I'd be free of concern for the soldiers in this Kaserne. More important, I'd again be an American, living in my own country, speaking English and planning my life and future. Here my life is on hold and there's always the threat that I'll be found out.*

Maybe I should talk with the tailor the next time I'm in town and see if they would smuggle me across with the next group.

Chapter Forty-Six

S everal days later a black sedan pulled into the compound and parked in front of the main office. Two men in black leather coats, boots and black leather hats walked up the steps and into the office. They both looked around the room, past *Oberfeldwebel* Schmidt. The taller of the two said but two words. "Major Decker."

Major Decker rose from his desk and extended his hand to welcome the two guests. They did not accept his hand. Instead they said, "Heil Hitler," bending their elbows only enough to approximate the typical greeting of Nazis. Decker returned the salute but with a little more feeling, as was expected.

Wilhelm observed that the higher the rank of an officer, the less he felt obliged to use the Nazi salute. If it was required, they said the words and bent their arms only enough to be noticed. It was the middle officers who were bucking for a promotion that were enthusiastic in their salute.

"May we talk privately, Major?" said the first.

"Yes, come into my office. Schmidt, bring the gentlemen some coffee."

Both declined the offer of coffee. The eyes of one of the men from the Gestapo conveyed to the major that Schmidt was not needed.

"*Oberfeldwebel*, why don't you take a break and have some coffee in the mess hall," said the major.

"Yes, Sir."

The two agents from the Gestapo spent a little over an hour questioning the major in his office. Then they grilled *Hauptman* Schlayer for approximately forty-five minutes, after suggesting that the major get some coffee and allow them to use his office. In the interest of being thorough, they requested *Oberfeldwebel* Schmidt to come into the major's office to answer a few questions.

When they were finished, they requested that Schmidt bring them to Schlayer's quarters and tell Major Decker he could have his office back. They were gone for almost an hour. They returned to speak with Major Decker and told him that Schlayer was being transferred. The major would receive the necessary paperwork by courier. Schlayer, however, was to leave with them. They told the major that it was the information that was given by *Oberfeldwebel* Schmidt that was most damaging to the captain. It had also come to their attention from a spy in Switzerland that a German officer had defected.

Both Decker and Schmidt breathed a big sigh of relief when the black sedan left the compound. It was just a few minutes before noon and this time, Major Decker didn't ask when he brought out two glasses and poured himself and Schmidt a glass of schnapps.

Decker lifted his glass and said, "To better days."

"And nights," said Wilhelm.

Chapter Forty-Seven

"**W**hat did you say that convinced them to transfer Schlayer?"

"I honestly don't know. They didn't seem concerned when I told them he was insubordinate and waited until you left to do what he wanted."

"I would have thought they would have pounced on that."

"They did seem interested in Schlayer's spying on the bakery girl. It was like they thought that was a very clever idea. When I told them it took many soldiers from patrol just to keep watch on the farmhouse they became interested all of a sudden."

"Did you tell them about the jewelry?"

"Yes. The first time I told them about finding the jewelry hidden in his drawer, they weren't interested. But after I told them about Hess going missing and the *hauptmann* from Belfort still not accounted for, they started to ask good questions. I don't know what I told them but something got their attention."

"Anyway, he's out of our hair. I hope the next *hauptmann* will be reasonable. Schlayer was unbalanced."

Several days later the German High Command sent *Hauptmann* Jon Reuter to replace Schlayer. He was younger than Schlayer, had black hair and was approximately six feet tall. He was pleasant and easy to be around. Nor did he salute or click his heels every time he entered the office. It was a pleasant change.

Reuter spoke with Major Decker to ask him what he believed the present situation to be. He asked if he believed people were getting across the border in this sector.

"We are fortunate and cursed in this sector. The mountains present a formidable barrier and limit where crossings are possible," Decker began. "They also make it difficult for patrols to go where the terrain is too rough."

"Have you any indication that people are crossing?"

"Once we found small footprints. They looked like a child's."

"Do you believe that the border is being penetrated in your sector?"

"No."

"Then you think *Hauptmann* Schlayer was wrong?"

"Yes, and I think he misused his position to promote his personal agenda, whatever that was."

"How can I best learn where the checkpoints are and how they are staffed and maintained?"

"*Oberfeldwebel* Schmidt can give you the most help." Decker called Schmidt to join them in his office.

"Schmidt, do you think our sector is being penetrated?"

"I have not walked the border, but have the ear of all the men who do. They do not believe that anyone has crossed into Switzerland. No one knows what to make of the footprints of a child, but if it happened that a child crossed, it would not be a daily occurrence. It probably only happened once. The only conclusion I can come to is that a child crossed the border from the Swiss side and was called back across the stream by his parents. The border is not guarded from that side. I don't believe the child came from the French side."

Wilhelm introduced *Hauptmann* Reuter to the various people he would need to know and finally to the *feldwebel* in charge of the patrols. "I suggest that you tour the entire border. I don't believe you will find it possible to cross the border at anyplace but the checkpoints."

When the two left for the checkpoints, Wilhelm returned to his desk. Decker came out of his office and stood by the window. "What is your opinion of our new captain?"

"This one seems reasonable." Schmidt got up and joined the major by the window. "Only time will tell."

Reuter was rational and thorough. He visited each checkpoint and walked the routes with the patrols. He asked about how often they patrolled the border and if they ever saw any indication of crossings. With one exception, they all said they didn't believe that anyone had crossed. Two soldiers said they saw small footprints in the soft earth near the narrowest part of the stream and they found a board nearby, hidden under some leaves.

"I saw the print of a child's shoe and I found the board hidden under leaves. For what it's worth, the child came from the Swiss side. There is no way the child could have come past us," was what the soldier told Reuter. His buddy nodded agreement.

Reuter even walked as far as he could west at checkpoint #2 until he couldn't travel anymore. He heard the waterfall and asked if anyone had tried to climb to the top. One of the soldiers started to laugh before he realized that the question wasn't meant to be funny. Reuter relieved the tension by smiling. At checkpoint #3, the *hauptmann* found that it was impossible to go any distance east. He would have bet his life that no one could get over those formations unless they were mountain climbers with lots of equipment. A huge formation blocked the way and behind that another could be seen. When he finished touring the three sites, walking the paths the soldiers walked, he felt certain the border was secure.

He did ask at each checkpoint how often *Hauptmann* Schlayer visited the checkpoints. Only those soldiers who were part of the original detachment could remember that he visited the checkpoint at all. Those that came later didn't ever remember seeing him at the border.

Reuter was a hit with the men after Schlayer's departure. His style was so different. Reuter paid attention to detail such as how often the men went on duty, what they did when they were off, how often they patrolled the border and what factors would allow fewer men to be on duty. When it snowed and he knew no one would attempt to cross because they would leave tracks, he told the *feldwebel* to reduce those on duty at the checkpoints.

Within a month, Reuter knew the area extremely well. He procured a map of the region and marked what he considered potential routes that could be used for smuggling. He would sometimes station two men at a spot on one such route where they wouldn't be seen. It was their responsibility to measure the traffic that passed that spot. They would record if it were a civilian auto or truck or a horse-drawn wagon. They would record the German military vehicles, bicycles and carts, the direction and the time. Then Reuter would look at their logs, searching for a pattern or something that didn't fit. Decker and Schmidt had to admit that he was thorough. He did admit to Major Decker that he didn't believe that visiting every farm in the area would be productive unless he had some indication that people were being led across. Decker couldn't help but agree.

It was late April when spring was starting to show and some trees were budding that Reuter attempted to make improvements to patrolling the border. The snow was all but invisible on the ground although there were some patches on the mountain and hidden between the rocks. Reuter had a crew install wooden stakes in the ground in areas he thought were potential crossing spots. The stakes were installed just allowing for about four inches to be seen above the earth. They were stained brown and not easily visible. Through a hole in the stake ran a wire that rang a small bell if it was tripped or stepped on. Reuter explained that if people were crossing at night they wouldn't see the stakes or the wire, and the patrol would know that the area was being penetrated. It was a low-cost way to be certain the borders stayed secure. The operation required two men to hammer in the stakes and string the wire and two soldiers to stand guard.

The stakes and wires were installed before the day was completed. The soldiers that came on for the evening shift at 1500 hours were told about the stakes and where they were installed. They were to pass on the information to the night crew when they arrived at 2300. Most of the men agreed that setting a trip wire was a good way to find out if anyone was crossing the border during the night when there were no patrols.

For the entire month of May, the men listened for the tinkle of the bell. Only once did they hear the bell tinkle and when it did, it tinkled lightly and repeatedly. In the morning they saw the footprints of a small four-legged critter. A raccoon or fox was determined to be the culprit.

Wilhelm asked *Hauptmann* Reuter how the wire and stakes were working.

"Wonderful if no one is crossing the border. If people are getting across, then the stakes and wire aren't working at all."

"How will you know if it is working?" Wilhelm asked.

"We'll have to catch whoever is doing the smuggling. This doesn't seem to be working."

"Have you considered posting soldiers in trees along the border?"

Wilhelm asked, searching for new information.

"My next experiment will be to place blinds off the ground and see if we catch anyone that way. So far, no one seems to be crossing, yet we have some information that numbers of Jewish children are seen on the Swiss side. We'll have to find out how they get there."

That afternoon, material to build blinds was moved to the checkpoints. Wilhelm watched as the trucks were loaded and looked for an excuse to visit the village. He had a shirt that needed an insignia sewed; he tucked that over his arm and took the car into town.

He had to wait a few minutes for the tailor to be available. They discussed the trip wire and the coming installation of blinds. The tailor told Wilhelm how much he appreciated the information and that it was extremely helpful in keeping those doing the smuggling from getting caught.

"*Monsieur Le Tailleur,* our security officer was told that children were somehow getting into Switzerland."

"I'm glad to know that. That confirms what we suspected. Spies on the Swiss side. I'll pass the word to our contacts and we'll find the source of that information."

While he was in town he bought a few pieces of fruit and some cheese and bought a loaf of bread from the older lady who ran the bakery from the lunch hour until closing time.

Chapter Forty-Eight

The blinds were in place during June and yielded the same results as the stakes and wire. The men reported at the end of each shift. The results were always the same: Nothing to report. *Hauptmann* Reuter was most anxious to hear something, but that wasn't to be. What concerned him most was that there was no attempt to cross the border. He considered that suspicious.

"*Oberfeldwebel* Schmidt, what do you think we should do now?"

"Maybe we should celebrate. The results have been good so far," said Wilhelm.

"That's what concerns me. I can't believe that there are no reported attempts at crossing. Maybe they know we had a wire hidden or that we had soldiers in blinds. Then they wouldn't even attempt to cross. I just can't figure it out."

"What does your source in Switzerland tell you?"

"That's another thing. We haven't heard from him for a while now, and

Berlin is getting concerned. I just don't like the way this situation is developing."

"I would have thought you would be pleased that no one is attempting to cross. That would be a good sign. No smuggling going on here. Makes your job easier."

"Normally, yes. But this is unrealistic. Every other Kaserne along the border has had some penetrations, and several who have attempted to cross have been captured. Airmen shot down try to reach Switzerland, and more and more Jews are attempting to cross these borders into Switzerland. Why are they not trying in our sector? It's not realistic."

"I'm sorry. It seems as if you have done all you can. The Resistance must have figured out that there are easier places to cross than in our sector. Is every border this secure?"

"Maybe you're right. They believe this area is well guarded and patrolled and that the mountains have formed a natural barrier. I'll just have to believe that for now. If we haven't learned anything by the end of the month, I'll take the blinds down. It takes a lot of manpower to staff them in addition to our regular duties."

"Good luck. Let me know if I can help."

Wilhelm thought about all he had learned and decided to avoid the village for a while. He wished he had a way to get the information to the tailor without having to visit the shop itself. He racked his brain but still was unable to find a way to get information to the Resistance.

It was in mid-July when he had his first asthma attack since coming to France. Major Decker noticed that he was having trouble breathing and was concerned.

"Wilhelm, are you having an asthma attack?"

"I think so. I started to become concerned last night, and now this morning, I'm quite certain it is asthma."

"Let's get you to the hospital in Audincourt. They'll take care of you. I can't afford to have you miss too many days."

Major Decker called the guard at the gate and told him to get someone to take Schmidt to the hospital. He was to tell the people at the information desk that the major would be there to make arrangements before noon.

The hospital was the best place for Wilhelm, and they did take good care of him. His breathing was labored but it never got as bad as on previous occasions. By the end of the second day, late in the evening, he got a visit from the local pastor, Father Robert Gilbert.

"How are you feeling?" They spoke in French.

"Better, Father."

"Good, we need you to be healthy."

"Oh?" said Wilhelm.

"You have provided us with much life-saving information."

"Then you are the one running the operation?"

"No. I am but one person in the operation."

"I want to tell you that my position is becoming difficult. I suspect that because no one has been caught they think someone is alerting the Resistance. When I return, I may be under surveillance."

"I'll stop by tomorrow night and we'll talk. I'll try to find a way for you to contact us."

"Father, would it be possible to smuggle me into Switzerland? I'm an American, you know."

"Not without tipping off the Germans and alerting them to the operation. You are so very valuable to what we do. Let me talk to some people. I'll know more tomorrow."

The priest laid his hand on Wilhelm's forehead and made the sign of the cross with his thumb and whispered a blessing in Latin. Wilhelm thanked the priest and soon fell asleep.

Chapter Forty-Nine

The following evening Wilhelm had already fallen asleep when someone touched his arm.

"Good evening, Wilhelm."

"Good evening, Father."

"I'm sorry to arrive so late, but it is safer this way."

"That's no problem. My asthma seems to be improving. I may be released in a day or two."

"Good. Wilhelm, I found a way for you to communicate with us. Every day they empty the wastebaskets into a large garbage can. They leave the can just outside the compound, and our trash pickup comes by around ten each morning. You know when they pick up your trash. Write what you want to say, put the paper in a manila envelope and fold it into quarters."

"What if they find the envelope?"

"I'm afraid that might shut down our operation and cost us our lives.

Can you be cryptic?"

"My parents wrote a letter to me and chose the first word in the first paragraph, the second word in the second paragraph and so forth. Why don't I do that? I'll make it look like I'm starting a letter to my parents who, everyone thinks, live in Saarbrucken. I'll put it in a manila envelope and fold it into quarters."

"Wilhelm, I think that will work. We'll check the garbage every day, as we do that already. We don't learn much but every bit helps. The tailor is still available, but it might be best if you don't visit the village, at least for awhile."

"Thank you, Father, for the visit. I feel certain this will work."

"I will write in print since my cursive writing is definitely not German."

"I'm glad you thought of that. Oh…about the question you asked?" He looked around to be sure no one could hear. "Smuggling you into Switzerland."

"What did you find out?"

"Since you are American, you have every right to seek refuge in Switzerland. We could arrange passage. That will have to be your choice. The Resistance believes that if we lose your services, it will only be a matter of time before the bakery girl will be caught and the airman with her. That will put an end to smuggling the Jewish children out of the country, at least in this section of France. It will also prevent us from rescuing airmen who have been shot down. This is the only successful operation that we have at this time. Wilhelm, I can't tell you what to do, but you have a decision to make. Think about it and pray over your decision. How you choose will affect many lives."

"I will. You've given me a lot to think about."

"I realize that. You have plenty of time to make a decision. Tonight, think pleasant thoughts."

"I will. Thank you for the information."

"Goodnight. God bless you and sleep well."

Wilhelm was released late the following day with instructions to rest for at least two days. Major Decker spoke with the doctor and promised that he would take care of him as though he was his son. Wilhelm was confined to his quarters the first day and came into the office for an hour the second. A *gefreiter* was lent to Major Decker temporarily, and Wilhelm let him do the work but with some supervision. The soldier said that working in the office was a nice change from patrol duty.

Wilhelm realized that they were no longer using blinds on the border, but he knew it was too late to pass on that information. One day *Hauptmann* Reuter pulled up a chair next to his desk.

"Schmidt, I heard that I will be going back to Berlin."

"I'm sorry to hear that. We've enjoyed your stay here."

"I've enjoyed it also. I was determined to find out why no one was crossing the border in our sector, and in that I have failed. I'm going to tell them that the reason is because we do an especially good job of patrolling and the terrain is extremely difficult. I have no other explanation."

"That makes sense to me," said Wilhelm. "Who will take your place?"

"It's not just me but Major Decker as well. I understand we are both being ordered back to Berlin. Decker is to be promoted to *oberstleutnant* (lieutenant colonel) and I'm told that the rank of major is waiting for me. Neither of us has been reassigned."

"Congratulations. When will you be leaving?"

"I am expected in Berlin by 18 August and the major will leave after 1 September. The new major and captain are due here by 1 September."

"Do you know who will replace you and Major Decker?"

"Yes. Major Frederick Oberdorf will be in charge and *Hauptmann* August Richter will take my place."

"Do you know them?"

"Not personally. The word is that they are hard line. Oberdorf is a protégé of Rudolph Hess and has risen very fast in army circles. I'm sorry, Wilhelm, but you are not going to like these two."

"I'm sorry to hear that. I like this assignment. With my asthma, I can't be in the woods. Major Decker seemed to appreciate my talents, and I did my best to keep the post running smoothly. There are a lot of details. I hope they don't mess up what the major and you have done to improve things."

"I hope not, also. I believe Berlin thinks I have failed in not finding out who is smuggling people across the border. They think that by sending these two they are getting tough and will get to the bottom of things."

"Will they find anything?"

"I don't think so. I thought there was smuggling going on but was not able to find any indication. I don't think they will either. They will try to find out by intimidation. That will not work. Believe me. I'm afraid things will change around here…and not for the better."

"I can honestly say that I'm sorry you're being transferred."

"Thank you, Schmidt. May I call you Wilhelm?"

"Yes, please, Major."

"You are the first one to honor me with that title, even though I don't yet deserve it. Thank you."

Chapter Fifty

Major Oberdorf and *Hauptmann* Richter arrived on 1 September, as scheduled. Major Decker remained to familiarize the new officers with the operation. It didn't take him long to find out that he was wasting his time. Oberdorf didn't want to know how things were done. He told Decker so in exactly those words.

"There will be some changes, Fritz. Some of the people here are not going to like them," said Oberdorf.

"Change is good sometimes, Frederick, but don't change what is working well."

"I'll determine what is working well and what isn't. It seems to me that you haven't been able to stop anyone from crossing the border. That will have to change."

"You can't stop what isn't happening. If no one is crossing the border, how can you stop them?" asked Decker.

"That's the problem, Fritz. You don't even recognize that you have a problem. That will soon end. There will be some changes, and we'll find out what is really happening."

"If you don't need my services, I'll plan on leaving in the morning," said the major.

"You're free to go, Fritz. Say hello to my friends in Berlin and tell them that we'll put an end to any border crossing in this sector."

"Frederick, I'll let you do your own bragging."

Wilhelm listened to this conversation between the two officers as he worked at his desk.

"Schmidt, would you stop by my quarters this evening? I would like to share a drink with you," he said so that Oberdorf wouldn't hear him. "Also, when you get a free minute, please order a plane to take me to Berlin. I'll also need for you to arrange transportation to the airport."

"I'll make those arrangements and I'll ask Major Oberdorf if I can drive you to the airport."

"Thank you, Wilhelm."

It was difficult for Fritz Decker to say goodbye to Wilhelm. *He reminds me so much of my own teenage son,* he thought. *I hope he will grow up to have the qualities and character of Wilhelm Schmidt. Schmidt had integrity and honesty and was energetic and clever. Not once did he find a mistake in the reports he had to sign and not once was he chastised for sending in a faulty report. The sergeant kept the post running smoothly and made it look effortless. That's because he delegated responsibility, recognized those who did a good job and followed up on what he delegated. The sergeant made me look good. What is more important, I like Schmidt and am going to miss him.*

Shortly after eight, Schmidt knocked on the major's door. A bottle of cherry schnapps was on the desk. The major showed him a chair and got two glasses. Fritz poured the *kirschwasser* and both men drank for a moment in silence.

The silence was broken by Wilhelm. "Major, I'm going to miss you."

"And I you, Wilhelm."

"I don't mean to be disrespectful to my new bosses, but I don't like them. If they are the face of the Third Reich, I don't want to have anything to do with them."

"Be careful, Wilhelm. Don't ever let anyone hear you say that. I can't help but agree, but you never heard me say that either."

The two men spoke of the times they had together and how it was made easier because of their friendship. Then Fritz asked Wilhelm. "Do you think the French are smuggling people across the border?"

"I'm not sure. Reuter didn't seem to think so."

"That's because they are too clever. I believe that Jewish children have been smuggled into Switzerland and are constantly being smuggled into that country across the border we are guarding."

"How can that be?"

"I don't know, but I hope these two idiots don't find out. I think Schlayer was on to something. I'm glad we caught him with Jewish jewelry in his desk. It gave me an excuse to get him transferred. Thank you, Wilhelm, for planning that. I have no idea how you did it and I don't want to know."

Wilhelm looked at Fritz, surprised. "You think I had something to do with that jewelry?"

"I know you did and I thank you for being so clever. Don't deny it now, Wilhelm. That was a noble thing to do. Schlayer was about to cause some real trouble, and I'm glad you found a way to get rid of him."

"Then I won't lie to you. Let's have some more schnapps."

Fritz poured another round and raised his glass. Wilhelm did the same.

"*L'Chayim*, to life," said Fritz.

"*L'Chayim*," said Wilhelm, astounded that Fritz would use the Jewish toast. For a moment the two men drank in silence, both with their own thoughts and sorrow that this friendship was about to end. Then

Wilhelm stood, placed his glass on the desk, said goodnight and departed.

Wilhelm returned with the help of the wall to his room, a bit tipsy. It didn't take any time before he was asleep. He did have a headache in the morning.

Fritz had to sit on the side of his bed because he didn't have the balance needed to get undressed for bed. He ate a few crackers before he attempted to get ready for sleep. He drank more than Wilhelm and knew he would have a headache in the morning. He did.

Wilhelm drove Fritz to the Belfort airport and was there but a few minutes before the plane arrived to take him to Berlin. "If you see our old friend, *Oberst* Dengel, send him my regards."

"I will."

Wilhelm could see that Fritz was starting to get emotional and so he shook his hand and hugged him with his left arm around his shoulder.

"Thank you, Wilhelm," Fritz said as he turned and headed for the plane. Wilhelm knew that the major was choked up, as was he. When he returned to the waiting room, he took out his handkerchief and wiped his eyes dry. He heard the roar of the airplane taking off as he walked to the car.

Chapter Fifty-One

When Wilhelm returned from the airport to the post, he immediately went to his desk to begin his day's work.

"*Oberfeldwebel* Schmidt, come here," ordered Major Oberdorf.

Oberdorf was about five nine and two hundred plus pounds. He had black hair that Wilhelm thought might be getting a little help from the bottle. He was thick in the stomach and looked like he hadn't missed a meal in a good while. He seemed to have trouble keeping his shirt tucked into his trousers and appeared slovenly.

When Wilhelm stood before the major, he wondered what the officer wanted.

"You don't salute when you come into the office of your superior?"

"I do if it is required. It has never been required," said Wilhelm.

"Schmidt, this post has never caught anyone trying to cross the border. Is that correct?"

"To my knowledge, no one has ever been caught."

"Why do you think that is?"

"The terrain is difficult and the mountains form…"

"Those are excuses, *Feldwebel* Schmidt. People are crossing and this post has been unable to stop them. That is, until now. We will stop them."

"Yes, Sir."

"I want a list of the schedule for patrols. I plan to double the number of people patrolling the border."

"The men have very little free time with the present schedule," Wilhelm began, "and there are other duties like kitchen and guard duty, trash pickup and…"

"They will find time. It seems like they have too much time. That will end. Bring me the schedule. Dismissed."

Wilhelm gave the major a salute, but the major had already turned away and most likely did not see the gesture. He turned on his heels and went to his desk to find the schedule for the patrols. He kept a schedule that was made up by the *feldwebel* in charge of the patrols. He took a moment to refresh his memory and could not help but be proud of the work that went into the planning. He was certain that Oberdorf would mess it up.

Wilhelm brought the major the schedule and returned to his desk. The major didn't even acknowledge his presence. Wilhelm also didn't like being called *feldwebel* instead of *oberfeldwebel*. There was the hint of a demotion in the use of the improper title. It was a long day and Wilhelm couldn't wait until it was time to quit. He ate supper and returned to his quarters. When he was sure that everyone was asleep he wrote a letter to his parents. It took longer than usual because he used print instead of cursive and had to compose plausible sentences. When it was finished he read it to see how it sounded.

3 September 1941

Dear Mom and Dad,

New changes are taking place at our post. The former major and hauptmann have returned to Berlin and we have two new officers.

These men are from Berlin and are used to a much more formal approach to soldiering than we have been used to. We'll just have to learn to adjust.

I am determined to supply all the support that I can since I have been here since the post was established. It is not easy to keep a post like this one running smoothly and efficiently. Maybe that's why they pay us so well. Sorry, that was meant to be funny.

Are you going to build that deck in the backyard like you suggested when I was last at home? That would be nice, as it would provide us a place to have breakfast during the nice weather. I can't wait to see it.

If I could just stop waking up at night I would be very pleased. The doctor at the hospital said that even when I feel great I'm not getting enough oxygen in my lungs and that is what keeps me awake at night.

The humidifier helps improve the flow of air to my lungs when I get an attack, but I do not have one at my disposal at this post. Since I am improving every day I've come to the conclusion that I don't need one. I hope I am right.

I have been reading more each night, doubling my monthly output. It's a great way to prepare for sleep and I enjoy it immensely. My only problem is getting a supply of books. We do a lot of trading here and I do appreciate the books you have sent me.

Well, it's getting late and the night patrols will soon be changing personnel. I'd like to be asleep by then. I'll close now, thinking of you and thanking you again for the books.

Love,

Wilhelm

When he was finished he felt that it wasn't a very warm letter from a soldier to his parents, but at least it wouldn't get him in trouble if it were found. He placed it on his nightstand and thought that he would get it into the trash in the morning.

The next morning he found an old manila envelope that Major Oberdorf had thrown in his trash bin and Wilhelm ripped his letter into quarters, placed it in the envelope and folded that in half and in half again, rubbing his fingers over the creases several times. He then put it back in the trash basket next to his desk. About ten o'clock a soldier came by with a cloth sack and emptied the three wastepaper baskets into it. Then he carried the sack to the trash can by the gate and emptied the contents into that trash can. One of the two soldiers on guard duty pulled the can to the street and left it there for pickup. Wilhelm worked at his desk with an ear for the trash truck. It came by about thirty minutes later and emptied the trash into the bed of the truck. He knew that at least he was able to get a message to the Resistance. He felt better.

In spite of what's happening, I have a decision to make. Can I leave Faymont knowing what might happen to those I've been helping? I so want to go home, see my parents and Greta, yet I don't believe I could live with myself if they were killed. And what about all the children who could not get to safety? And the airmen who would have to spend the rest of the war in a POW camp? With these two new officers running things, my information might be more critical than previously. I just can't walk away until the situation changes. Now is not the time.

Chapter Fifty-Two

Wilhelm was asked to type up a decree in both German and French. Then it was written in both languages in large print on a poster board. It said in big bold letters that all Jews in countries under German control were required to wear the yellow Star of David on their outer garment. It was signed by Major Oberdorf. This decree was posted in the town square, and the merchants of the town were told to make sure every member of the village read it. The villagers claimed that they had no mayor. Oberdorf said that he would be back next week to make sure the decree was being obeyed.

When the major returned from the village, he was furious that they acted as if this didn't pertain to them. They read the decree silently and moved on. No one seemed upset or angry that the German occupiers were taking away their freedom. He asked *Hauptmann* Richter why the villagers were not upset by this action. Richter had no explanation.

"They act as if they don't care. Well, they will care. I will see to that.

Next week when I go into town I want to see Jews wearing yellow stars. And I will."

Hauptmann Richter made it his business to visit the businesses in town during the following week. He asked the owner of every store to tell him who the Jews were in town. He wanted to know where they were employed and why no one was wearing stars on their outer coat. He got the same answer from everyone. We have no Jews living here. He reported his findings to Major Oberdorf.

The following Saturday two trucks filled with soldiers and a vehicle with Major Oberdorf and *Hauptmann* Richter rumbled into town shortly before noon. The soldiers sealed off the town so that no one could leave. Then Oberdorf, using a bullhorn from his vehicle, ordered everyone out into the main street and to the town square. When it appeared that everyone was gathered, he spoke through the bullhorn from the back of the truck. His words were translated by another soldier into French.

"Where are your yellow stars?" he bellowed. No one answered.

"You there. Come forward," he said pointing at an elderly gentleman who was nicely dressed. "Why aren't you wearing your star?"

"Because I'm not Jewish," he answered.

Oberdorf put down the bullhorn and released the strap across the pistol that hung from his belt. He then removed the pistol and drew back the hammer. Pointing the pistol at the man's head he asked again. "Why aren't you wearing your star?"

The answer was the same. "Because I am not Jewish."

Oberdorf pulled the trigger and the man's head exploded as he fell in a heap. "Drag his body over to the wall," he said to two elderly men from the crowd. "Nobody is to touch the body until this time tomorrow. Let that be a lesson to everyone that I mean business." He climbed down from the truck, walked to the car and told his driver to take him back to the post. He told *Hauptmann* Richter to remain in the square to observe how the villagers react and to hear what they had to say. One of the trucks filled with soldiers was to remain with Richter.

Richter was shocked when he saw Oberdorf pull out his gun and aim it at the head of the old man. After the incident, the soldiers wanted to leave as soon as they could, not wanting to be a part of this injustice. Richter overheard some of the villagers' remarks. Many of the villagers blessed themselves. Several said that God would surely welcome him. He then heard one old lady say, "What will we do for a sacristan? He has been at the church for so many years."

"Who was a sacristan?" asked Richter.

"The old man you just shot. He was the sacristan at St. Jeanne D'Arc Church for at least thirty years. We have no Jews in Faymont. This is a Catholic village. You should know that." With that last remark she turned away from him in disgust, mumbling something under her breath.

When Oberdorf returned from the village, he immediately went to his office and shut the door. Wilhelm knew something was wrong and knew he wouldn't get the answer from the major. He waited in silence until mess at noon and sat with the men to hear what had happened in town. They all told the same story, almost word for word. It wasn't until several days later that the word got out that the old man who was shot was the sacristan at the Catholic Church and had been for over thirty years. This village was considered a Catholic village. If they didn't attend the Catholic Church they didn't go to church, but there was only one denomination in town. That's the way it had been for centuries. Oberdorf should have known and would have known if he had asked or believed what he was told.

Hauptmann Richter said that he was going to visit every farm in the area to find out who would be potential smugglers. He began in sector one. Wilhelm wrote a short note to his parents that he sneaked out in the trash. He began the first paragraph with the phrase, *"Visiting this area of*

France…" and the second with the phrase, *"The farms in this part of the country…"* He wanted to alert those doing the smuggling to be prepared.

Wilhelm overheard Richter's comments about his visits to the farms. Each evening, Richter would tell Oberdorf what a bunch of hicks these people were. He would tell him that all they know or want to know is farming. Most of the people couldn't smuggle anyone across the border even if they wanted. He mentioned that an exception would be the bakery girl, who is young and smart. He said that his visit to her farm yielded nothing. He also remarked that the mountains behind her farm are very difficult to cross. He mentioned that they spent a whole day looking for a way to cross to the border but met only dead ends and drop offs.

"So you think she could be smuggling people across the border?" asked Oberdorf.

"No, but I think she should be investigated. She keeps very strict hours at the bakery but maybe has time to smuggle in the late afternoon or early evening. We'll send patrols past her house to make sure she doesn't engage in anything illegal."

Major Oberdorf still hadn't learned his lesson. He would drive into town and the people would all scatter. Yet he never saw a Star of David. The only people who couldn't hide were the merchants who had to stay in their stores. He would ask them if they hired any Jews and they would always answer that there were no Jews. This infuriated him, but that was all they would say. If he wanted to instill fear in the hearts of the townspeople, he succeeded. They weren't sure what he would do next.

Chapter Fifty-Three

Major Oberdorf received a visit from his superior the first week in October. It couldn't have come at a better time as it was the only thing that kept Oberdorf from becoming completely out of control. *Oberstleutnant* Carl Steinbrink was visiting the posts along the Swiss border. Finally, he showed up at the one in Faymont. He arrived with his driver in a staff car. As the driver, *Feldwebel* Johann Hass introduced himself and the *Oberstleutnant* to Wilhelm. Oberdorf came from across the compound. Wilhelm introduced the colonel and sergeant to Oberdorf. The colonel then asked for a private meeting with the major.

Wilhelm took the liberty of showing Hass the compound. While they were walking, Hass asked the secret of the success this post was achieving in preventing smuggling. Wilhelm said that he thought the mountains were able to take much of the credit. It also made patrolling the rest of the border much easier.

"There are other posts that have mountainous terrain, and they still have attempted crossings. I understand you have not apprehended even one person," said Hass.

"Then maybe it can be attributed to Oberdorf's shooting of the church sacristan," said Wilhelm.

"I didn't hear about that. Tell me."

Wilhelm told Johann Hass the story of Oberdorf accusing a man of being Jewish. When he said he didn't wear the Star of David because he wasn't Jewish, Oberdorf shot him and left him on the street by the hardware store wall for twenty-four hours.

"That is not good. We've seen that pattern before. Once an injustice is performed by one side, the other side commits a greater injustice. Soon there is undeclared war and the locals start to resist. That makes them prime targets for the Resistance. The task of controlling the border then becomes more difficult."

"I believe that is what we are starting to see," said Wilhelm.

"Keeping good relations with the locals is important. The task of preventing smuggling grows when the relationship with the villagers breaks down."

"I agree with you. We had no trouble when Major Decker was here. Now I am afraid to go into town, especially alone."

"We have a village just north of here that is a constant problem because a villager was shot. Then the father of the young man who was shot killed the soldier who shot his son. The son was deaf, by the way, and didn't hear the command to stop. Then the major ordered that the father and ten villagers be shot. We've had a constant battle ever since. Many villagers have been killed and we have lost a dozen soldiers to various ambushes."

The two sergeants were at the mess hall, so Wilhelm suggested they get a cup of coffee. Hass agreed and the two sat at a table by the window. After they were seated, the conversation continued.

"Then Major Oberdorf's headed for that kind of relationship," said Wilhelm. "He thinks there are Jews in this village and it has been a Catholic village for centuries. There are no Jews here and never have been. The businesses have been handed down from father to son for generations. Maybe we have too many soldiers here and Oberdorf is spending more time than he needs to on matters that aren't important."

"Look, Schmidt. You have provided me with very good information that I'm certain we will not get from Oberdorf and Richter. Maybe the answer is to cut the number of soldiers in the garrison, although the major will scream like a stuck pig if we do. Or maybe he will give us assurances that he will improve the climate with the villagers."

"It will be better for the soldiers here if he improves the climate with the village. The number of men patrolling such a long border is none too many. If you make a visit to the checkpoints you'll see how the mountains aid us in keeping the border safe. That's not to say that the border doesn't have to be patrolled and the checkpoints staffed, it's just that other border spots make for easier crossing."

"I'll suggest to *Oberstleutnant* Steinbrink that we visit the checkpoints. Would you show us where they are?"

"I think it would be wiser if I send a *gefreiter* with you and the colonel. I don't want Oberdorf to think I've been supplying you with all this negative information. You may also want to talk with some of the men and get their story of the major's killing of the sacristan. Remember that I will have to stay and work for Oberdorf and Richter after you're gone. If you can keep me out of this, I would appreciate it."

"I understand and I will. Now let's talk about other things. Where's home?"

Wilhelm and Carl spoke of their hometowns and how they happened to advance to the rank of sergeant. He had to remember that his fictitious hometown was Saarbrucken. Wilhelm shared his problem with asthma and his shorter leg as being the reason he was given a desk job, something he was well suited to handle. He admitted that he liked organizing a post and having authority over all the non-commissioned soldiers. He also spoke of the good relationship he had with Major Decker and *Hauptmann* Reuter.

"I take it you don't like Major Oberdorf and *Hauptmann* Richter?"

"Let's just say that their methods are a bit high-handed and not calculated to get cooperation from the men. That makes my job much more difficult. I have to get results or my neck is on the block. Aggravating the soldiers doesn't make that job easier. Treating the townspeople like he does is only going to make matters worse."

"*Oberstleutnant* Steinbrink leans to your style of management. Let's see what we can do to make things better. We don't need another situation like we had at the post that was decimating the civilians," said Hass.

"How did you resolve that situation?"

"We sent the major and *hauptmann* to a concentration camp…to Dachau, outside of Munich. It was a lousy assignment, but somehow I think they are enjoying it. They like seeing people suffer. They live to show off their power and want others to believe that they are superior. Plenty of opportunities for that pomposity at Dachau."

The two men walked across the compound and joined Major Oberdorf and *Oberstleutnant* Steinbrink in Oberdorf's office. Wilhelm suggested that now would be a good time for Steinbrink and Hass to visit the checkpoints if they thought it would help them understand the situation. All agreed. Wilhelm asked one of the men to get *Gefreiter* Zimmer to drive the *oberstleutnant* and *feldwebel* to the checkpoints.

"I'm glad to get rid of those two even if for only a few hours. Can you believe it? He wants me to coddle the villagers and he chastised me for shooting the sacristan. He's driving me crazy."

"Did he have any positive suggestions?"

"None that I can use. You're free to leave, Schmidt. All these dumb French peasants understand is the use of force." He continued to mumble as Wilhelm left the room.

Wilhelm could only shake his head and wonder how people learned to think like that. *Didn't the major have any experience dealing with people? Didn't he learn that if you push people too far, they would push back, regardless of the consequences? Doesn't he understand that the end results are what count and not satisfying one's need to be the boss?*

Finally, he wondered how people like the major could advance to that rank when they were so obviously unsuited for the job. All he could do was wonder and hold his tongue.

The guests stayed in quarters set aside for visiting officers; in the morning they once again spent some time with the major. During that time Hass sat at Wilhelm's desk and the two talked about their time in the military. Hass had been in the university for a year when he was drafted and his dreams of being an engineer were shattered.

"Maybe you can continue your education when the war is over," suggested Wilhelm.

"If there is a university. The British are doing a job on some of our cities. Once the Americans declare war against us, we'll probably have no country to return to."

"Do you think it will be that bad?"

"I've seen some of the devastation that has taken place in our industrial cities, like Hamburg. Wait till they really get going. I think Germany has made a terrible mistake, and we will pay dearly for it."

"I hope you're wrong, Johann. My insides are telling me that you may be correct."

At that moment *Oberstleutnant* Steinbrink came out of the major's office and announced that it was time to move on to the next post. The two sergeants shook hands and wished each other good luck.

When Oberdorf got a chance, he called Richter into his office and they discussed the visit of the *Oberstleutnant*. Wilhelm could hear them chuckle when they thought their visitor was unrealistic. What I didn't like," said Oberdorf "was that he actually threatened me. He said that if I was going to act like a dictator, he would find someone to replace me and have me sent to someplace, like Dachau, where I could be a dictator."

"Was he serious?"

"I believe so. I'd rather stay here than go east. Maybe we can back off the rough stuff for a while until they forget about the sacristan."

"Did you find out who was telling him all this stuff?"

"I presumed all the soldiers mentioned the killing. For now, we give all our attention to the border and avoid antagonizing the villagers. What annoyed me was the information given to Steinbrink was so accurate, and he wouldn't tell me who was giving him the information."

"Maybe we have a spy in our midst," suggested Richter.

"More likely, many people spoke to the colonel. He knew much more than one soldier could provide. Next time, I may not let them go to the checkpoints alone. That was a mistake."

Wilhelm overheard most of the conversation but especially the last comment. He was thankful that they didn't suspect him of giving negative information to the *oberstleutnant*. In fact, he gave the information to the *feldwebel*. He hoped that maybe there would be a lull in the boot-jacked tactics for a while.

Chapter Fifty-Four

The last three months of 1941 began quietly. One reason was that Oberdorf decided to take some of Steinbrink's advice and back off the rough stuff. It wasn't that he wanted to follow his suggestion but, most likely, believed it wasn't in his best interests to antagonize Steinbrink. An assignment to the eastern front did not appeal to him. He ordered the men to stay close to the barracks; visits to town were severely restricted. While the number of patrols was increased, they were not too burdensome. The weather also cooperated with fairly frequent snowfalls during December, making smuggling—if there was any—difficult and lessened the need for increased patrols.

During the first few days of December the bad weather continued. Patrols at the border had nothing to report. Richter remained suspicious and constantly spoke with his spy people in Berlin, but so far they also had nothing to report. Oberdorf remained frustrated that he couldn't find anyone he could punish.

Then on December 7 the Japanese attacked Pearl Harbor in Hawaii and the United States declared war on Japan and Germany and their allies almost immediately. Oberdorf said that it wouldn't make much difference since the Atlantic Ocean would keep America on that side of the ocean and what ships tried to cross would be stopped by German U-boats.

Most of the soldiers had a different opinion. They believed that this could make a difference in the balance of power because American bombers would eventually bomb German factories and cities. They feared for their families.

Wilhelm was still wrestling with his decision. *Why am I having so much trouble making a decision? Maybe I have decided, because I didn't request to be smuggled across the border? Or am I just postponing what I need to do? Who am I kidding? I can't bring myrself to put others in danger. I know what will happen to the children if they are caught. I have no doubt that Oberdorf will place the bakery girl and airman before a firing squad in the town square if their presence and activity became known. I cannot be responsible for all that.*

Winter turned to spring and still no incidents at the border were reported. The spring and summer remained quiet even though the patrols remained on duty until darkness fell. In October 1942, Richter was asked to fly to Berlin and a plane was sent to Belfort for that purpose. Wilhelm could have arranged for a driver but preferred to drive him to the airport himself, to learn what he could. The best he could find out was that Berlin was getting information that smuggling was going on. That small bit of news didn't seem worth the trip, but Wilhelm suspected that more drastic measures would follow.

"*Hauptmann,* when you know you will be returning, please let me know and I will have a driver here to pick you up. If one is not readily available, I'll come myself."

"Thank you, Schmidt. I'd appreciate that."

"I know it is a long trip and those planes aren't comfortable. We'll try to get you back to the post as soon as possible."

"I'd appreciate you coming to pick me up. As you said, the planes are uncomfortable and cold during these winter months. It's nice not to have to wait for a ride."

Richter didn't say anything more and seemed slightly preoccupied on the ride to the airport. *Maybe Richter thinks he might be getting a change in assignment, which would not bode well for him,* Wilhelm thought. *He will just have to wait and hope that he could find out what was happening.*

After he dropped off Richter at the airport, Wilhelm drove past the barracks and continued on into town, where he stopped at the tailor's shop. The tailor was busy sewing a pair of trousers but was pleased to see Wilhelm. He told him that everything was going well and that they received both his messages. Wilhelm grinned, pleased that he was helping the cause. He told the tailor that *Hauptmann* Richter was on his way to Berlin and he suspected that some changes would be on the way. He would try to get out a message if he learned anything.

Richter was gone for a week before he called the post for transportation from the airport. Wilhelm made sure that all his drivers were on duty or busy and so was able to tell Oberdorf he was the only one available to get Richter.

He arrived at the airport about ten minutes before Richter's plane landed.

"How did everything go?" Wilhelm inquired as he took one of Richter's bags.

"Fine."

Richter refused to say more, and Wilhelm thought it wiser to remain silent.

They drove along in silence for about fifteen minutes until Richter spoke. "They suspect that someone is tipping off whoever is doing the smuggling."

"How can that be?" asked Wilhelm.

"I don't know, but our new source in Switzerland is convinced that airmen and Jewish children are crossing in that sector. It is just too quiet on our side and much too busy on the Swiss side."

"I'm sure you'll find whoever is behind this activity.

"I'd better find out or I'll be headed for the eastern front. Wilhelm, you may not know it, but Adolph Hitler has taken over the army. He is now in charge of the military and he is a fanatic when it comes to killing Jews. He wants them eliminated. Letting them escape into Switzerland is not eliminating them. He wants our border with Switzerland to be secure, and I assured those in Berlin that it would be. Do you have any suggestions?"

"I'm afraid that my skills run in the direction of organizing and handling paperwork. It seems that you are doing everything that should be done."

"And yet we haven't caught anyone."

"Maybe you'll have better luck next month before the snows begin."

"Wilhelm, keep your eyes open. If you see anyone—anyone at all—speaking with the villagers or with shopkeepers, please let me know."

"Are you going to stop the men from going into town?"

"For now, yes."

"Maybe you'll be able to surprise whoever it is doing the smuggling."

"I hope you're right," Richter sighed.

They were approaching the post when the conversation ended. Wilhelm thought it best to be silent.

Richter went immediately into Oberdorf's office to tell him he was back and to give him the results of the meeting with security in Berlin. At one time they closed the door, so Wilhelm couldn't hear the conversation. He felt he knew all there was to know.

The next morning Richter was busy getting a large group of men together. Finally he came to Wilhelm and told him that they were going to search the border from in front of the mountain, looking for a way through the mountain from the French side.

"Good luck, *Hauptmann*. What area are you searching?" Wilhelm asked nonchalantly.

"That area behind the bakery lady's farm. We searched the farm, and the house and the woods behind her place but never went looking for a way through the formations. Maybe we'll have some success this time."

Wilhelm's heart was beating fast as his brain tried to think of a way to pass this information on. He kept typing as he did so and finally had to admit that he couldn't do it without exposing himself to detection. He said a silent prayer as his fingers moved over the typewriter.

Richter loaded two trucks with soldiers and rode in the staff car with a driver and another soldier. It was 1130 hours when they left and the men were told to take mess at eleven, as they might be out all afternoon. At least the weather was cooperating and had provided a beautiful late autumn day.

Wilhelm could do nothing but wait. He was anxious to know what the soldiers would find since he knew that a passageway through the mountains did, in fact, exist. He was surprised when at 1430 the two trucks returned and Richter was dropped off at the office.

"How did it go?" Wilhelm asked.

"We came up with nothing. We have searched the barn, the woods, the mountains and the house and have come up with absolutely nothing. Schlayer searched her place three times and spent over a week in surveillance. We have spent all sorts of attention on her. It must be someone else. And she doesn't seem the least bit shaken with our presence. She gives no indication that she is involved. I'm puzzled."

"Maybe it is because she is so obvious that we are spending so much time on her. Who else is there who is not so obvious or who is it that couldn't possibly be doing it? Maybe that is who we should be looking at," Wilhelm suggested.

"You're probably right. That bakery girl is just so capable and her farm is the closest to the border. That's what makes her so hard to ignore. But she lives alone and arrives at the bakery early and works till noon. Then she takes care of the chickens and a small garden and keeps to herself. Maybe we should be looking elsewhere. I just don't know where," said Richter.

Richter went into his office and started to rifle through some papers. When Wilhelm left for a cup of coffee at the mess, he saw Richter studying maps of the area.

Chapter Fifty-Five

The order from Berlin came in November. Twelve men were being taken from the garrison and moved to another post. It was the decision of the German High Command that the French Vichy Government was not cooperating to the fullest extent with the German Occupational Forces and that they couldn't be completely trusted. So these dozen soldiers would be assigned to patrol a village formerly controlled by the Vichy regime. Two officers would be sent from Stuttgart to run the post.

That put a bit more stress on the soldiers who had to take up their duties. Yet as the soldiers heard stories of what other German soldiers were enduring, they were grateful for their assignment, in spite of Major Oberdorf's harsh ways. At least they weren't facing the enemy in a bitter cold foxhole or being shelled by bombers. Several of the men even expressed the opinion that their parents living in Frankfurt or Mannheim were in much more danger than they were. That turned out to be true.

With fewer soldiers to patrol, Wilhelm was asked to make up a duty roster to utilize the soldiers as efficiently as possible. He would put more soldiers at the #1 and #3 checkpoints and put some of the lazier men on #2. *They would make fewer patrols and they would probably be careless and sloppy in the performance of their duty,* Wilhelm thought. *Anything he could do to make it easier to smuggle children across the border was worth the effort. With snow on the ground, their task was considerably easier since everyone knew it would be suicide to cross when snow would present good tracks.*

With the spring of 1943, Richter was getting information from Berlin that people were still crossing from his sector into Switzerland. He couldn't believe it. He sat down one afternoon with Wilhelm and asked him what he could do that he wasn't already doing.

"I just can't believe that people are coming through our sector," he began.

"How can they be so sure?" asked Wilhelm.

"I don't know, but they have their ways. And they're usually correct."

"May I make a suggestion?"

"I'd love to hear a new idea. Go ahead."

"Suppose you patrol farther back from the border. I don't mean that we should take people away from the checkpoints, but we could watch the road or roads going to one of the checkpoints. Each week we could watch a different road and if there is smuggling going on we might just catch them where they least expect to be caught."

"That's not a bad idea. We don't have enough men to watch all the roads, but if we watch one for a week and then move to another we might just get lucky. Move around. Change our pattern. It's worth a try."

"*Hauptmann,* let me draw up a schedule since this is going to really stretch our personnel and interfere with all their other duties. I would also like to ride over the roads and might have some suggested places to set up roadblocks or checkpoints. Do you mind if I do that?"

"No, Schmidt. It's your idea and you have a handle on how many men could be spared to do what needs to be done. If you have the time, I'd be pleased if you would plan it. Let me talk with Major Oberdorf and get the necessary permission."

"If I could borrow your maps so I have a better idea of where we need to place our troops. I'll get on this right away."

"Thank you, Schmidt. I'll speak with the major."

Oberdorf approved the plan and thought it had a good chance of working. He praised Schmidt for being so clever. Wilhelm studied the maps and saw where it would be best to locate checkpoints. With the shortage of men, only one area could be covered at any one time. While Wilhelm was studying the maps and the roads, he came up with another idea. *Suppose a fairly large number were to cross into Switzerland in an area beyond our patrols, say a distance from our last checkpoint #3. It would be a diversion, and if they left a sufficiently large number of footprints, the spies watching that area might just conclude that was the porous sector. That would take pressure off Hauptmann Richter, and German Security might just decide to beef up that area of the border.* Wilhelm thought it was worth a try.

Wilhelm also had to think about how he would notify the Resistance. He felt reasonably secure that, once the plan was adopted, they would stick with it. He could control the number of men available and could make it difficult for Richter to change the plan. He would find a way to visit the shops in town and pass on the information to the tailor.

Wilhelm spent several hours each day traveling the roads between Faymont and the border. He checked out every little dirt road and possible road to the border. It took him the better part of a week to locate the best place to set up a checkpoint and determine the number of men needed. He also tried to place the checkpoints at spots where they wouldn't be easily seen, and those doing any smuggling would not be able to turn back or around. Richter thought the plan had a one-in-three chance to catch someone trying to cross the border. Surprise would return to those guarding the border.

Having access to the maps of the area allowed Wilhelm to do some long-range planning. *I wonder which way the Allies will come when they get around to liberating France. Their best chance would come from the south. I'll have to make mental notes of the main roads.*

He was already planning his escape from the German Army but needed to memorize his options. Who knew if he would even get the opportunity or if he would have to shoot someone to get free? He'd cross that bridge when he came to it.

The schedule was arranged with Checkpoint #1 being the first to be targeted. Once the dates were established, Wilhelm plotted how he could get Major Oberdorf to send him to town. At night Wilhelm made a copy of the map and located the spots where the checkpoints would be. He also gave the dates and times when the checkpoints would be manned. When several months of planning were completed and a duplicate copy made, he asked *Hauptmann* Richter if he could present the plan to Major Oberdorf. Richter told him he would set up a meeting and he wanted several of the other *feldwebels* present since they would be involved.

The plan was well received by everyone. Wilhelm explained that if this didn't catch someone in the net, then there were probably no crossings in this sector. All seemed to agree, including Major Oberdorf.

"I would like to propose a toast, but I'm afraid we have nothing to toast with," suggested Wilhelm.

"That's a good idea, Wilhelm," said Oberdorf. "If you have a reason to go into town, maybe you could bring back a bottle of wine. I understand they make some great red wine in the area."

"I know just the wine. Suppose we meet back here at five, just before evening mess, and we'll have our toast."

Wilhelm changed his jacket and took the staff car into town. He picked up two bottles of good red wine and paid for it with his own money. Then he visited the tailor. "The soldiers will be patrolling the roads leading to the checkpoints."

"That will make it difficult for us."

"Not if you know where they'll be and when. Here's a map and the dates and times they will be at those checkpoints."

"That will be extremely helpful."

"May I suggest the Resistance set up a diversion beyond checkpoint #3. That might take some pressure off our checkpoints and explain for the German High Command how people are getting into Switzerland. In any case it will be a diversion."

"Good idea."

"Since you would only be doing it once, the chance of getting caught would be small."

"We thank you for this very useful information. If they decide to change things, use the trash can to communicate."

Wilhelm nodded that he understood as he walked to the staff car.

The wine was a big hit and Wilhelm refused the money offered by the major. The six men who would be conducting this new tactic praised how well it was planned and thought it had a good chance to catch anyone trying to sneak across the border. After finishing off the two bottles, the men joined the rest of the garrison in the mess hall. Wilhelm was pleased with his work.

Chapter Fifty-Six

The plan went into effect the very next week, allowing time for everyone to adjust their schedule and for new duty assignments to be rearranged. There were three roads leading up to checkpoint #1. The first was just outside the village of Della at a bend in the road. The soldiers could stand under the trees and would stop any vehicle that passed that location. They didn't bother those on foot or on a bicycle. The second was on a dirt road in a very remote spot where a grove of trees provided shelter to the soldiers.

In the first week, they didn't see anyone come down the road except several farmers from town on their way to their farms. The third checkpoint was just west of the area known as Croix. It was a crossroad with farms nearby, and the only people traveling on that road were farmers and several children who lived in the farmhouses. They also didn't witness any suspicious activity.

The two soldiers outside of Della got the most action. In the morning, several vehicles drove into Audincourt or Mount Beliard. Those same vehicles were inspected on their return in the evening. During the day, several vehicles would pass by and were stopped and inspected. There was nothing suspicious that first week.

The second week, a new crew was assigned to the second section, leading to checkpoint #2. Two soldiers took up a position on a dirt road that ran parallel to the border, one on the main road to the checkpoint and the third sentry past the farmhouse occupied by the bakery lady. They were dropped off in the woods about a half kilometer from the barn. They could see the farmhouse in the distance. The only vehicles on the main road were the soldiers going to the checkpoint. The other two soldiers had no sightings.

It was during the second week that *Hauptmann* Richter got a call from Berlin. He finished his conversation with the security section and asked to meet with Major Oberdorf and Schmidt. He told them that something interesting had happened.

"Last night a large number of people crossed into Switzerland. From footprints left by the group they seemed to be mostly adults, both men and women. There were several children. They crossed in the area to the east of our checkpoint #3 near Vaufrey and went north to the road leading to Porrentruy. It looks like there may have been twenty or so. That surprise shower last night provided us with good footprints. Possibly they may have been using that route all along and, because our sector is to the west, they just assumed that the smuggling came from our sector."

"So Berlin thinks that maybe that is the porous border site. Are we in the clear?" asked Oberdorf.

"That's not what they're saying. They are saying that we may have been right all along: that the mountains have formed a good barrier and have helped us. They are considering that we take over another checkpoint to allow more men to cover that sector," said Richter.

"That would put a strain on our forces if we have to patrol these areas in addition to those we have been assigned," argued Oberdorf.

"That's true. But it looks as if we have no choice. I believe you'll be getting an order later in the day. That's how Berlin works. They don't ask us. They tell us what we will do."

"That's the way they do things," echoed Oberdorf. "Schmidt, get with the *feldwebel* who makes up the patrols and make up a new schedule. I don't think we'll be able to follow your plan, especially if we have more border to patrol. We may have to put fewer men on each patrol. See what you can do."

"Yes, Sir," said Wilhelm.

It took most of the rest of that day to reassign those who would be patrolling the roads to the border to patrolling the new sector. True to expectation, an order came that afternoon to do just that. Wilhelm suggested to the *feldwebel* in charge of patrols that it would be wise to visit the new checkpoint. The crew already on duty would teach the soldiers from Faymont.

"I'm certain we would all like to see where they crossed the border," said Wilhelm. They will probably cross there again soon if they don't suspect that we know."

In speaking with *Hauptmann* Richter, Wilhelm learned that the spy who was supplying information to security in Berlin was living in Porrentruy. He thought that was information that should be passed on to the Resistance so that they would be able to trace who was supplying Berlin with this information. Getting rid of that spy could be helpful to the children crossing near Faymont. That evening, Wilhelm started writing a letter home. He knew that if the town of Porrentruy was mentioned and the letter was found, they would be able to crack the code very easily. So he decided to write a letter not being cryptic, telling them everything he knew. He would just have to make certain that it was not intercepted.

That evening he wrote the letter and put it in an envelope, placing it in his briefcase. When he went to the office in the morning he found a brown envelope, placed the letter in it and put the envelope in his briefcase, unfolded. When the soldier who had cleanup duty came to get what was in the wastebasket, Wilhelm folded the brown envelope into quarters and placed it in his wastebasket while the soldier went into the major's office. He watched the soldier return, empty the trash into the large cloth sack while Wilhelm engaged him in conversation. He then continued on his route.

Using the pretext of stretching his legs, he walked to the window several times and was rewarded by seeing the soldier empty the sack into the trash can near the guard gate. He watched as the guard dragged the can to the road, ready for the trash pickup. Wilhelm knew that this was the most dangerous thing he had done, only because he wouldn't be able to come up with an excuse for his behavior. He knew he would be shot if Richter or Oberdorf even suspected that he was supplying information to the Resistance. When he heard the trash truck come by, he walked to the window to see the trash emptied into the back of the truck. He was greatly relieved as he walked back to his desk. Now he would be able to concentrate.

Chapter Fifty-Seven

The next few months were relatively quiet. Richter spent much of his time overseeing the security at the new border. His communication with Berlin seemed to suggest that everything was quiet. Summer turned into autumn and autumn into winter. While the weather caused problems for the patrols and those at the checkpoints, the job was much easier since it often made the task of smuggling impossible.

The soldiers didn't talk about the war now since it was not going well for Germany. 1943 saw them driven out of North Africa. They were also stopped and beaten back on the eastern front. Germany's successes, if you could call them that, were in defeating the defenseless Jews in the ghettoes of Poland and in putting millions into concentration camps for eventual extermination. The only other bright spot was the success of German submarines against Allied shipping in the North Atlantic.

As the year went on, Wilhelm heard that the Allies invaded Sicily and then landed at Salerno on the mainland of Italy, moving toward Rome.

The Soviets continued to advance and had reached the Polish border. Those managing the war were starting to run scared. That meant doing something, anything, to look good. The non-commissioned soldier often bore the brunt of the frustration of commissioned officers.

By the new year of 1944, it was difficult to disguise how poorly the war was going. Anyone who knew anything about geography could tell that Germany was being pushed back on every front. The men talked about what was happening among themselves but not with the officers. They did express their concerns to Wilhelm, and he felt free to talk openly with them that Germany was not winning the war. He also spoke somewhat guardedly with the officers, since they had no one to speak with except each other and their superiors in Berlin. They, too, were concerned and had strong criticism for those conducting the war.

While the soldiers had radios at their disposal they were expressly forbidden to listen to the BBC. But it seems as if one or another of the enlisted men would take turns listening to the evening broadcast when others were at evening mess. That soldier would then pass on the news he heard. They didn't believe the German propaganda but did believe the BBC.

One evening Wilhelm wasn't feeling good and so left the mess hall and headed for the nearest latrine in the barracks. In the sleeping area, he heard the noise of a radio and came up behind a soldier with his ear pressed to the radio speaker. The man dropped the radio then tried to turn it off. Wilhelm told him to find a better place to listen, where he wouldn't be heard or seen. He suggested the warehouse.

No sightings had taken place since the large number that crossed the border the year before. *Hauptmann* Richter communicated frequently with Berlin and was told that either those who were handling the smuggling operation into Switzerland had stopped or they had moved their operation. Richter came to the conclusion that his efforts had halted any smuggling. Wilhelm voiced the opinion that they had moved their operation. Major Oberdorf wasn't sure if Richter was correct, but he liked the fact that Berlin wasn't criticizing him for not catching those trying to cross the border.

On June 5, the Allies entered Rome and the following day the Allies landed at Normandy in France. Even the most patriotic of German soldiers knew that it was not good for their forces. They were being pushed north in Italy, pushed west on the eastern front, pushed east on the western front and bombed to pieces from the air.

Yet Hitler insisted on continuing his program to exterminate the Jews.

Throughout the summer the men heard of one defeat after another. They were no longer afraid to listen to the BBC but were careful to do so only in the presence of other enlisted men. They kept a guard posted to watch out for Oberdorf and Richter. There was very little expression of emotion as each man listened with his own private and silent thoughts, wondering what would be his fate. They also listened to the German broadcasts and found it increasingly impossible to believe what they were being told. They all knew the news was exaggerated or an out-and-out lie.

It was on August 15, during the evening broadcast of the BBC, that the men heard that the Allies were in southern France. Several asked Wilhelm if he had a map of this part of France, as they wanted to know where the Allies were. He told them that he would get one for them.

The following morning, Major Oberdorf called a meeting with Richter, Wilhelm and four of the *feldwebels*. "It has come to my attention that the Allies have landed in Southern France. And while that area is controlled by Germany, I don't believe the Allies will meet much resistance."

"Is there anything we can do to stop them?"

"Yes, we can be prepared. This garrison hasn't fired a weapon since we've been here. Some of them are probably rusty, as are the soldiers. I mean, they probably couldn't hit the front of the *Bahnhof* from fifty meters. We need to find a site to practice."

"Could we practice here on the compound?"

"No. That would be too dangerous, as would the woods around here. The noise would not be good for the villagers to hear."

"Wilhelm, could you find a place to practice that will be suitable and away from any population centers?" Wilhelm nodded that he could. "*Feldwebel* Gruber, could you arrange the site, procure the ammunition and targets? We should be ready if we are attacked." Gruber also nodded.

It was agreed that small groups of men would be taken to the range for an hour each day and Wilhelm was to set up a schedule. Oberdorf said that training in rifle practice was the first priority and patrolling the border would now become the second priority. Gruber was to do the training.

It took the rest of that week to find a place suitable for target practice. It took several more days to set it up. Wilhelm used his maps to locate potential sites. He finally found a spot that had a flowing meadow beneath a hill at the western perimeter. He climbed the hill and saw nothing but pine trees as far as he was able to see. A road led into the woods for about a kilometer before it opened to the meadow. No village was anywhere near the site, as far as he could tell from observation, as well as by studying the map. It appeared to be ideal for rifle practice.

The first group of soldiers was scheduled to begin practice immediately. Gruber seemed to enjoy his new responsibility and his enthusiasm was contagious. It was also a delightful change from patrolling, a task that they had long since found boring and repetitive. Four years of walking the same trails and standing in the same guardhouse, looking at the same scenery, had long ago lost any charm it might once have held.

Chapter Fifty-Eight

As news filtered down to the troops, it became clear that the Allies were advancing rapidly into all parts of France. Wilhelm constantly planned how he would hook up with Allied troops without getting shot by either the Germans or the Americans. Oberdorf and Richter were on the phone communicating with Berlin, trying to convince their superiors that there were no natural positions they could hold. The general consensus of the commanders of the posts along the Swiss border was to go north and hold the land on the other side of the Rhein.

Each day the Allies advanced farther north, and by the first week in September it was obvious to everyone, except possibly the High Command in Berlin, that it was time to pull out and retreat to a line that could be defended. Oberdorf spoke with several of the commanding officers along the Swiss border, who all shared the same opinion. Each expressed the need to move now before everyone became a prisoner of war. Finally, the word came that they would retreat across the Rhein.

Now the problem became one of logistics. Trucks were needed and gasoline was in short supply. It was decided that the posts in the south would be moved first and then, each day, new posts would be moved. It was easy to calculate that at that pace less than half of the troops would be moved before the Allies advanced beyond them. The officer in charge of each post was making the decision to leave as soon as possible, regardless of what Berlin ordered. They would take only what was absolutely essential. Papers that weren't needed were to be burned. Only men, guns and ammunition would be transported north.

Wilhelm listened to the broadcasts and located the towns on the map that the Allies were supposed to occupy. He became convinced that if they didn't leave within a day or two, they would be overrun. Wilhelm thought it would be better if the troops were captured on the road rather than being forced to fight or be taken prisoner. He asked to speak with Major Oberdorf.

"Major, the Allies will be here within three days. If we leave now we can walk to the Rhein. It is just over one hundred kilometers, and I'm confident our men can easily do forty kilometers a day. If we wait for the trucks, they may or may not be here tomorrow or the next day. Then there's the matter of fuel being in such short supply. If they don't come or if we run out of fuel and are stranded, we wouldn't have time to cross back into Germany."

"Schmidt, I believe you're right. I've been waiting for Berlin to tell us to abandon the post, but I think we'll be prisoners when we get the word. We're sitting ducks here. I think the men would rather be walking for their life than sitting here waiting for it to end. What is your plan?"

"Here is a map to Mulhouse and the bridge across the Rhein. If the men carry food and a rifle, I believe they can make the trip in two and a half days. If we stay to the main road we'll be able to climb aboard any empty or half empty trucks," Wilhelm said, even though he knew that last statement was a lie. He also knew that they didn't need their rifles, but if they took them they would be slowed down considerably. Wilhelm thought that was all the more reason to take them. Rifles would be next to useless when confronted with heavy artillery.

Oberdorf conferred with Richter. They would announce their decision to the soldiers at evening mess. The men, hearing the news, were not surprised that they were retreating to the Rhein. Most would have asked why it took them so long to make that decision, but they said little, grateful that at last they would be leaving. They were told to take their rifles and ammunition for the march, as much food as they could carry and their canteen. Streams along the way would be used to supply water. The route was posted and the men were told to memorize the route. Basically, they were to go north to Belfort, then east to Mulhouse. They would leave before dawn.

"Herr Major," said Wilhelm. "What records do we need to burn? That should be done first thing in the morning if you will tell me which are important."

"Schmidt. Thank you for reminding me of that. I'll mark the files that contain sensitive material. Burn those first and whatever else you have time for."

"May I choose two men to help with that chore? It should not take us long with a little help. Then we can catch up with the rest of the men."

"Of course. Choose whom you wish. Make certain the important material is burned."

"Yawohl, Herr Major."

This is exactly what Wilhelm wanted. He was being ordered to stay behind, separate from the rest of the garrison, and was being asked to destroy all sensitive information. He was thrilled with the prospect of this assignment. It was even better than he'd hoped.

Later that evening, a communiqué arrived from Berlin telling Oberdorf to prepare to retreat to the Rhein as soon as possible. Both Oberdorf and Richter were angry that it took the High Command so long to understand what was happening. While Oberdorf was marking which files were sensitive, he was mumbling about the stupidity of his superiors. Wilhelm received a certain amount of pleasure listening to his superior's displeasure.

In the morning, Oberdorf and Richter lined up the men one last time and saw to their departure from the Kaserne. Then the two officers climbed into the staff car and, in a puff of exhaust, drove from the post. Two trucks followed, filled with machine guns, grenades, ammunition and heavy supplies. The trucks were to cross the Rhein, drop off the supplies and return to pick up the first group of soldiers. Unless petrol was waiting for them, they would not be able to return to pick up troops and Wilhelm was quite certain petrol was in short supply.

The men left the post after a good breakfast, just as the sun was rising over the forest. When they were gone, the post was like a morgue. Wilhelm handed the two soldiers boxes of papers that had little value, which they carried to an empty oil drum. These papers were lit and in short order created a blazing fire. Wilhelm made certain the important papers were left in one cabinet. The soldiers made trip after trip, burning useless paper, until Wilhelm told them that all the important documents were destroyed. Then he wrote a brief note in English on the file cabinet. The note said, "THIS MATERIAL MIGHT BE USEFUL TO THE AMERICANS." Wilhelm strapped on a pistol and told the men to get their food and water, and the three of them left the compound. They were about an hour behind the main body.

So far, everything was going as planned.

Chapter Fifty-Nine

The three men trudged along on the deserted road north toward Audincourt. It was not perfectly north but bent to the west for about a kilometer before it continued on its northerly route. The weather could not have been more perfect, and except for the uniforms, it looked like three men were walking to the nearby fishing hole. Wilhelm was excited about what was about to happen but was forced to keep his excitement from his companions.

In an hour they reached Audincourt and passed through the town without incident. The villagers stayed inside, but those soldiers on the street managed to find a store that had something they wanted. When they reached the road from Mandeure, they found it filled with German troops walking north as they were. Wilhelm spoke with a *feldwebel* and found out that these men came from the post just south of Faymont. This would cause a problem, and he would have to adjust his plan. He didn't expect to be on the road with all these troops when he found the right place to ditch his two fellow soldiers. All he could do for now was walk and attempt to find out where the Allied forces were.

"We estimate," said the *feldwebel*, "that the Americans are a day or two away, at the most, south of us."

"Have you seen any indication of them or heard any trucks?" asked Wilhelm.

"We haven't seen our trucks, the ones from our post. We have all our light artillery and ammunition piled up in the compound waiting for trucks to take them back over the Rhein. If they don't get here soon, all those weapons will be lost."

"How long have you been walking?"

"We left mid-morning yesterday. We slept by the side of the road, as best we could, and got started early this morning. We're hungry, tired and morale is low."

"We're a good distance closer to Germany than your post. Our men left this morning, and the three of us left several hours after they did. Someone had to stay and burn the sensitive files," Wilhelm explained.

"I hope the men can last without food and sleep."

"Good luck. While my men are fresh, we'll move out a bit faster. We would like to catch up to our unit." Wilhelm picked up his pace to join the other two men walking a hundred meters ahead.

Wilhelm caught up and kept pace with his companions, telling them what he was able to find out, all the while deciding to devise a new plan. He and his two companions were walking faster than the main body of troops and so could see the front of the column ahead, several hundred meters. If he could get ahead of them, possibly a full kilometer, he would feel free to complete his plan. He looked behind and saw soldiers as far as the road stretched and thought that another post may have joined this northerly migration. It was essential to get ahead of the column.

He met the *oberfeldwebel* in charge of the group that they joined. "How long have you been walking?"

"This is the second day. My men are tired, and I'm not certain where to go."

"That's no problem. Just follow the road to Belfort. There you'll go east. There will be so many troops there you will have trouble finding room on the road. Don't worry. You won't get lost."

"It's nice to have another sergeant to join our group."

"I'm afraid I won't be walking with you. We're trying to catch our unit. They're about an hour ahead of us. My men are fresh and we'll be marching faster than your group." With that last remark, the three stray soldiers increased their pace and moved in front of this unit.

When they were in front of the slower unit, Wilhelm spoke to his men. "There is a good chance these men might not make it back to Germany. They are hungry and tired and should have been released several days ago. They feel betrayed by their officers."

"If we catch up to our unit, we should be all right," one of the men stated. It was more a question than a statement.

"If we join our unit, we should be fine. We'll reach the Rhein by tomorrow afternoon," Wilhelm assured him.

After another hour of walking, they separated from the main body of troops by a half kilometer, now on a straight road to Belfort. As they came over a rise, they saw an empty road in front of them. Wilhelm decided it was time to put his plan into action.

"Men, I need to use the woods but don't want to hold you up. Keep walking and I'll put in a little double time to catch up with you. It's a straight shot to Belfort. The road to the Rhein and the bridge at Mulhouse is to the east. It will be well marked. I should be up with you in about an hour."

"*Oberfeldwebel* Schmidt," said the taller of the two, "we don't mind waiting. We'll take a break."

"No, we won't catch our unit if we do. I'll catch up to you. Just keep walking north. If we stop now we'll just get further behind. Keep walking and I'll catch up with you."

The men didn't like it, but Wilhelm had more rank than they did. They did what they were told. Wilhelm scooted into the woods, not wanting to be seen by the soldiers coming over the rise a short distance back. He hoped that they wouldn't notice that only two soldiers were ahead of them. When they did, it wouldn't matter, as Wilhelm would be deep in the woods.

In three strides he was off the road and into the woods. At long last he was separated from the German Army. As he made his way through the underbrush he prayed that soon he would again be an American.

As the sun climbed higher in the sky, he made his way west through heavy forest and bushes. The dense underbrush scratched his face and hands, not deeply but enough to draw blood. Eventually the bushes became less dense and gave way to a friendly pine forest with layers of soft pine straw. The air smelled of pine. He could see a good distance as the tall pines blocked the sunlight from the floor of the forest. There was little new growth. He now found it easy to move through the forest. For that he was grateful.

His departure from his two fellow soldiers would not be suspicious, at least for awhile. He was an *Oberfeldwebel*. No one would question his order. When he didn't return, they might wonder why he was slow catching up to them, but they could truthfully report they were ordered to go forward without him and that is what they were doing. They didn't want to be caught by the Americans.

Wilhelm went deeper and deeper into the forest, always moving toward the west. The sun remained over his left shoulder or on his back. According to his plan, he was headed toward a major road, if the map in his office could be trusted. The problem with the map was that the scale indicating kilometers had been folded under, forcing him to estimate distances. As morning turned to afternoon and then to mid-afternoon, he hadn't come across a highway. He began to believe that he might have to spend the night in the woods.

By late afternoon, with the sun getting low in the trees, he made a decision to seek a spot to bed down for the night. Spending the night in the woods, sleeping on pine straw and experiencing some discomfort from the cold would be a small price to pay for his freedom.

The spot he chose was near a small stream. The water appeared to run clear and clean. A short distance from the stream was a big rock with smaller rocks nearby. He laid some pine boughs on the ground and some others against the big rock, making himself a shelter. He gathered some smaller stones and placed these in a circle to contain a fire. A small fire gave him light and some warmth. He gathered a good supply of wood to keep the fire going all night. Weathered pine branches were plentiful. With the loss of daylight, Wilhelm fell asleep.

Chapter Sixty

The first sign that something was wrong with Wilhelm occurred during the night while sleeping on the bed of pine boughs. He awoke several times and found himself taking several deep breaths before returning to sleep. He wanted to believe it was the cool night air. When he awoke in the morning and experienced shortness of breath, he knew he was experiencing the beginning of an asthma attack.

At first he ignored it and wanted to believe it was nothing, but when his breathing became more labored and he was forced to rest, he knew he would soon be in trouble. It had been quite a few months since he'd had an attack. He failed to take this possibility into account as he was planning his getaway from the German Army. He really believed that his time in the forest would be but a few hours, at most. Now he realized that a day among the trees breathing pine pollen was most certainly the culprit. Sleeping on pine and being covered with pine surely didn't help. He knew he would have to reach the highway to team up with the

Americans. They would help him. There was nothing to do but push on, regardless of how short of breath he would become.

By mid-morning he reached a stream where he drank deeply and refilled his canteen. The water gurgled as it splashed over pebbles, making a pleasant sound. It refreshed his spirit as well, because he knew he was near his destination. The brook had been swollen by a recent rain. He washed his face and hands and felt better for it. In the distance, as he moved away from the gurgle of the stream, he could occasionally hear voices. He was certain they were the voices of a retreating army on the main road going north. He didn't want an encounter with them.

Refreshed by the cold water, he moved closer toward the sounds, to verify they were German. He had reached his destination but would have to wait until the road was free of soldiers. He withdrew back into the woods and rested behind an evergreen bush, which he believed was a spruce. He didn't wish to be seen or taken by surprise by a stray soldier.

An hour later, hearing only the sounds of the forest, he crept toward the road. From behind a healthy rhododendron he saw a dark grey ribbon of highway. In both directions the road was devoid of activity. His strength was depleted and he was having difficulty dispelling air. His voice was a whisper. He found a shady spot by the side of the road, propped himself against a tree, removed his revolver and canteen, placed them next to his knapsack, loosened his collar and promptly fell asleep.

It was mid-afternoon when Wilhelm, bathed in sunlight and perspiration, was awakened by a soldier in a brown uniform kicking his boots. Standing over him were two GIs with rifles pointed at his chest. His pistol was nowhere in sight. Nearby was a Jeep, idling.

"What'a ya think, Sergeant? Should we shoot the Kraut bastard?" the younger of the two said.

"No. We have his gun and he looks like he's sick," said the sergeant. "Maybe he can give us some information. I'll notify the captain that we have a prisoner."

Wilhelm tried to speak but his passageways were swollen and he had trouble making words. His asthma was more severe than it had ever been. It was at that moment that he made a decision. In his thoughts he remembered that he was no longer a German sergeant. He was Billy Schmidt, an American, and it was time for him to start acting like he was an American.

He made a gesture like he was writing and they just looked at him. He did it again.

"Hey, Sarge. I think he wants to write something?"

"I wonder if he can write in English?" said the sergeant.

"I'll get a piece of paper and a pencil," said the corporal as he headed for the Jeep, not waiting for permission.

While the corporal searched for a pencil and paper, Wilhelm pointed to the collar of his uniform and with his index and middle finger made the motion of walking on his arm.

"What are you trying to tell me?" asked the sergeant.

Billy again grabbed the lapel of his uniform.

"You're telling me something about Germans."

Billy nodded and made the walking gesture again.

"You're telling me that German soldiers were walking down this road?"

Billy nodded and continued his game of charades. He held up five fingers and pointed to his watch.

"Are you saying that it was five hours ago?"

Billy nodded again.

As the corporal came back with the paper and pencil he said to the sergeant. "Hey, Sarge. He seems to understand English."

Billy nodded as he took the pencil and paper. It was an effort but he wrote in block letters.

I AM AMERICAN ASTHMA NEED HOSPITAL

"You've gotta be shitting me," said the corporal as he took the paper and handed it to the sergeant.

"I'll be damned. Are any Krauts in the area?" asked the Sergeant.

Billy shrugged.

"What the hell are you doing in a German uniform?"

Billy asked for the paper again and wrote.

VISITING COUSIN ASTHMA TAKEN FROM HOSPITAL

"Can you believe that, Sarge? An American dressed in a Kraut uniform."

"I'll bet he has one hellava story to tell," the sergeant said. "Where did the Krauts go?"

Billy saw the map in the back of the Jeep and pointed to it. The corporal brought it to him, and he traced the route to Belfort and showed them the road to Mulhouse. The sergeant asked him how many and Billy was forced to shrug again. Then he held his hands out wide to indicate a large amount, The sergeant understood.

"Corporal, get me the walkie-talkie."

The sergeant spoke with his captain back in Mont Beliard, several kilometers south. The captain told the sergeant to bring the German soldier to him and he would decide if he was an American. Billy, breathing with great difficulty, got in the back of the Jeep.

At the crossroad in Mont Beliard the captain leaned against a pine tree, his shirt open, waiting by the side of the road for the Jeep to arrive. A cigarette hung from his lip as he expelled a puff of gray smoke. It looked as though he hadn't shaved in several days. He assessed the soldier dressed in a German uniform and then read the paper that the sergeant gave him. He handed the paper and pencil to Billy and asked him where he was from.

Billy wrote NEW YORK.

"Where in New York?"

BROOKLYN NORTHPORT NEED HOSPITAL AUDINCOURT

"Sergeant, get one of your men to drive him to the hospital in Audincourt. I think he has been there before," said the captain. "Post someone outside his door." He looked at Billy and asked him if he knew the way. Billy nodded that he did.

"Oh, one last thing. Which way did the Germans go?"

The sergeant spoke up and told the captain that they went north to Belfort and would go east to Mulhouse from there. Billy reached for the map and showed them the route the Germans would be taking. Then he pointed to the captain and showed him a shortcut to Mulhouse. He asked for the paper and pencil again and wrote.

NO ARTILLERY NO OFFICERS HUNGRY TIRED RIFLES ONLY

"Thanks, soldier," said the captain. "Get him to the hospital. He earned it."

As he rode to the hospital in the passenger seat at a most unexpected speed, he wondered how this all happened. He remembered that this odyssey had started with an asthma attack and was ending the same way. Relief was the word that best described his feelings. He was remembering the events that led up to this strange journey as the Jeep pulled up to the hospital at Audincourt.

Epilogue

The corporal drove somewhat recklessly to Audincourt, or so it seemed to Wilhelm, who pointed when he needed to make a turn. He helped Wilhelm into the reception area and tried to explain to the receptionist, believing that everyone understood English. She ignored him and summoned a nurse and wheelchair and rushed Wilhelm into emergency care.

An hour later Wilhelm was resting comfortably in an oxygen tent with an IV in his arm, breathing easier. Outside his room was posted an American soldier with orders to keep the soldier safe and to call the captain when he was awake and able to speak.

Two days later, the captain visited Wilhelm, accompanied by a corporal.

"What's your name, soldier?" the captain began.

"Wilhelm Schmidt, sir," he said. "I was Billy Schmidt before this all happened."

"Well, first of all, Schmidt, let me tell you that because of you we were able to capture over a thousand German soldiers without firing a shot. We just waited for them outside of Mulhouse and they walked right to us. Most were exhausted and hungry. I think they were happy to be captured. We put them in trucks and they are now in a POW camp. That's a thousand krauts that won't be killing American soldiers. We have you to thank for that."

"Glad I was able to help."

"Where did you say you were from?"

"When we moved from Germany we lived first in Brooklyn, then moved to Northport."

"Where d'ja live in Brooklyn?" asked the corporal. Wilhelm recognized the accent instantly and lapsed into Brooklynese.

"Flatbush, about six blocks from Ebbets Field on Berry Street. How'bout'ju?

"Bay Ridge, near 38th and 6th."

"My sister and I would swim dere at Sunset Park. I loved da pool dere."

"Hey, Captain. He's real. I'll bet he knows the line up for the Dodgers."

"I do, if we can put the 1938 team on the field."

"Who's your favorite player?" asked the soldier.

"Dolph Camilli. I like Leo Durocher, too. De're both good."

"I'll betca can't wait to get home."

"I can't wait to have a Coca-Cola."

"We'll see what we can do about that," said the captain. "Look, kid. Get some rest and we'll be back tomorrow. There are still a few officers higher up who have questions about you. Maybe we can satisfy them now that we've spoken with you. Get some sleep."

"There are some people in the village of Faymont who can supply information. They are members of the Resistance. I supplied information to them to help them in smuggling airmen and Jewish children into Switzerland. Why don't you speak with them?"

"We will. We didn't know that you came with references. Who should we see who can give us some information?" asked the Captain.

"I consider it safe to tell you who I've dealt with. The tailor, Monsieur Girard and the priest, Father Robert Gilbert at St. Jeanne D'Arc Church in Faymont," said Billy.

"Look, Schmidt, or whatever your name is…"

"Call me Billy. Wilhelm is gone forever. And before I forget again, stop at the Kaserne north of town and get the records in the file cabinet. They were all considered top secret. I saved those and burned the meaningless files."

"Thanks. We'll check it out. Look, Billy. We'll be back tomorrow. Get some rest."

And while he was feeling better, he was happy to get some rest.

True to his word, the captain returned the next day accompanied by a lieutenant colonel. "How are you feeling today, Billy?" the captain began.

"Fine, Captain. Much better. I can breathe easier today."

"Billy, this is Colonel Edward Scott. We spoke with the priest in Faymont and the tailor and both told us all you did to help the Resistance. They are most grateful for your help and they had nothing but praise for providing them with good information."

"Honestly, I was just trying to be a good American. It was not my idea to be drafted into the German Army."

"Why you didn't get caught is beyond me," said the colonel. "Can you tell us your secret?"

"Nice to meet you, Sir. Thanks for visiting. My secret is that I found out that officers hate paperwork. I learned that if I could take care of the paperwork for them, they would think I was a genius. None of my superiors wanted to lose me."

"In other words, you've made yourself indispensable," said the captain.

"Since I have asthma I've had to learn how I could be useful in the office so as not to spend time in the woods and in trenches. While escaping from the Germans, I had to go through the woods. I didn't intend to spend that much time in the forest."

"You did a wonderful job sneaking out German plans to the Resistance and keeping them informed of any major changes," said Colonel Scott. "That allowed the only successful smuggling operation to take place in this part of France. We were able to smuggle dozens of airmen back to England. You also helped hundreds of Jews, mostly children, avoid the concentration camps. A lot of people are grateful to you…owe you their lives."

"You make me feel so much better. Being in the German Army when I was an American really bothered me until I found a way to help the Allied cause. I was afraid that everyone would consider me a traitor because I spent the war in a German uniform. Did you find the files I left for you?"

"Yes. We've turned them over to Intelligence. We'll know more about them in a week or two. Intelligence believes they will be useful and may help us crack some codes."

"When can I get that bottle of Coca-Cola?"

"We have something better than that. First of all, I am privileged to present you with this Silver Star for gallantry in action for the work you did during these five years. And we are making you a Master Sergeant in the United States Army. You will walk out of this hospital in a United States Army Uniform. I do believe that there is some back pay involved."

"Thank you. More than anything else, I wanted my name cleared. And now you have done that. I'm grateful."

"One last thing," said the captain. "There is a Coca-Cola in the refrigerator with your name on it."

Billy was released into the custody of the Army that afternoon, but not before a news conference with the military newspaper *Stars and Stripes* was arranged.

"Could we postpone the publicity?" asked Billy. "There are too many officers in the German Army who would put my relatives in prison just to get even with me. Once we liberate Saarbrucken, they would be safe and you could print the story then."

"I don't see why we can't postpone the story for awhile. We'll set up the session, write the story while it's fresh and hold it until your relatives are no longer in danger. Would that be okay?"

"Yes, just as long as I'm certain it won't be released."

"You have my word," said Colonel Scott. "I guarantee it will not be printed until we cross into Germany and make certain Saarbrucken is under Allied control."

"That's good enough for me," said Billy.

Just before the conference, after he had put on his new uniform for the first time, the priest and the tailor visited him. "*Bonjour*, Wilhelm," said the priest.

"*Bonjour, Mon Pere.* Monsieur Girard."

"*S'il vous plait. Comment vous appellez-vous?*" asked the priest.

"*Je m'appelle* Billy Schmidt."

They continued to converse in French and both men thanked Billy for making sure they knew what the Germans were planning. They told him that the baker had started smuggling Jewish children across the border because he knew a passageway through the mountains. He died of a heart attack and an airman from Canada became the person who filled in for him. He lived with the baker's daughter and while the Germans were watching her, he was ferrying the children into Switzerland. Eventually they got married. "They are now taking their honeymoon in Bern with no fear that they will be stopped at the border," he said, smiling broadly.

"What about the soldier who turned up missing, yet his car turned up at the border checkpoint?" asked Billy.

"He tried to rape the baker's daughter shortly after her father died. He didn't know the airman was in the house. He met an untimely death. The airman had to get the car away from the farm and needed to bury the soldier."

"And the *hauptmann* from another post? The one who posed as an English airman?"

"The airman saw immediately that he was a phony. When the baker's daughter came home the airman tied the German up and held him at gunpoint while she went into town and notified me. I notified two of our members and we took him away and disposed of him. We put out the word that he defected."

"But your best work," said the tailor, "was in framing *Hauptmann* Schlayer with the jewelry I gave you. Putting it in his desk so that he looked like he was smuggling was clever. You knew he would be sent to another post. He was getting too close. Thanks to you, he was transferred out."

"And we told all of this to the American colonel and captain," said the priest.

The captain interrupted them to say that the reporter was here to ask some questions and take some pictures. Billy had to translate for the priest and tailor and had to explain what they said to the reporter. Pictures were taken and the journalist left to complete his task of getting information for his press service.

Billy was examined by an Army physician and, after consulting with several others, recommended that he be given an honorable discharge because of his asthmatic condition. Upon his release from the hospital, a call to the states was set up and Billy was able to talk with his family for the first time in six years. Hearing his sister Greta squeal like a teenager when she answered the phone made it all worthwhile.

A year and a half after returning home he received a call from the airman, Paul, and his wife, Annette, the baker's daughter. A visit was set up and they eventually became friends when the airman and his wife decided to start a business and live on Long Island.

CPSIA information can be obtained at www.ICGtesting.com
Printed in the USA
LVOW13s2342241013

358296LV00002B/98/P